The Garden
Tour Affair

Ann Ripley

BANTAM BOOKS

New York Toronto London Sydney Auckland

THE GARDEN TOUR AFFAIR

A Bantam Book / January 1999

Translation of *Henry von Ofterdingen* by Novalis, from *The Blue Flower*,
by Penelope Fitzgerald. Houghton Mifflin Company, New York,
April 1997. (First published in Great Britain by HarperCollins, Ltd.,
trade paperback, ISBN 0-395-85997-2.)

Book design by Dana Leigh Treglia
Border design by Joanna Roy

Library of Congress Cataloging-in-Publication Data
Ripley, Ann.
The garden tour affair / Ann Ripley.
p.   cm.
ISBN 0-553-10693-7
I. Title. PS3568.I598G3   1999
813'.54—dc21   98-19490
CIP

Published simultaneously in the United States and Canada

Bantam Books are published by Bantam Books, a division of Random House, Inc.
Its trademark, consisting of the words "Bantam Books" and the portrayal of a
rooster, is Registered in U.S. Patent and Trademark Office and in other countries.
Marca Registrada. Bantam Books, 1540 Broadway, New York, New York 10036.

PRINTED IN THE UNITED STATES OF AMERICA

BVG   10   9   8   7   6   5   4   3   2   1

TO TONY

Acknowledgments

I was inspired to write *The Garden Tour Affair* after reading Penelope Fitzgerald's book, *The Blue Flower*. I thank her for the use of excerpts from her beautiful translation of German Romantic poet Novalis' *Henry von Ofterdingen*.

Thanks also to the many people who assisted me with this book: Stephanie Kip, my editor at Bantam Books; Jane Jordan Browne, my agent; Trux Simmons, KRMA-TV, Denver; Jon W. Galloway; Enid Schantz; Jim and Jessie Lew Mahoney; Irene Sinclair; Margaret Coel; Sybil and Mancourt Downing; Karen Gilleland; Nancy Styler; my husband Tony and my patient daughters. For generously sharing their botanical expertise, I'm grateful to Catherine Long Gates, Long's Gardens, Boulder, CO; Panayoti Kelaidis and James E. Henrich, The Denver Botanic Garden; Biology Professor Gloria M. Coruzzi, New York University; John W. Pohly, former county agent for Boulder County, CO; Professors Harrison Hughes and Whitney Cranshaw, of Colorado State University; and Ramon Jordan, the U.S. National Arboretum. Other valuable background came from Dr. Sarah Conn, of Cambridge Hospital, Cambridge, MA; former horticulturalist for White Flower Farm, David J. A. Smith; Rick Ernst, Cooley Gardens, Silverton, OR; bee expert Thomas Theobald; Randy Burr, B & B Laboratories, Oregon; Lynn Lewis, resident trooper, Litchfield, CT; Gerald Present, New York University; Karl Lauby, The New York Botanical Garden; Andy Ocif, former Connecticut state trooper; Cathy Field, Litchfield Historical Society; and Allan Williams, Acting Director, Natural Resources Center, Connecticut Department of Environmental Protection.

Gardening Essays

by Ann Ripley

I have no craving to be rich, but I long to see the blue flower. It lies incessantly at my heart, and I can imagine and think about nothing else. Never did I feel like this before. It is as if until now I had been dreaming, or as if sleep had carried me into another world. For in the world I used to live in, who would have troubled himself about flowers? Such a wild passion for a flower was never heard of there.

—— HENRY VON OFTERDINGEN ——

by the poet Novalis, 1772–1801

The Garden
Tour Affair

Prologue

THE TWO CLIMBERS WERE crouched not five feet apart on the mountain summit—a disorderly heap of boulders thrown together in Paleozoic times and made slippery today by a fine mist of summer rain.

"Ah, here we are at the top," said the first.

The other didn't answer, only stared.

"Is something wrong? Why are you looking at me so strangely?"

"I want you to recall some pretty silly things you've said. These are your words, your exact words—do you remember? *'It takes so very little, just your hand warm against mine and our fingers entwined, and I feel as if I'm connecting with your very soul.'* You *said* that."

Silence for a long moment. "I *see* . . . now I understand. I *did* say that once, I admit it. I'm not ashamed." His green eyes held a kind of pagan innocence.

"And you said, *'You are my very heart's heart.'* "

"I said it, yes. They're quotations from a poet, but they expressed how I felt. Why are you going into this now, for God's sake? Let's discuss that at another time, in another place . . ."

"It's all down in writing, you know."

"I—didn't know that."

"But I'm going to *destroy* it. That it happened at all is bad enough. I know it will get out. And if it does, it will be the biggest disgrace of my life." The first climber lunged at the other, like a rattlesnake striking. But also skillfully, with one booted foot wedged in a crevice between the rocks.

The totally unexpected push easily unbalanced the other climber. In the man's green eyes there was horrified surprise, as he fell far, far down to the rocks below.

Chapter One

It was hot in northern Virginia—98, with the comfort index at 120. Tropical Washington's heat monster was loose again, devouring people imprudent enough to step out of air-conditioned buildings. Louise Eldridge got out of her air-conditioned car, and hurried up the mossy walk through deep woods where even the trees seemed to be sweating. Within ten steps, she herself was dripping like a stevedore. Quickly, as if evading an attack, she slipped in the front door of her low-slung, modern house and slammed it shut. With a swipe of a forearm she got rid of the heaviest perspiration on her brow.

For a minute, she just stood there, trembling with relief in the chilly-feeling seventy-five degrees. Life was going to be okay as long as she didn't absentmindedly open the glass sliding doors and let the beast in.

"Hi, Ma." A light voice floated to her from the living room.

There, her seventeen-year-old daughter Janie was slumped on the couch, as limp as a piece of raw liver. She wore shorts and a halter top and little else. Her blond hair was splayed over the cushion behind her, her bare feet propped up, a glass of iced tea equipped with a bendable straw clasped in her hands. Her dark-lashed blue eyes were fixed warily on her mother. Louise went over and gave her a kiss. "Hello, darling."

Janie said, "I'm boiling: I just came in from hanging out my undies."

Louise could see two lacy brassieres strung on a collapsible wash line in a sunny spot amidst the tall trees. "It's beastly, isn't it?" She went to the refrigerator and poured herself a tall glass of iced tea, then returned to the living room and perched on a sturdy antique chair opposite Janie. "Maybe your hair would be better off in pigtails."

Janie's mouth turned down, as if Louise had failed a test. "We're not going to talk about the weather and hair, are we?"

"No." The only thing on the girl's mind was the trip with her parents that she didn't want to take. They had started this debate last evening, and gone to bed with the winner uncertain.

Janie said, "I'll be okay by myself."

Louise didn't answer. She thought, *Oh, no, you won't.*

But the girl's statement hung in the air, waiting like an anxious atom to bond with another to make a conversational molecule.

"I'll be okay by myself," she repeated.

"Probably," Louise said carefully. "But you might enjoy coming on this trip with us, seeing how your father wants to come, and Chris's mom has invited herself, too. Connecticut's interesting. You can go on a historic garden tour, hike the Appalachian Trail, raft on the Housatonic. Your father will have just come back from Vienna, and I know he would love to have your company."

And besides, the alternative was alarming: Janie alone with boyfriend Chris, while Louise and Bill and Chris's mother Nora went off together for the three-day weekend. No way.

The teenager was as cool as Louise was trying to be. She gave her mother a calculating look from under dramatic dark brows, then took a long slurp of iced tea. Only after that was she ready to launch her opening argument. "Ma, I'm not nearly as earthy as you are. Garden tours are just not my scene. Anyway, why would you want me there? The three of you can have a nice, quiet weekend together. You and Dad can—you know—do the things you like to do when you're alone. Nora—why, she can knock off a few poems sitting by one of those rivers. When you're in the car, you can groove on Dad's tapes of *The Iliad* and *The Odyssey*. Frankly, I wanted to do some things around the house—you know, clean out my closet, pack up the clothes that no longer fit me and give them away . . ."

Really—is that what you would be doing? Time for the trump card. She had just spoken with Nora. "What if I told you Chris wants to come."

Janie sat upright on the couch and swung her legs to the floor. "He *does*? But what *for*?" Louise could see the young woman's visions of an unchaperoned weekend vanishing like a cloud of vapor.

"I guess he heard about all the neat things to do—mountains to climb, waterfalls to photograph, craggy rocks to hop about on . . . Being away for his first year of college, he hasn't seen much of his mother and he thought it would be fun to spend some time with her."

"And his dad—what about Ron? Won't he be home alone then?"

"He's been called away to Singapore on business."

Janie's eyes widened angrily. "I can't believe it. Now you and Dad expect me to go because Chris is going, right? That way, you don't have to worry about the two of us hanging out together without the 'rents and doing all sorts of terrible things, like having *sex*!"

"Janie." Louise was hurt. Neither she nor Bill deserved that—or did they?

"Now that you've engineered everything the way you want it, I guess I have to go. Or else I'll be alone in this dank house in the swamps of northern Virginia for three whole days."

Granted it was hot in Washington, but did Janie have to describe their home in such a contemptuous way? The size of the mortgage alone gave Louise deep respect for this house in the northern Virginia woods.

Now the girl was facing her, sitting on the couch like a thin Buddha filling in the ignorant parent. "You realize, Ma, Chris and I could have sex any time—in a closet over at his house, in their garage, in his room—his mother never intrudes, you know—she's way too busy sending her poems off to little magazines in hopes someone will buy them. We could be doin' it in the car on the way to the movies, or when you send us out to help you with *grocery shopping*. Why do you think we need a weekend alone to manage it? After all, it only takes *minutes*!"

"That's all true. But this is our house, and you're our seventeen-year-old daughter. Both are our responsibilities. And we prefer that you don't stay alone. It's called, in the words of your father, who after all was raised Catholic, 'avoiding the near occasions of sin.' Or substitute 'temptation,' if you don't believe premarital sex is a sin, which most likely you don't."

"I don't, you're right. Okay, Ma. But let me tell you something."

Louise sat up straighter and wiggled her back against the old wooden chair, a Detroit chair that had been her grandmother's and which she found particularly comfortable. "Go ahead, tell me."

Janie looked right at her and narrowed her eyes a little, as if she were looking at something unpleasant under a microscope. *Very odious specimen: Manipulative Mother.* Louise could feel the goodwill draining out of their mother-daughter relationship like water out of a leaky pail.

"You always have to manage everything. You can't just let Chris and me develop our relationship in a natural way and let what happens happen—you have to put these enormous road-blocks in the path."

"As I said before—"

Janie was not to be stopped. "You're a control freak, but you don't *have* to be, you just *choose* to be. Life isn't an eternal crisis here. But you had to manage everything when we came from overseas because Dad got stationed in the States—to make sure nothing went wrong. Then, you're just a Foreign Service wife in America with nothing to do. So you have a big job crisis: 'Oh, dear,'" she mimicked, in a falsetto voice Louise found particularly objectionable, "'I must find a career right *now!*'"

Louise reddened. "So that's how you think I acted."

"Then"—and her gaze veered away from Louise, toward the living room's big glass windows—"that first crazy murder happens and you, unfortunately, get involved. You did good, Ma, don't get me wrong . . ."

"Thanks."

"And then the PBS station hires you for that garden show, and you even get a job as a mouthpiece for some screwy lawn-mower company. How would you like kids teasing *you* about your mother advertising *lawnmowers?*"

"It's a *mulch* mower . . ."

Janie ignored her and continued in a low, menacing voice.

This must be the bad part, thought Louise. "All it's been since you started working is control, control, *control*. You get involved in more crazy, dangerous things. Nobody else's mother stumbles on crimes left and right. And you're traveling to all those botanical gardens and nurseries all the time, so everybody has to do everything you say while you're out of town—or something will go *wrong*. But when you are in town, you don't even get home in time to cook dinner. Sometimes I have to cook, and even *Dad* has had to cook."

"Poor Dad."

"Worst of all, you have a constant fear that I'll jump in the sack with Chris, when you don't even know the first thing about how we feel about each other. Why, I might have a love interest in French class. Chris might have a girlfriend at Princeton . . ."

"I don't think so, from the way you two act."

Some of the wind had gone out of Janie's rhetorical sails. "Act, schmact, Ma. All I have to say is that you can't control everything. You can't control my life. You can't control my *love*."

"Honey, I'm not really trying to. But it's my job to be your mother until you come of age. I believe that's next year. Then you can call your own shots. As for the other things, well, I'm sorry I'm not managing my life very well."

Janie waved a careless hand, but Louise had no idea what this casual gesture meant—another slam, or a reprieve? It turned out to be a reprieve. "Oh, you're really not that inadequate," said her daughter. "Just sometimes." She threw both hands out, in the same gesture the Pope used when blessing crowds. "Actually, it might be kind of fun to go with you and Dad and Chris and Nora to Connecticut."

Louise blinked. Did she hear that right? Was that speech real, or just something aimed at driving her mother crazy? Cautiously, because she didn't want to let her guard down completely, Louise threw in some travel information: "Litchfield County's a beautiful corner of the world. The town is a gem: the prettiest in all of New England, they say. Old colonial houses, old barns, a covered bridge or two. We'll be staying at a wonderful old inn. You and Chris can go off on your own there and do whatever you want."

"Will there be anyone under forty at this place?"

"I'm afraid the youngest people will be a newlywed couple."

"What will you guys be doing?"

"A PBS crew's driving up from New York, and we'll be taping a show, but it won't intrude too much. We want to feature the Litchfield garden tour and Wild Flower Farm, which I'm sure you've heard me talk about: It's a great nursery. They'll still have their new red iris in bloom. It's known as the Sacred Blood iris." Louise smiled. "A gory name, isn't it?"

"So that's the big attraction for you—a red iris with a religious moniker? You plant people must be really sick. What else?"

"Otherwise, the weekend's free. We can swim, too: there's a natural pool on the property of Litchfield Falls Inn where we can take a dip any time we want."

"Cool," said Janie. "Though it sounds like your program will be the usual garden pablum—irises, roses, probably."

Zapped again by the daughter's verbal ray gun.

"I beg your pardon?" Louise's voice had a chill in it. "Since I took over the show I've bent over backward to do a more serious job than my predecessor—"

"You mean your *murdered* predecessor."

Louise could feel herself reaching the boiling point. "Yes, her. You know what they called Madeleine Doering at Channel Five? 'Lady Madeleine,' because she liked lightweight programs where all she had to do was wander up and down the flower borders. *Gardening with Nature* is serious, in case you've never noticed. It focuses on practical, organic gardening. And we've covered every environmental issue there is that's related to gardening." Sarcastically she added, "After all, there has to be some reason why the President appointed me to the National Environmental Commission, hasn't there?"

Coldly, she looked at her daughter, still snuggled in the comfort of the couch. "And you call that garden *pablum*."

"All right, all right." Janie put her hands up in front of her, as if to ward off a blow. "Your show is not all pablum. But *this* place—Litchfield—sounds totally white bread. Anglo-Saxon all the way. The white hinterlands of America."

"Not true," said Louise, losing hope. "That area is a real mix of people."

"But mostly Europeans, Ma."

She gave her daughter a good once-over. A stint as a volunteer in Mexico last summer, plus a summer job this year working with underprivileged kids in Alexandria, was making its mark on the teenager. What was more, Janie's twenty-year-old sister, Martha, also into social reform, was advocating that the family move out of the Virginia suburbs and into Capitol Hill in Washington, so they could experience life in an ethnically diverse neighborhood. Louise tried to smile at her younger daughter and failed. Dryly, she said, "Connecticut is where the British settled in colonial times, so it can't be a surprise to find a few Anglo-Saxons still hanging around the place. But our next two shows are on urban gardens—one in Newark, and the other in Wilmington. So there's no reason why we can't do one program in the white hinterlands." She got up from her chair stiffly.

"I've hurt your feelings, haven't I?"

"Maybe you have." She didn't want to look at her daughter right then. She went into the kitchen, wondering what on earth she could conjure up for dinner without running out to the market. Maybe macaroni and cheese? But the cheese, a soft, not-very-good cheddar, had a thick coat of green mold. She caught a glimpse of herself in a tiny Mexican silver mirror hung up with other gimcracks on the kitchen wall next to the stove. Her long brown hair looked straggly; she gave it a remedial smoothing. And there were alarming, drawn-down lines around her mouth, about which she could do nothing.

The conversation with Janie seemed to have aged her about twenty years.

The girl, looking like a particularly pretty blond-haired waif, trailed her to the kitchen and leaned on the door frame, one bare foot twined around the other. "Ma, it's good we're having arguments. It's part of my growing up. If we got along too well, it might hamper my development into a grown woman."

Louise couldn't restrain a tired laugh. "I don't think there's any danger of that."

Chapter Two

SHOVING A STRAND OF pale hair back into her bun, Barbara Seymour hurried through the first-floor rooms of Litchfield Falls Inn, headed for the living room. She was a little harried, for she had a busy day ahead getting ready for the arrival of seventeen weekend guests. It was nine o'clock already, and high time she got organized so she could issue orders to the staff.

She stopped short midway into the living room, her gaze caught by a reflection. She forgot her work for a moment. The morning sun was firing its rays through the tall windows and hitting the mahogany highboy against the far wall of the room. In the process it cast Barbara's shadow onto the highboy's rich wood, reminding her of something. *That fuzzy shadow could be the image of a young woman,* she thought. Instinctively, she raised her proud chin a little higher and stared at the reflection again. It awakened memories of what she had once been: not a wizened creature of seventy-five, aging like an old turtle, but twenty, and a beauty in men's eyes. A ripe, passionate, strong-willed girl. After a long look, she turned away, and her bony shoulders sagged.

No, that passionate girl was gone. Her vitality and youth had been drained away, as she spent her years helping her widower father run his inn and his other businesses. In the end, she discovered, there was nothing more sterile than a lifetime of business with no husband or children. What she *did* have was a flourishing mansion inn, and two relatives whose ardent regard for her she sometimes questioned. Was the affection for her, or for her money?

With a shake of her head, she dismissed these thoughts, for before her on the eighteenth-century table was the work of the day: the job assignment list and the guest list, neatly typed by her assistant Elizabeth on mansion stationery.

She heard Teddy coming, and her heartbeat quickened. He was humming a peppy tune under his breath and snapping his fingers in time. Full of life, full of energy, Teddy Horton was the person who made her life worth living. In the past three years, he had become almost like a grandson, forgoing college to work for her at the inn. At twenty-one, he had finally quelled his adolescent acne and the awkwardness following a growth spurt that shot him up to well over six feet. Anyone might have thought him an ignorant country bumpkin, for he had all the attributes: a longish face, washed-out blue eyes, uneven teeth, turned-up nose, and an unruly cowlick atop his brown hair. But Barbara knew differently: The smart Teddy was her trusted right hand.

She hoped he hadn't noticed her admiring her reflection in the highboy.

"It's a full house, Teddy. Look at this list so you'll know who's coming. That way—"

He crossed over to her in three strides. "That way," he said, finishing her sentence for her, "I can take care of the *sticky* problems." To dramatize his words, he bent down and executed a drumbeat flourish on the tabletop with his long fingers. Then he straightened up and gave her a big grin. *You have nothing to worry about with me around here,* the grin said. And it was true: Teddy would go to any lengths to meet the most outrageous guest demands. Paying special attention to the lonely and unhappy ones. Deftly separating quarreling children. Tossing in a quiet, remedial joke when he saw a couple suffering from the strain of vacationing together.

She looked fondly up at him. He was standing there in homely splendor, seeming to flex every muscle in his body. His whole being exulted in being alive and young and strong. Barbara suspected that, besides being the result of his natural enthusiasm, this was due to the weight lifting he did in the inn's basement when he was between household duties.

Again, she was reminded of her own sorry physical state: still shapely, to be sure—actually, too thin—but with honeycombed bones, and now this new blow: a nerve infirmity in her legs. She didn't mind aging; she simply wasn't used to being *decrepit*. She unconsciously pushed at her bundled mass of whitened blond hair to be sure it had not gone askew again. At least her *hair* remained healthy, although her legs would give out as the day wore on. By dinnertime, they would be trembling with fatigue.

"Well, Teddy, a number of the guests this weekend are relatives. Stephanie, of course—"

"Uh-hmm," he said appreciatively, leaning in to look at the list, shoulder to shoulder with Barbara. "I like your niece."

"Such a lovely young woman. I only wish she could come more often." Her tone grew more reserved. "And, of course, her husband will be along again."

"Neil, the developer." He turned his head away, as if to avoid a bad smell. "Well, the man's handsome, all right, and he's got a happenin' head of blow-dried hair."

Barbara giggled. For a moment, the years seemed to melt off her. "By a happenin' head of hair, I assume you mean good. Neil Landry *does* have good hair, if nothing else." Her eye returned to the list. "Now, here's someone you like: my nephew, Jim Cooley. He'll be accompanied by Grace, of course—"

"Oh, yes, Grace—I mean, Mrs. Cooley."

"He's also bringing his business partner and his partner's wife, Frank and Fiona Storm. So they're a foursome." She slanted a look at her young companion. "My guess is that they've come to ask me for a new infusion of money to run their schools."

Now Teddy stood quite still, all seriousness. "Those schools, huh? Not to be the least bit disrespectful, ma'am, but I—I bet you've given Jim Cooley a ton of support already—"

Barbara pressed the knuckles of one hand against her chin. "I *shouldn't* begrudge them the money—they do so much good. Why, they've even been written up in the papers; *The New York Times* did an enormous story. Neil and Frank run three schools now in the New York area, you know."

" 'Higher Directions.' "

"Yes. And they do such a wonderful job with those young people, who otherwise might land in jail. I understand Fiona Storm is in on the business, too. It has been a very positive thing for the schools, to have the Storms in on them—to have minority leadership alongside my nephew's." A little frown creased her face. "I admit Jim's philosophy is a bit hard for me to take. It's that tough-love business . . ."

His eyes began to twinkle. "Isn't that where you just"—he

made a slashing gesture across his throat—"get rid of your kid if he misbehaves?"

"Higher Directions demands a lot." She inclined her head. "Maybe that's why the schools work."

"Miss Seymour, you are a very generous person." He gave her a look that warmed her heart. The young man truly cared about her, and that's why she intended to care for him, too, in her will.

"Thank you, Teddy." She looked back at her list. "Grace, as you know, might need special attention. Though I will say she was a bit happier when they visited in April. She'll have her usual supply of pills, vitamins and herbs and such, but stand by with the smelling salts: Jim says that she's been suffering from faintness. The garden tour in town and the summer tea at Wild Flower Farm should certainly please her—that young woman is crazy about gardening."

"I remember."

She looked at Teddy, wondering if he knew Jim's delicate wife better than she thought.

But he explained before her thoughts could wander too far. "I helped her do some planting in the kitchen garden last time she was here. She and I put in all those baby herb plants for you."

"Bless her—and you—I'd forgotten. Now maybe we can fatten her up a bit—she's frightfully thin." Her finger traced a downward path on the paper. "Now the others, whom I am disinclined, of course, to call 'outsiders,' just because the others are 'insiders.' There's a rather odd couple driving up from Pennsylvania—the Gasparras."

Teddy looked over her shoulder. "I suppose they're coming for the garden tour."

"I'm not at all sure about *that*. I had the sense they had some other agenda. They're growers—big producers of perennials." She laughed. "Maybe they're going over to Wild Flower Farm to steal plants."

She made two more checks on the list. "Then we'll have some newlyweds, the Posts. Apparently *she's* quite a sportswoman. And they already have a house in Darien." Not sure if he understood the implication, she added, "Darien property is extremely pricey. Oh, and they *had* to have a garage for their car. Guess what kind of car they drive?"

Teddy scratched his cowlick. "A Porsche, maybe?"

Barbara smiled. "Better than that, a car fancier might think: a *Bentley*. My father once had a Bentley, but he got rid of it because no mechanic in Litchfield at that time was able to fix it when things went wrong—which they did frequently."

"Did you tell them they'll have to leave it out in the weather?"

"Elizabeth informed them they could drive it into the old horse barn down in the hollow, but that there were certain drawbacks . . ."

He grinned. "Barn swallow doo-doo . . ."

"And a brisk walk back up the hill to the inn."

"Miss Seymour, none of the guests sound like much trouble."

One of her eyebrows arched upward. "Oh? I'm not finished. There's more. A couple of singles. Teddy, don't forget this little piece of advice: One never knows as much as one should about singles; they can be *very* troublesome. Whereas there's something comforting about couples, even the ones who don't get along very well."

"So who *are* the singles?"

"There's a woman named Bebe Hollowell. Just widowed, from a little farm town in northwest Massachusetts. Doesn't sound ominous, does it? But she wouldn't even deal with Elizabeth when she called—had to talk to me. Went on and on and *on* about her husband's death. She's pretty down, Teddy. I'm hoping we can jolly her out of it."

"Who's the other troublemaker?"

She looked at him quickly and could tell he was making gentle fun of her. That was because Teddy didn't find anyone a burden. His good humor seemed to sweep away other people's foibles.

"A science professor from New York University named Freeling. Elizabeth said he's well known in the field of genetic engineering."

He flicked his hand, as if swatting away an insect. "Genetics? Aw, no problem. Probably wears glasses, drinks herbal teas, and spends his time thinkin' up new ways to clone sheep. But Miss Seymour, that's only seven rooms. Leaves you with three empties. Who else is makin' the scene at the inn this weekend?"

She smiled at the way he tried to glamorize their staid old country inn. "This group is interesting. I liked the woman: Louise Eldridge. She's perfectly charming on the phone, but I have some misgivings." Her brow showed deep worry lines. "Trouble seems to follow this Eldridge woman everywhere she goes; she's been involved in more than one *murder*."

"Murder?" said Teddy, his eyes shining. "Neat! Is she a private eye? Is she on a case?"

"Of course not. Apparently she just stumbles into violent situations."

"What does she do—I mean, when she's not involved in a murder?"

"She hosts a Saturday morning garden show on public television."

Teddy broke into a big guffaw, revealing a set of snaggly teeth untouched by city orthodontists. "A Saturday morning *garden* show hostess? What kind of a detective would *she* make?"

Barbara looked at him disapprovingly, at which point his laughter subsided. "You're wrong on that, Teddy. And her show is quite successful, too. Her station is sending her to Litchfield to film both the garden tour and Wild Flower Farm. She's bringing a whole entourage with her."

"A TV crew?"

"Not exactly. The TV crew is mostly from New York; they

won't be staying here. She'll be with her husband, her daughter, her neighbor, and the neighbor's son. He's about your age, maybe a little younger."

Teddy's face took on an anxious expression, and she knew he was worrying again on her behalf; that's why she liked him so much: She was *sure* he cared—about both her and her inn. "Sounds like more than three rooms to me, ma'am. Are you sure this is going to work out?"

"It will," Barbara explained, "since the husband will share a room with young Radebaugh. Mrs. Eldridge will sleep with her daughter. Mrs. Radebaugh will sleep in a room alone. That makes our full house."

"Wouldn't it be cool if she stumbled into a crime when she was here?" said the young man.

"I'm afraid that is something we can't provide, with the low crime rate in Litchfield. The only thing we have to worry about is that everyone shows up for work. We'll need absolutely every staff member on hand, especially as all the guests will be eating at the inn on Friday." She bit her lip thoughtfully and jotted some quick notes at the bottom of her list. "Don't forget now: We need an occasional fire in the library fireplace, to keep down the damp—especially since they predict rain this weekend. We'll order flowers from the florist's to supplement the garden supply. And we'll use the European sterling and the best linens. I daresay the guests will reserve for Saturday night's dinner as well, especially when we post the menu. I plan to feature rack of lamb."

Teddy smiled, the assured smile of a young local man who knew and understood local truths. "They've heard we have the best food in Litchfield County."

"And the most wonderful grounds."

He put a gentle hand on her shoulder. "Now, now, Miss Seymour, you're familiar with the sin of pride. The priests always told me to avoid it. I know we're good, but we can't be the best at everything, can we?"

"Nonsense, Teddy, there's nothing wrong with being the best," she said jauntily, and swirled out of the room, casting a final glance at the shadow on the highboy as she went.

Teddy followed her, mimicking a drummer marching the troops to the day's combat. "B-r-r-r-rump-pump-pump, b-r-r-r-rump-pump-pump . . ."

"Teddy," she chastised gently, "you're *outrageous*!"

The Joys and Sorrows of
Garden Tours

GARDEN VISITING DATES BACK to very ancient times. It probably started when a Cro-Magnon man dropped over to his neighbor's cave and admired his vegetable garden. All the while, he was snickering behind his hand because he knew *his* crops were better: They were treated with mammoth droppings.

Garden tours can be as informal as visiting the neighbor's backyard, or as formal as doing the English garden circuit—the Chelsea Flower Show, Kew, Wisley, Gertrude Jekyll's Hidcote Manor, Sissinghurst, Tintinhull, Kiftsgate Court, and Jane Austen's and John Brookes's places. It is not a cut-and-dried thing: There are protocols, and primitive urges that we gardeners must curb.

While Americans' lack of established, systematic garden tours has been likened to the lack of a "developed muscle," Britons are just the opposite. Garden tours there are as well organized as the peerage, and they are listed in the famous Yellow Book published by the Benevolent Society for Gardeners. A Britisher is especially honored to be in the book, with the potent words, "GARDEN OPEN" alongside the name. The listing is about as important to a gardener as being knighted.

When an American horticulturalist commended a Britisher on the beauty of his lawn, the Britisher drolly replied, "Thank you. We've been at it for four hundred years, so we've had a chance to work out the kinks." In terms of gardening, the United States is young, and sometimes a bit gauche about the results. Nevertheless, there are plenty of U.S. garden tours, in every state.

Your best American garden visit might be to one of the 500 public gardens. Here, in contrast to the crowds that jam places like Disney World or action movies, you will find beauty, tranquillity, and relative quiet amidst acres of trees and flowers.

Some people have trouble with garden tours, according to an expert tour guide. They become self-conscious and very arch, as the spirit of competition rears its ugly head. The tour guide is thinking, "I have something very good here in this rose bed," while the visitor is thinking: "His roses are good, but mine are better."

There are unspoken rules for garden visits:

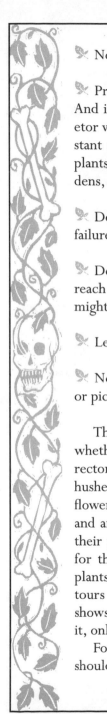

※ No stealing of plants.

※ Praise a plant: This means you covet it. And in the private garden, the smart proprietor will dig you a division, knowing that constant movement and division will only make plants prosper. This won't work in public gardens, of course.

※ Don't comment loudly on the garden's failure to fulfill your expectations.

※ Don't point out weeds, or, heaven forbid, reach down and pluck a weed, as a nosy guest might pick up a dust curl in someone's house.

※ Leave unruly children and pets home.

※ Never leave the path and damage plants, or pick flowers.

The tour guide wants to make an impact, whether it is a backyard gardener or the director of a public garden. He or she wants a hushed reaction to the utter beauty of the flowers and trees. It is a combination of hubris and an altruistic desire to inspire others. For their part, garden tour visitors are on a hunt for the Holy Grail—looking for the perfect plants to put in an idealized garden. Garden tours can be likened to a show, and like most shows, the audience doesn't care how you do it, only that the effect is magic.

For the latest on touring in America you should consult garden magazines or get a

special book on the subject from your public or botanic gardens library. Such a book will give you a comprehensive look at garden events, from orchid shows to month-long house-garden tours. Certain subgroups of gardeners who are interested in one species or specialty, such as rock or water gardens, are very active: They talk back and forth over the Internet and make field trips together. Members of the International Water Lily Society, for instance, recently went to Brazil to do research on the DNA of the gigantic water lily, the Victoria. With these people, garden tours are not aesthetic idylls, but a higher calling, namely, the preservation of plant species.

Chapter Three

LOUISE HADN'T BEEN ENTHUSIASTIC about dragging the whole world with her on this location shoot—despite her determination not to leave Janie and Chris home alone. Now there were Bill, Janie, Chris, and Chris's mother, Nora—voluptuous, dark-haired Nora, who was not the happiest of women these days. But then that was probably why she had invited herself on the trip. Nora's problems were so numerous and diverse that Louise almost thought of her as a female Job:

menopause, failure to publish lately in those little poetry magazines, severe marital problems—and on top of that the recent
discovery that her widowed mother suffered from Alzheimer's.
All this made Nora's behavior erratic: Louise didn't know what
to expect of her friend and neighbor on this trip. Having Chris
and Janie along made it even more awkward.

Once they had picked up their rental car and left behind the
hustle and bustle of the city, she began to feel better. Everyone,
even Nora, was cheery and full of little jokes. The countryside
rolled by, covered with thick woods and dotted with quaint,
neat villages. With only the cars on the road updating it to the
present, it was perfect, like a Currier and Ives print. So different from Washington, D.C., with its shaggy overgrowth and
jungly vines. By the time they neared their destination, Louise
was in love with the Litchfield hills.

"Bill, wouldn't it be great to buy a little place and come here
during the summers?"

Her husband looked at her and shook his head in disbelief.
"Seventy miles into the state and you're ready to become a
Connecticut Yankee."

He was a picture of comfort behind the wheel of the car, a
little smile on his face, seat tipped comfortably back, blond
head resting lightly on the headrest. Both his posture and his casual traveling clothes bespoke a man who looked forward to a
vacation. He had just returned from Vienna, where his once-
secret undercover work with the CIA continued. Now he handled the problems of strayed and stolen nuclear and biological
materials from the former Soviet Union countries. *Nothing too
serious,* she reflected wryly. *Just the future safety of the world.*
Louise was glad to see he had put his work behind him for the
moment.

"A little summer place," she mused, "like that little farm we
just passed."

"Louise, I hate to disillusion you, but that place probably
wasn't a *farm*. This countryside has an element of a Potemkin

village about it, from everything I hear. There are few farmers left, and those fields are kept mowed simply to preserve the feeling of old New England countryside. I doubt we could afford a property around here—I know for a fact Steve Forbes just moved into the neighborhood."

Her enthusiasm retracted like a camera lens. "Bummer."

Bill's blue eyes glittered with mischief. "Unless, by chance, you want to acquire another big mortgage." He knew she hated the mortgage they already had.

"No way. But we could rent a place for a couple of weeks." She looked with a different eye at the visible parts of the unassuming farmhouses peeking from behind the enticing hills.

"I read that book you gave me on Connecticut on the plane ride home. I know you must have picked up a lot of history while you were researching your show—did you run across the fact that Litchfield was the home of the first law school in the United States, before even Yale and Harvard . . ." Still a history major at heart, Bill loved to act as the family's Arthur Schlesinger, Jr.

His little chronicle was interrupted, however, when they saw a colonial-era sign announcing Litchfield Falls Inn. He swerved into the wooded driveway, and from the moment they saw the mansion, Louise was smitten. It was immense, gleaming white, its Georgian architecture marked by graceful, round-topped windows. A wraparound porch on the first floor with steps pouring off it in all directions gave the impression of a user-friendly building with easy access to the grounds. When they walked inside, they were surrounded by the smells of fresh flowers, old wax, and fine food. This somehow made her feel quite at home—though her home, she had to admit, didn't smell anywhere near as good as this well-tended place.

They were greeted by a trim, middle-aged woman named Elizabeth, who introduced herself as proprietor Barbara Seymour's assistant. Elizabeth did a good job of masking her surprise. "Of course it's no bother that you're early," she assured them with a little too much vigor. Of course it *was* a bother: The rooms weren't ready, but they could wait on the veranda with tea. Instructing them to leave their luggage in the imposing two-story foyer, Elizabeth guided them through the first floor, pointing out objects of interest. Louise thought the mansion looked unchanged since its construction two centuries before, but Elizabeth informed her that it had been remodeled at some point from a huge home to a country inn.

"We'll just peek in the library," Elizabeth said, as they reached the first room off the foyer, "and then you can return at your leisure." They came in and stood at the edge of the Oriental carpet. The collection of books covered the walls from floor to ceiling. Scattered among the furniture were pedestals holding vases and humorless marble busts. A fire, unusual for July, blazed in the huge fireplace, apparently to fight the rising New England damp.

Then they saw the cat. Louise, Nora, and Janie all emitted joyful noises, as if they had discovered a baby on the premises. "Ooh," cried Janie, "what a cool cat!" It was an enormous gray and black-striped tabby, sitting in its old wicker basket near the fire. As they watched, it majestically rose, stretched its back into an unbelievable arch, then drifted behind a leather couch.

"Don't mind Hargrave," said Elizabeth, laughing. "He has sort of an attitude—thinks he owns the library. Not too social, and quite old, in fact. But he seems to have lost most of his sense of curiosity, so he won't bother you." Then she led them into the living room.

Dull gold wallpaper with simple designs of pineapples and flowers covered the walls there. It made a fine background for the eighteenth-century pianoforte and other antique furniture, which included a magnificent mahogany highboy. The woodwork, with double-mitred corners, was the labor of a master carpenter, and the walls were hung with dark oil paintings depicting drama and drownings on the Atlantic seas. Scattered artfully about were several lovely old vases and bowls, some filled with bouquets of verbena, petunia, and scabiosa in quiet pastels. Despite this beauty, Louise felt a chill.

"It's almost spooky, isn't it?" she said to Nora.

Nora gave her one of her Mona Lisa smiles. "Yes. There could be ghosts here."

Overhearing them, Bill said, his eyes twinkling, "They can't be that scary: They're probably Congregational ghosts, since they made up a good part of the population back in the old days." Louise rolled her eyes.

Beyond the living room was a sunroom. It was filled with overstuffed furniture covered with gently faded chintz and strewn with plump matching pillows, in what Louise knew was the most venerable East Coast decorating style. Beyond that was the huge veranda. Scattered with an array of antique wicker chairs and tables, it obviously served as the outdoor dining room in good weather. Now it served as a waiting room.

Elizabeth had tea brought to them and refused to accept any more apologies for their early arrival. Barbara Seymour was still nowhere to be seen, but there was a hum of activity within the enormous mansion. Louise could smell, even from the veranda, delightful food aromas that whetted her appetite for the evening's dinner.

The five of them sat on the wicker chairs in their rumpled traveling clothes, clutching their cups of tea. "Don't *we* make an interesting picture," said Louise. "The other guests will never figure us out. Janie, you and Chris are so tall and blond that you look like brother and sister." She grinned. "Wait 'til somebody sees you with your arms around each other!"

Janie frowned her disapproval, and Chris looked embarrassed. On a roll now, Louise said, "And Nora and I, with our dark hair, might pass for sisters. Since Ron's not here, we'll share the attentions of Bill and raise more eyebrows. And Bill, you're so blond they'll think both Janie and Chris are your kids, of course."

"Sounds incestuous to me," he said, and then lowered his

voice. "The real question is, what kind of people are we going to meet here—or do we care?"

Louise shrugged her shoulders. "I don't think it will matter. My guess is we'll be so busy we won't get a chance to get well acquainted. And we can always go out on the town tonight."

Nora looked skeptical. "I wonder about that. Small towns like this roll up the sidewalks at the fall of darkness."

As fifteen minutes stretched into a half hour, they consumed a steady supply of cucumber, watercress, and pimento-cheese sandwiches off a frequently replenished tray. The restless Janie and Chris explored some of the thirty acres of grounds attached to the inn and returned. By then, two other guests were drifting toward them, looking as if they had stepped out of the pages of a fashion magazine.

"Dressed to kill," murmured Nora.

"From the way she's hanging on him, they have to be the newlyweds," replied Louise.

Mark and Sandy Post introduced themselves smoothly, then made the rounds of the table, schmoozing individually with each member of the group. Sandy was small, with a perfect figure and a feathered blond hairdo, and wearing a honey-beige, wide-legged St. John knit pantsuit. Her smart, blocky shoes clacked gently as she crossed the wide floorboards. On her shoulder was an enormous, flawlessly coordinated leather bag big enough for anything—a small arsenal, perhaps, or enough clothes for the entire weekend.

The tall, self-assured Mark had a thin face and aquiline nose, and his brown hair had been styled by an expert. His body was muscular but slim, as if he were a runner. Louise was surprised to find out that *Sandy* was the jock. "I hardly had time to plan my wedding," she complained, "because I was training for the Olympics with the U.S. women's biathlon team." In that outfit, it was hard to imagine her cross-country skiing while shooting a gun. Particularly eye-catching was the little bee pinned to Sandy's jacket; its body was made of one enormous pearl, its wings of many tiny diamonds—probably a throwaway item from Tiffany. Mark held up his end of the image, decked out in sports clothes with expensive logos.

"We, like, *just* returned from Italy," Sandy told them, shedding most of her mystique with the one sentence. "We wanted to keep the romance of Tuscany alive by spending a few days in charming Litchfield hills." Her blue eyes widened. "You know, they say there's a similarity between the two places."

Mark turned his birdlike gaze on them. "But not between the profits they make. In Tuscany, it's fifteen-dollar lattes in the piazzas, and thousand-dollar Ferragamos." By accident, probably, his glance rested on Louise and stayed there. He gave her a slow grin, as if he were saying, "I'm cute, and so are you." Ah, thought Louise, is this the kind of guy who must prove his manhood at every turn?

"Like, you wouldn't believe the crowds near Florence," Sandy continued, her voice grating on Louise's ears. Although Sandy was grown up and married, she had not left behind her Valley Girl vocabulary that, thanks to television, had come into universal use even among the allegedly educated. Louise was suddenly thankful her daughters hadn't picked it up.

"*Everybody's* doing Tuscany this summer," Sandy continued, "in addition to wherever else they might be going—it's kind of, you know, an obligatory stop. Of course, Mark had to get back to Stamford to his computer company . . ." She gave her new spouse a look that would have dissolved most men, but which did not seem to penetrate Mark. When the new bride went on to tell them she worked in marketing with Calvin Klein in New York, Louise and Nora discreetly shared a look that said, "Tell us something we couldn't already guess." It was the kind of job that would fit Sandy like a glove.

The pair good-naturedly sat down at an adjoining table with Janie and Chris, and the four soon found something in common, despite a decade's difference in their ages: cars. With this proximity, it was easy for Nora and Louise to overhear the details of Mark Post's problems garaging his Bentley in the horse barn on the inn's property—the only option available. And the car *needed* garaging because—after all—it was brand-new. Mark and Sandy fervently hoped bird droppings wouldn't land on the car's pristine roof.

"Young love takes many forms," Nora told Louise, sotto voce. "One is working together to ward off bird guano."

Louise giggled. "This may be Janie and Chris's chance to absorb Yuppie life and learn to love it."

"Or better still, learn to hate it."

When another—older—couple arrived, getting acquainted with them was more difficult. They were shy, Louise guessed. They sat at a table by themselves and sipped iced tea, determined to appear too busy refreshing themselves to speak. But Louise was more determined to include them. She sauntered over and asked them straight out if they were interested in the garden tour. And they finally opened up: The Gasparras were growers from southern Pennsylvania, their specialty, the iris.

"We didn't come here for the tour, you can bet your life on that," said Rod Gasparra, a short, stocky man with dark heavy eyebrows sheltering his brown eyes. Louise guessed his ancestry included some Middle European—Romanian, perhaps—blood, plus an assortment of other nationalities. He wore a sober business suit. If this was to be a vacation weekend, the man hadn't gotten into the mood yet. "We might do the tour, we might do something else, like hike. *Viewing* flowers is not our top priority," he added, his tone rising. "I have some serious talking to do with that fellow who owns Wild Flower Farm." During this little burst of emotion his fists balled up and his face turned a dull red; Louise would hate to see the man really blow his top.

Dorothy Gasparra put a restraining hand on his arm, her face wary. Her rosy cheeks were framed by wavy, attractive brown hair caught back in a no-nonsense bun, and she had spectacular brown eyes that reminded Louise of gypsy nights. "Dear, Mrs. Eldridge doesn't—"

"Just call me Louise."

"Louise doesn't want to hear about our problems."

Churlishly, he replied, "Okay, then, that's enough: I won't tell her."

Bursting to know what was bothering the man, Louise nevertheless was loath to get in the middle of a husband-wife struggle. After a few tactful words, she returned to the table where Bill and Nora waited.

Four more people arrived on the veranda, a white couple and a black couple. Jim Cooley was in his mid-forties, big and muscular, with wavy dark blond hair, strong features, and smiling hazel eyes. Louise felt an immediate sense of comfort in his presence; perhaps it was his warm baritone voice. Frank Storm was a black man in this white world, perhaps a little older than Jim, but it was hard to tell. He was a standout as well: virile, dignified, and even more solid than his companion, but with a more aloof manner.

Jim's small, pretty wife was appropriately named Grace. She was at the very least ten years younger than her husband, and the aura of youth about her was accented by her short, many-pocketed cotton dress with flowers so delicate and pale that they appeared faded. *Child bride?* wondered Louise.

Grace timidly waved at the Posts, as if she had met them before; Sandy Post smiled back in a flush of recognition.

Frank's wife, Fiona Storm, stood out all the more beside the pale Grace. She was a classic dark beauty with a touch of Asian lineage in her slightly slanted eyes, and wearing a well-cut pantsuit, with perfect posture. Her expression was almost confrontational: It said, "I am not only black, I am smart and competent."

Jim Cooley brought four chairs to the table where Louise, Bill, and Nora sat, then cajoled the reticent Gasparras until they, too, drew their chairs into the group. Immediately they began to look more at home, and Louise saw how clever Jim was at bringing people together.

It turned out Jim and Frank ran the cluster of New York—

area schools for troubled young people called Higher Directions, about which Louise and Bill had recently read several newspaper articles. Fiona was the school's fund-raiser. If Grace had a role in the business, nothing was said of it.

"I hope you all feel as at home here as I do," said Cooley, casting his eye around the veranda, where *Clematis montana* 'Rubens' rambled in and out of the white wooden porch railing posts. "I'm Barbara Seymour's nephew, and I've visited this mansion since I was a little boy. Used to help around the place every summer. I'd sit out in the kitchen garden at night with the help and we'd play folk music on guitars. What a long time ago that seems. This has always been like the family's country home. It was turned into a hotel in the late thirties, well before I was born, but there were always rooms set aside for family members."

Only minutes later, they were joined by another of the innkeeper's relatives, Stephanie Landry, a porcelain-skinned young woman with long, dark-brown permed hair that stood out as boldly as the Afro hairdos of two decades before. Louise judged her to be in her mid-thirties. She caught everyone's eye, even that of some of the kitchen help, including a homely young man watching from the edge of the veranda. After effusively kissing her cousin Jim and bear-hugging his thin wife Grace, Stephanie felt it necessary to apologize for the absence of her husband Neil, who was apparently in town picking up something from the store.

"I'm the bearer of good news," she said, her eyes shining. "My aunt has just told me our rooms are ready, and we can go upstairs. You can use the lovely staircase, but you might prefer the elevator; it's certainly easier with luggage." With Louise lagging behind to examine each interesting piece of antique furniture she passed, the group slowly drifted back into the house.

At the large front door, there appeared two late arrivals. They were obviously strangers to each other, the man holding himself apart from the older woman as if she had permanently

34

disenchanted him on their brief walk together from the parking lot.

Since Elizabeth had disappeared on other duties, Stephanie and Jim stepped up to greet them. The woman was in her early sixties, and large in stature, with a face bronzed by the sun. Louise noted her hair was dyed that ambiguous blond-beige color that sixty-year-old women seemed to favor. She wore big gold hoop earrings. In a rasping smoker's voice she announced that she was Bebe Hollowell and had had "one devil of a time getting here from Massachusetts." Then she began her litany of complaints. "First, I got a late start. Then, the traffic on Route Two—why, it was *terrible*—some funeral. And it's impossible to make up for lost time once you get to Connecticut, which in my opinion has very poor road signage. Especially near Litchfield . . ."

"Oh, I agree," said Stephanie placatingly, "very confusing."

"I took a wrong turn to Kent: That delayed me for at least half an hour." Bebe Hollowell granted them all a big smile, as if they had passed a test just by listening to her tirade. "Anyway, sorry I'm late. And I see you're all waiting, anyway. Is everything all right here?"

"Oh, quite all right," said Jim Cooley, stepping in to introduce her to the others. The man who had arrived at the same time was no more than forty-five, tall, with sandy hair and a Vandyke beard, wearing small, effete glasses with wire frames. While he stood waiting for Bebe Hollowell's conversation to subside, he looked around with keen eyes. Louise noted that his gaze was like a butterfly's flight, resting for a moment on the fragile, bright-eyed beauty of Grace, then on Janie and Chris, moving on to encompass the rest of the group, but pausing lengthily when it reached Nora, and then stopping dead at the Posts. The man exchanged a shocked look with the newlywed husband.

Sandy Post gave an involuntary cry, then put her hand quickly over her mouth.

The new arrival gave her a measured look, then announced

in a quiet voice, "I'm Dr. Jeffrey Freeling. Some of you obviously know me from NYU." A few deft questions from Jim Cooley established that Freeling was a botany professor at the university who specialized in genetic engineering; naturally, he was "intensely interested in gardening." Jim started to mention a prestigious science award the professor had won for discovering the gene that allows plants to bloom at will, a fact his aunt apparently had told him about Freeling. The professor brusquely interrupted. "Please—it's not important to these people."

During the introductions, the Posts acknowledged knowing the professor, their embarrassed facial expressions indicating they regretted the fact. Dr. Freeling seemed equally discomfited. *Is it love or hate that inspires such emotion,* Louise wondered.

As the amenities progressed, Louise noted the crowd was, in a manner of speaking, deteriorating. The delicate Grace had donned her dark glasses and sagged onto a velvet-cushioned side bench. Frank and Fiona Storm waited near her, and Fiona put a hand on Grace's shoulder, as if consoling a tired child.

After their cool greeting to Dr. Freeling, Mark and Sandy eyed each other as if they were going to burst, from suppressed anger, full bladders, or a surfeit of love's passion, Louise wasn't sure. Both Gasparras shifted nervously from foot to foot, and Rod Gasparra was giving Dr. Freeling what Louise could only describe as dirty looks. Chris and Janie were leaning on the balustrade at the foot of the stairs, waiting for the signal to go to their respective rooms. On the far edge of the crowd, the young man from the kitchen waited, also, for the signal to carry up the baggage.

Swim, unpack, take a nap—it didn't matter—everyone was anxious to get settled and do something. Delay was not a popular word among American tourists seeking a getaway weekend in the country. Louise herself was so impatient to get this vacation started that she was thinking of biting off a bothersome hangnail, something she normally did only during horror movies.

And she had serious doubts about this group: Everyone was polite, but there was a tension here she couldn't define and didn't like. It was a diverse bunch, with not a lot in common. The only impetus that appeared to drive them all to Litchfield County, Connecticut, was the Litchfield Falls Inn.

She stifled a sigh. So much for expecting the weekend to be bucolic and laid-back. She found the hangnail and removed it in one bite.

Then their hostess appeared, as suddenly and dramatically as a Broadway star. Barbara Seymour stood at the top of the tall, winding stairs. The woman had a royal air, and even from this distance Louise identified her aristocratic bearing with old New England tradition and wealth.

She called out to them in a strong, low-pitched voice: "Good afternoon. My regrets for the delay. But all is ready now. I am pleased and honored that you all have come." At that, she descended the first stair, which obligingly declared the antiquity of the house by creaking loudly. The stairs were carpeted in patterned wool that Louise guessed was an authentic reproduction of an earlier time, for pictures, draperies, moldings, and wallpaper were either the original fixtures or careful copies of the eighteenth-century accoutrements of the mansion. Even Barbara was like an authentic reproduction, as Louise beheld her through the flattering golden light of the chandelier that hung in the atrium lobby. She was an aged beauty, with fine, distinctive English features, whitish-yellow hair bound up gracefully in a bun, wearing a maroon dress with a period look in its gathered skirt and billowing sleeves.

Barbara's feet had descended the second stair and the third, when Louise saw something bulging out slightly on the fourth. At the same moment, the older woman's slim body flipped out into the air, as if she were attempting an outrageous aerial trick that even the most experienced circus performer would not have dared, and she began to fall.

Chapter Four

"Help!" screamed Louise, and lurched toward the stairs.

But Chris and Janie were already standing there, staring up in panic at the body sailing toward them. Instinctively, they both grabbed for the skimming heap of maroon fabric. It was over in an instant, and Janie and Chris were sprawled onto the stairs themselves, part of a clumsy mélange of arms, legs, bodies, and seemingly endless yards of cloth.

"Ohhh," groaned Barbara, a deep, painful sound, as she and her full, flowing gown were gently disentangled. Jim Cooley rushed to her side and took charge.

There was a hubbub of concerned talk as everyone gathered around to look in awe at the still body. Janie and Chris got shakily to their feet. "Man, talk about flying objects," said Chris, laughing nervously. "That lady was really flying." He put an arm around a trembling Janie. Without speaking, she closed her eyes and leaned her head against his chest.

After a few seconds, the woman's eyes opened, and there was a grateful murmur from the onlookers. "Oh, my," she moaned, "where am I?"

"You took a tumble, Aunt Barbara," said Jim Cooley, "but these young people were able to cushion your fall. I'm going to call the ambulance to take you to the hospital." His wife Grace was now kneeling, head bowed, at the old woman's feet, as if revering a religious statue, while Stephanie Landry sat on the stairs at her side and cried quietly, her big hairdo trembling with the sobs.

The young man from the kitchen had somehow wangled his way through the little crowd to Barbara's other side, and was holding one of the fallen woman's hands. Barbara, her age-bleached hair now loose like a young girl's, looked at him as if he were an anchor in a storm. "Teddy," she whispered. The tone of her voice startled Louise. This plain young man was more than just kitchen help at Litchfield Falls Inn.

Then the old woman turned to the others and said more forcefully, "I do believe I am all right, my dears. No need to call an ambulance." The group continued to watch quietly. For a few minutes she simply reclined on the bottom stairs, then slowly sat up, gingerly checking herself for damage. "I am still here. And what's more, magically, I'm in one piece."

Stephanie's voice hitched as she said, "You're not hurt. I am so *grateful*." Her hazel eyes were wide with relief.

Barbara Seymour stroked Stephanie's hand. "Thank you, my dear. I'm fine, and you say it's because of these two young people." Her eyes went to each of them, first, Janie, then Chris. "How can I thank you both?"

The two teenagers demurred, and with assurances that, except for minor bruises, she was uninjured by her fall, Barbara allowed her nephew to help her to her feet. Accompanied by Grace and Stephanie, she disappeared down a dark, meandering hallway into the private recesses of the huge mansion.

Spooked by the near-tragedy, the guests went through a short period of catharsis. Only natural after a crowd has seen an accident, thought Louise, although this one ended with the victim unharmed. There was a buzz of relieved voices, commending Janie and Chris for acting so fast, speculating on what could have happened had they not been standing in that exact spot at the foot of the stairs.

"You are two very quick-thinking young people," commented Jim Cooley.

"Any time we can help." The tall Chris grinned, his blond hair falling boyishly in his eyes.

Then, to Louise's relief, Cooley broke up the chatter. He divided the guests into groups, signaled Teddy to come and help them, and sent them up on the elegant 1930's elevator to their rooms.

On the second floor, the elevator opened into a small uncluttered area, from which two long halls extended in opposite directions. The same charming woodwork and wallpaper was in evidence here, but without as much variety in the appointments, Louise noted. A solemn parade of paintings of the illustrious Seymour clan lined the walls. Handsome people, but way too grim-looking for her taste. Of course, she reasoned, everyone put the dull furnishings in the hallway, because nobody spends any time there.

The rooms had been updated, and each bedroom now had a modern bath with Jacuzzi. The replicated woodwork within the bedrooms was not quite as complex as it was in other places, but each room was done in a special decorating theme, and had its own name. Louise and Janie's was called the Bronze Room. It was done in muted orange and brown, with heavy mahogany furniture, including a high-standing, comfy-looking bed. On a marble-top side table was a bouquet of orange gazanias, yellow marguerite daisy, and white Queen Anne's lace, casually tucked into a brown-and-white antique pitcher.

First, Louise unpacked her travel pillow, the one creature comfort she couldn't do without, and tossed it onto the bed. The family had nicknamed it "Puny" because of its skimpy down filling. Since Janie had traveled light, Louise claimed the top of the dresser to lay out what Bill asserted made her suitcase weigh a ton: a few novels, two books of poetry, a half-dozen garden books, and the scripts for her *Gardening with Nature* shoot, which she would know by heart by tomorrow. She couldn't forget that for her, this weekend was work, as well as fun.

"Not a bad place," said Janie.

"It takes you back in time, doesn't it?"

Janie didn't answer. She had unzipped her bag and put it on the antique luggage rack, which apparently was to be the extent of the girl's unpacking. With lightning speed, she changed into shorts and T-shirt. She looked at her mother distractedly. "I'm unpacked. Chris and I are going to explore."

"You two were great down there," said Louise, sitting in a chair slipcovered in light yellow chintz. She was ready for a chat. "You probably saved that woman's life. Think of what would have happened if her head had hit the stairs."

"Yeah, it worked out," Janie said quickly, shifting from foot to foot like a runner anxious to start a race. "I'm glad—and Chris is glad. But we're tired of people talking about it so much. Like I said, I'm leaving now. Are you going to be *okay*?"

"Of course I'll be okay."

"All right," she said breezily. "Then g'bye." And she trotted out.

Louise rubbed her hands idly against the smooth chintz covering the chair arms. The girl, of course, did not have to hang around the room and make small talk with her mother—there was no need for that.

Louise began unpacking her suitcase, trying to deny the hurt she was feeling. Janie was growing further away from her every day. In desperation, she turned her thoughts away from her younger daughter, and remembered Melissa McCormick, whereupon a little curl of hope began to grow in her heart. Melissa, thirteen, daughter of an old friend, had lived through a trauma no teenager should have to face: She was virtually an orphan. She was coming to visit soon. And unlike Janie, she *needed* Louise.

Finished hanging up her clothes, Louise wandered into the hall and leaned over the railing. She spied Bill talking to someone below. Hearing something closer at hand, she automatically checked the view down each of the two upstairs hallways. There was a bank of windows along the right-hand hall with a long, carved bench beneath it. Beyond that point, darkness, as the hall bent to lead into another wing. In the other direction, a length of hall ended in a magnificent Georgian window with rounded top.

Two men emerged from the darkness to the right: Jim Cooley, holding a metal box under his arm, and a shorter man with a handsome head of hair and a youthful face. Louise guessed it was the missing Neil Landry. Cooley was speaking quietly, gesticulating in an angry way. Then he saw Louise, and hurried up to her, leaving his companion to turn and go back the way they'd come.

"Uh, better be careful going down those stairs."

She chuckled nervously. "That thought had already crossed my mind."

"I need to fix the carpeting—it's gotten loose. That's why my aunt fell." He spoke in a deep, gentle voice. With his large, calm presence, she could see he was a natural leader, a conveyor of reason in unreasonable situations. Opening a small toolbox, he descended the stairs ahead of her, kneeling to examine the rod that held the carpet in place. "Ah, just as I thought," he said. "The rod isn't secured properly."

Louise's proverbial antennae were up. Something was not right. Why, with a full house of guests expected, was the carpeting so dangerously loose in a house where every detail was managed so carefully?

She took a long, deep breath, trying to ward off the heart palpitations that she knew would come if she didn't calm down. Jim Cooley's mood also was grim, though he said little. With the expertise of a trained carpenter, he took a couple of nails and with a few accurate bangs, secured the offending rod back in its proper place. "There you are—all safe and sound."

She started to say something about her suspicions and then thought better of it. "I guess I'll go join my husband."

Bill was looking up at her now, beckoning her with an index finger. Louise walked slowly down the stairs. By the time she reached the marble floor of the foyer, she had been swept back a couple of centuries to when this house was first built, and ladies descended those stairs in long gowns.

Her husband's blue eyes were filled with merriment. "I saw that—walking like a grand lady down that staircase."

"Just getting in the historical mood," she said, tucking her arm in his. "Where's Nora?"

"Don't worry about Nora. She's come and gone."

"With Janie and Chris?"

"No, she's wandering the grounds with someone else. She should have waited, though, because it turns out those two women in the library"—he nodded to the open door of the large room where Sandy Post and Grace Cooley stood together, examining a book—"are real poetry buffs. They took a course in it together, apparently. Sandy's college career was stuffed in between spasmodic Olympic training and international travel. Grace takes a college course now and then, she informs me—and thus the two did meet. They're deep into—you'll never believe it—German Romantic poetry."

He opened his eyes wider, and she could tell something funny was coming next. "Like, you know," he said, in an imitation of Sandy Post's annoying mode of speech, "Goethe's influence on the poetry of Novalis, Goethe's metaphoric use of the colors blue and yellow—and how prescient *that* was, Novalis' influence on the work of Coleridge, and so on and so on." He shrugged. "What's more, they seem to know what they're talking about."

"I'm more familiar with the British Romantics."

"So is almost everyone," said her husband. He nodded his head toward the library. "People tend to look at German literature and art—even that genius, Goethe—through the lens of two world wars and Nazism; it doesn't do much for their luster. Keats and crowd are a heck of a lot more popular—though Grace Cooley told me that Novalis is gaining popularity, largely due to a book that's come out about his life."

Louise smiled at the inadvertent history lesson and they wandered out the front door. In the front yard, she paused to drink in the pungent smell of the tall hemlocks. "You know, this place is *quintessential* New England," she said, realizing as soon as she said it that she would release the historian in him again.

"Very true. The Beechers were its most famous residents, of course. Righteous, God-fearing reformers. Lyman Beecher was the pastor of the Congregational Church here, and Congregational churches really kicked booty—I mean, they really ran things: helped make the laws, wrote the school curriculum, and acted as moral arbiters for everyone."

"So I've learned."

"And Lyman had notable children: Harriet Beecher Stowe, who helped turn the country against slavery when she published *Uncle Tom's Cabin*. A daughter who was a well-known educator. Son Henry, the preacher, who sent guns, hidden in shipments of Bibles, to the abolitionists in Kansas."

"Yes—but isn't there a lurid story about Henry Beecher and—"

"Victoria Woodhull, the feminist. If you call being tried for adultery lurid, yes. It was probably the trial of the century back then. The funny thing is that it didn't hurt Henry's reputation very much. Now, Woodhull herself didn't believe in marriage; she brought the case against Beecher just to prove a point, because she thought adultery was quite all right. Reminds me a little of—" He cocked his head toward the grounds beyond the mansion.

"Nora?"

"Yeah. Nora. We both know she doesn't always take her marriage vows seriously."

"And that's a problem for me, Bill. It bothers me that Janie admires a woman like that." She clutched his arm more tightly. "Though I have come to love Nora dearly, don't think that I don't . . ."

"I know," he said, eyebrows arching, "just like Jesus loved Mary Magdalene."

"Oh, Bill, she's hardly a Mary Magdalene . . ."

"All the easier to forgive her, huh? Well, don't worry about Janie. Both she and Chris understand his mother, and that doesn't mean they approve."

She looked up at him. "How on earth did you know that?"

He tried not to look smug. "The thing you have to remember is that I've had long talks with our daughter, too—until she recently began not *wanting* to have long talks. We discussed this very thing." He tossed another glance over his shoulder. "By the way, Nora and the professor just disappeared down that back hill."

"The *professor*? She went off with that professor? Isn't the horse barn back there?"

"They're only *walking,* Louise. Anyway, she's a big girl, and she's discreet." A grin broke over his face. "That means they'll close the barn door first."

Her tone was rebuking. "Don't tease me."

"Then stop worrying: This is supposed to be a vacation. I'm hoping you'll get into the romantic spirit of this place. Then, we can get Janie and Chris to take off some evening and you and I will have a few hours alone in your bedroom."

"Hours?"

"If there aren't hours, I'll take minutes—say fifteen?"

She laughed and brushed her lips against his cheek. "Hardly long enough, my dear, to enjoy your carnal charms, but I suppose we could manage it."

"And no more fussing," he told her. "I saw you conjuring up dark thoughts when you stood there with Jim Cooley and saw that loosened stair rod."

"You believe that woman's fall was just an accident."

"My dear, I sincerely hope so or this weekend isn't going to be fun for either one of us. Now let's do a little exploring, ourselves. I can hear the river from here, and I want to see if it's as good as it sounds."

Bells, Burbles, and Rustles: The Sound a Garden Makes

THERE IS A YEAR-ROUND rhythm to a garden. In springtime, it is filled with promise, as whorls and spikes of leaves in colors from chartreuse to deep red emerge from the ground. In summer, it is as bright as the palette of an artist, with flowers in full-blown color. It remains a continued comfort in the fall as hues slowly fade; seed heads and flower heads in peach and tan and jet black are echoes of the garden's former splendor. And then winter comes: Baby evergreens, red and yellow dogwood, the grays of *Artemisia, Eryngium,* and *Santolina,* and the naked arms of woody perennials give it form and beauty.

But what is missing from this garden picture? Something not seen, but heard. For

there is another quality needed in a garden that few of us think about. That is, the *sound* of the garden. Through all four seasons, sounds can give our garden a charm that will draw us to it like a magnet.

The chirping of birds, the persistent call of the whippoorwill, the gentle hum of the bees, and the flutter of hummingbird wings are sounds we delight to hear when we garden in summer. And we hear the plants themselves. The rattle of the leaves of the aspen and the cottonwood. The sighing of the pines. The restless agitation of the bamboo branches. The gossipy chatter of the low-slung sedge—and even the rustling of seedpods we leave behind in fall.

When nature's helpers have fled for the winter and noisy leaves have fallen from the trees, we can still create sound. One way is to install a canvas shade on the porch. When it catches breezes, the flapping noise is reminiscent of a ship's sail fluttering in the wind. Such a shade can stay out through the year. Care should be taken to anchor it at the bottom so that it does not wear unduly.

Antique cowbells hanging on the patio or garden fence are another sound-maker, but cowbells are hard to come by. Chimes are better: They have long been at home in the garden. Some people are content with a cheap set of bells that clang pleasurably when shaken. Relatively new are wood-crowned sets of chimes available in tones from the massive base set costing several hundred dollars to a small set ringing in the highest registers for less than thirty dollars. Kept under the cover of a porch, these chimes can stay outside and herald changes in the weather. Even fancier are cast-brass "wind" bells. They are mounted on a stone base and brave the weather, catching the rain in their neat, round little bell cups.

Some prefer old-fashioned models: wooden wind chimes, funky-looking hanging shells, or glass chimes.

But the wind does not always blow and fill our desire for constant garden sound. Only falling water, in either a fountain or waterfall, can do that. Its sound is contentment itself, and on the quietest day, the noise of water falling can mask the clamor of passing autos and make us think we're in a place far removed from urban life. Both the height of the fall, its volume, and what it strikes—stone, wood, or water—will affect its pitch and resonance. Even the smallest homeowner-created fountain, however, will supply a pleasant cacophony.

Circulating fountains can be built rather simply and housed in a traditional fountain, in a large rock that has been drilled out to hold the fountainhead, or in a custom- or home-built backyard waterfall/pool. For about five hundred dollars, the gardener can buy a motor, PVC to line the pool, and enough rock to fashion a six-foot-long water pool with small recirculating falls at the end. Ideally, this and any other water feature should be incorporated in the original garden design, but life is not always programmed so neatly. It is quite easy to add fountains and small waterfalls and

have them seem to have been there forever. It involves the art of joinery, in which we either integrate the different garden materials, or contrast them. To integrate a natural little waterfall, for instance, a small berm could be constructed near the existing garden; the waterfall would emerge out of the side of this small hill. Graceful cascades of ornamental grass are excellent for naturalizing the area around a water feature.

Though some people construct larger fountains and waterfalls, this size would overpower the average yard. A small one is enough. With it, we can enter a sounding garden whose watery clatter shuts out the noises of the everyday world.

Chapter Five

"IT NEVER HURTS FOR a place like this to serve good food," said Chris, shoving his tall, rangy frame back from the table on the veranda.

"That's the understatement of the week," snapped Jeffrey Freeling. "This food is four stars according to *The New York Times*."

Bill, ever the peacemaker, said, "*I* didn't know that, but I'd gladly have thrown my two cents' worth of commendations in, if the kitchen hadn't already heard them from the critics."

The professor, having escorted Nora on a two-hour journey up and down the hills of the property, had joined their
party for dinner, making it six. He was an aloof man, distracted
and almost crabby. Louise could see her husband was doing
his best to extricate what civility he could from the noted
academic.

But the atmosphere was certainly propitious: Newly arrived
clouds were flying picturesquely over a bright moon in the New
England sky, giving a sense of electric movement in the firma-
ment. Down on the veranda, handsome hurricane lamps cast
romantic shadows on baskets overflowing with blooms in mauve
and purple, dramatically accented with blue-leaved, scarlet-
flowered 'Queen of the Nile' nasturtiums. In the background,
Chopin preludes could be heard.

It was definitely the people who were the problem. There
were three tables of six, plus a dozen or so smaller tables for
outside dinner guests. By virtue of their late arrival, Mark and
Sandy Post, Rod and Dorothy Gasparra, and Bebe Hollowell
were forced to sit together at a larger table. The third table was
occupied with Barbara Seymour's relatives and their friends:
the Cooleys, Storms, and Landrys.

Though all was peaceful on the surface, Louise noticed that
each group seemed edgy. Bebe Hollowell, like all the women,
was dressed up, wearing an attractive sleeveless white dress to
emphasize her dark tan. Unfortunately, from the moment she
sat down, she overwhelmed the conversation at her table, talking primarily about her deceased husband, Ernie. The tension of
the Posts and the Gasparras was evident. Bebe appeared to be
everyone's cross to bear this weekend—both her excessive
talking and her cigarettes.

Jim Cooley had a stern look on his face which seemed to
dampen conversation at his table, Louise noted. But while
Frank and Fiona Storm, as well as Stephanie and Neil Landry,
were clearly subdued by Jim's mood, Jim's frail-looking wife
rose to the occasion, quietly carrying the conversation on her

own. And she was talking, if Louise was hearing right, about flower metaphors in poetry. ". . . The blue flower, for instance, was the symbol of yearning in German Romantic literature," Louise overheard her say.

Louise was sure the reason for Jim's bad humor was the presence of the skulking Neil Landry, who was joining the group for the first time since Barbara Seymour fell down the staircase.

Sighing, Louise took another bite of the scrumptious meal. Even at their own table, Dr. Freeling's formal manner discouraged a free flow of conversation and squelched the usually talkative Janie and Chris.

When Louise questioned him about his projects in plant genetic engineering, the scientist would touch only on generalities. "Mrs. Eldridge," he told her quietly, raising a graceful hand to adjust his glasses, "I am a scientist. Surely you can't expect me to reveal what's going on in our laboratories. There are some projects to alter major crops, and thus deeply impact the American economy. It's premature, and indiscreet, to talk about them, since it can affect all sorts of things . . ."

". . . even crop futures, I suppose," she said breezily. "It's funny how forthcoming a business like Monsanto Chemicals will be: It's heavily into this field. I'm just anxious to do a program on it for my show, and I can't do it without specifics."

Freeling smiled in what Louise thought was a rather supercilious way. "I'm sure that Monsanto will tell you everything you need to know."

"And that implies that your work is so secret that you can't even mention it."

"It does, doesn't it," he said, and then turned to Nora, who was sitting to his right. She had on a show-stopping red silk dress. As if to be sure he was rid of the inquiring busybody, Freeling bent deliberately toward Nora and asked her more about her poetry.

Louise had seldom felt so rebuffed.

Janie had drifted away from the dinner table, but now she returned, swinging back into her chair with blond hair and light pleated skirt twirling after her. Louise noticed she had been talking to the personable young employee, Teddy, who, it turned out, ran the dining room. He made it a point to introduce himself fully—first name and last. Teddy Horton. This cowlick-haired individual looked as if he should be munching on a hayseed: He was straight out of a Norman Rockwell magazine cover. Yet he had handled the crowd with the panache of a Parisian maître d'hôtel. Now, he followed Janie's movements with his eyes, and Louise suspected that it was a case of love at first sight.

"Guess what, folks?" Janie told them. "After dessert and coffee, there's going to be dancing, right out here in the evening air."

"Good," said Freeling. "I like to dance." *Ah,* thought Louise, *the man has an Achilles' heel, a genuine human weakness: He likes to dance.*

The professor also had his eye on Janie, not covetously, but as if she were the image of someone he knew. Louise suspected he was the kind of man who had had a wife who died young, rather like one of the great tragic figures in literature whose true love died of tuberculosis.

Yet if she was wrong and the man was a bachelor, she had certainly caught a glimmer of why: Though attractive enough, Freeling had an irksome quality about him. It was almost as if he wanted her to dislike him. Conversely, he was finally beginning to open up to the others, especially Bill and Chris. Maybe he was more comfortable talking to men—but if so, why had he spent two hours with Nora?

As the twilight deepened, the tables were cleared and pushed to the side. Inside the large adjacent sunroom, someone turned on 1940's music that reminded Louise of World War II movies. She could hardly imagine the impact of that war, but her mother had told her how the music had somehow unified people emotionally. Through multiple speakers the songs flowed out to them: "I Had the Craziest Dream," "Don't Get Around Much Anymore," "Sentimental Journey," and "Lili Marlene." The music worked its magic on her, too, bringing tears to her eyes.

"Aha," noted her observant husband, "the music's got to you."

She clutched his hand. "I feel a great need to kiss you." And she leaned over and pressed her lips gently to his. But their romantic moment was interrupted by a clamor of greetings at the next table. Barbara Seymour had arrived to join her family group. The guests gave a little round of applause as the tall woman entered the porch area, wearing a gleaming blue taffeta dress that was another stroke of good fashion sense for a woman playing the part of historical dame.

"This is a little sick, isn't it?" Louise murmured to her husband.

"Sick—why?"

"To clap for her. It's as if we're celebrating—as if Barbara is some kind of Evel Knievel. She didn't cavort through the air off those stairs for our pleasure."

"Honey, that's not it: Everyone is happy because she's okay."

As the mansion owner sat down with her family, she gave an especially warm wave to the day's heroes, Chris and Janie. Louise noticed Neil soon excused himself from the table, after appearing to have a problem looking the matriarch in the eye. He hurried down the stairs of the veranda and disappeared into the cricket-loud night. Shortly after this quick departure, the Storms left the family table and joined her and Bill. Quite right, Louise thought: That family needs to talk things over.

The music swelled, and the action began. The professor snared the lady in red and led her to the dance floor. Soon they were locked in an embrace, moving slowly to "These Foolish Things." Janie and Chris joined them there, awkward, but enjoying the close bodily contact. In the shadows, Louise could see the earnest Teddy, standing with an arm hooked snugly around a veranda pillar, as if he wished it were Janie. His eyes were riveted on the girl; he might have been dying for a dance, but he knew it wasn't appropriate. She was beyond his reach. The princess and the commoner.

Louise's eyes widened in alarm as she watched Nora, her smooth dark hair falling over one cheek as she practically swooned in the arms of the professor. For his part, he looked quite dashing, those weird glasses tucked away somewhere, his sandy hair falling casually across his forehead, his eyes half closed. Heads turned as he gracefully guided his alluring dance partner through the slow two-step.

Was Nora feeling the chemistry that was evident even to the wallflowers? Was she going to yield to temptation again?

Stop it, Louise thought to herself. *As Bill said, Nora's a grown woman and I am not her keeper. The only ones I have to keep an eye on this weekend are Janie and Chris, and that shouldn't be too hard, since Janie is sleeping in the same room with me.*

"They make a nice pair, don't they?" said Frank Storm in his deep, mellow voice.

"Indeed, they do," she agreed hoarsely. Then she turned determinedly toward Frank and tried to forget the potential waywardness of her friend. "But now tell me more about your work at Higher Directions."

Just then, Bebe Hollowell tapped Bill on the shoulder and requested a dance. Bill was a prince of a man: He would do his best to make whole this flawed woman. Bebe, who must have weighed in at two hundred pounds, danced as lightly as a feather.

Louise adjusted herself comfortably in the chair as Frank opened his story. He and Jim had joined forces ten years ago to set up a unique school for troubled kids. They had become acquainted in graduate school studying education. Both were religiously inclined, and thought an ethics-based high school would help the difficult cases who often dropped out. "We started on a shoestring," said Frank, "but with substantial help from people like Barbara Seymour, we set up our first school in Brooklyn. And it succeeded.

"The school's philosophy," he said, "is an amalgam, but it's all laid out in our motivational manual. There's an element that some call 'tough love.' We are absolutely ruthless about disciplining people who won't follow the rules, or who exhibit disloyalty."

"Disloyalty," repeated Louise.

"Yes. From our research, we've found that loyalty and obedience to a group are the two most important factors in getting kids through the teen years."

"And what does disloyalty include?"

"Our creed bans cheating of any kind, premarital sex, homosexuality, adultery . . . But the message is presented positively, not mired in negative language."

Soon she was sitting on the edge of her chair, arguing vigorously about their "one-strike-and-you're-out" policy. "I think young people need chance after chance. Tough love or not, it would take more than one mistake for me to kick a child out of my school."

"Oh, but the child has plenty of forewarning of what's going to happen."

She pursed her lips and tried to think of a rejoinder that would adequately display her disapproval while still being fair to Frank. He explained that the schools were incredibly sensitive to their young clients' educational needs—much more so than almost any public school, for instance. They employed methods like mental imaging to quicken the learning pace. And they had been so successful. Who was she to criticize their way of doing things?

"And, of course, when punishment is needed," Frank said, giving her a calm smile, "the punishment fits the crime, as the old song goes."

"That sounds like the code of Hammurabi to me—an eye for an eye, a tooth for a tooth."

"The ancients understood many things," he said solemnly. As he went on talking, she realized her shoulders ached from sitting forward in rapt attention. Her mind was numb from an overabundance of information. But the discomfort was worth it, for now she had some insight into the enigmatic Frank and Jim. They had developed a nondenominational, evangelical creed called, fittingly enough, "Higher Directions," just like the school. It was a loose church structure set up when the first school opened. No doubt about it: Frank and Jim were true believers, in the tradition of the evangelicals of old. Of course, she reflected, evangelicals had burned witches in Salem, Massachusetts, just a hundred miles or so to the north, and stirred up national religious revivals across the United States. Powerful people, those evangelicals.

And the lovely Fiona Storm believed just as strongly. She chimed in occasionally to add to Frank's earnest words, gesturing with graceful hands that flashed with a large diamond. "We are making these youth into *new people,*" she declared. The woman might have deferred to Frank earlier, but now she was having her say. It was a brief speech about her "raison d'être," as she called it. "I was raised on Osage Avenue in Philadelphia. It was a deprived childhood, let me assure you. But someone back then gave me a chance: In my case, it was the Sisters of Mercy. But that chance enabled me to boost myself out of the ghetto and transform myself into a successful, contributing member of society."

Louise looked at the woman. She was so attractive that Louise couldn't imagine her remaining in a deprived environment for long. Movies or television would have claimed her, had not Frank Storm come along first—and even if she weren't as smart as she obviously was.

Perhaps Fiona read her eyes, for there was a barrier there: She did not like Louise. Maybe Louise was too upper-middle-class? Too associated with the establishment? Her husband *was* with the State Department. Or was it because Louise was connected to the great Mammon television? "I'm *part* of television, so sure, I watch television," Louise had confessed to the woman. "I watch everything, just to see what's being offered to the public."

"Wouldn't it be better to spend your time on more serious pursuits?" Fiona had asked.

The conversation, Louise realized now, had been like a boxing match. Why hadn't she just sat there and listened, instead of arguing every point?

Now Fiona concluded her little speech: "So I made a chance for myself and I didn't muff it. And that's what we do for these kids: We allow them to have a chance. Then, if they blow it, it's blown. There's no room for—"

"Failures," finished Louise.

"Yes, failures," said Fiona coolly. Then, with a lift of her magnificent chin, the woman signified she was done. Frank picked up the promotional pitch again, talking about their plans for a fourth school. Putting on her most interested face, Louise let her attention wander to the riveting discussion at the next table.

In a quick, sideways glance, she saw three dominant faces, highlighted by the hurricane lamp as if in a picture by Rembrandt. Barbara Seymour looked serene and happy: Tonight, she must be particularly grateful just to be alive. The light touched dramatically on Jim's angular features and Neil Landry's bland countenance and perfect hair. Stephanie Landry and Grace Cooley were leaning back in their chairs, their faces outside the halo of light.

The conversation was a verbal thrust and parry: the two men and the timid Stephanie against Barbara Seymour. Grace was silent. Louise heard something about a development. Something about how the waterfall would enhance the property so that profits would be "at the maximum." Something about acting *"now."*

". . . an idea we're throwing out for discussion, but with a pressing time frame . . ." Jim was saying.

". . . a plan Stephanie and Jim and I have developed over the years, when you no longer want to go to all the trouble to run this place," said Neil.

". . . no terrible need for new housing that *I've* seen," she heard Barbara reply.

". . . perfect for when you need to quit all this work . . . and one of the homes, a prime home, just for you," said Stephanie.

". . . still thinking of turning it over to the Connecticut Trust for Historic Preservation," said Barbara.

Dead silence from the others.

Louise didn't need much more to realize that this property, with its magnificent acreage, was being discussed as a site for a new housing development—or, alternatively, for remanding to the state of Connecticut. It was quite apparent that Jim Cooley, as well as Neil and Stephanie, favored development over deeding the property to the state government—prosperity over posterity. She hadn't heard Grace utter an opinion, one way or the other.

No one but an aging woman stood between these heirs and a rich haul of money.

Now the niggly little suspicion in Louise's mind had substance: There was a motive for that stair carpet to have been loosened with malicious forethought. And since the incident, Jim Cooley had treated Neil like a misbehaving schoolboy. But now Neil was back in the bosom of the family. Maybe Jim simply needed Neil to be on his side in this debate over the disposition of the mansion. It sounded like a moment when all family votes would be counted, from good guys and from guys who weren't so good.

Chapter Six

LOUISE BIT INTO AN after-dinner mint, and savored the cool rush inside her mouth. Why was she fussing about a family con job on a wealthy old woman? It happened every day, she was sure, somewhere in America. But it was depressing to see it close-up. On the eve of a difficult location shoot, where they would be short-staffed, and she would have more responsibility than usual, the last thing she needed was to be depressed. For the camera never lied: Either she would come across as alert, focused, and prepared, or not. No sense in getting bogged down in someone else's problems.

Resolutely, she turned her attention back to the dance floor. It was not the usual scene, with soporific partners lazing in each other's arms. Instead, it was rife with tension. Each of the dancers seemed to be painfully aware of the others, creating nervous currents and cross-currents, furtive glances, and careful jockeying for position on the floor. As she watched, Louise remembered reading about fish behavior: The more robust females swim in the middle of the school, waiting to be fertilized by male fish. And there were Nora and Janie and the luscious Sandy Post, swirling confidently in the middle of the room, with men spread out around them.

Everyone had switched partners —well, almost everyone. Chris was now dancing with his mother, who was guiding him through the old-fashioned steps that suited the music of the evening. Yet he kept one eye on Freeling and Janie, while Freeling had at least half his attention on the beautiful Nora as he wheeled Janie about the floor.

Mark and Sandy still had their arms clasped around each other, like a little romantic island unto themselves, but the illusion was spoiled when Mark shot suspicious looks at the agile-footed professor. *What on earth is going on between those two?* Louise wondered.

Teddy had apparently given up hope of ever getting closer to Janie, knocked off work, and gone home. Somehow, Louise missed him; he seemed like a grounded, sensible person.

As another tune ended, Freeling pulled the delighted Bebe Hollowell to her feet for a dance to Glenn Miller's "String of Pearls." The woman danced like a pro, and together, the unlikely pair would have won any dance contest. Bill, with a little urging from Louise, took Nora and swung her around the floor. The Storms joined them and, like Bebe, made the rest of them look like amateurs. Fiona had an amused smile on her face, as if to say, "We're fulfilling your expectations that black people can really shake it."

The next song started, and Jeffrey Freeling was suddenly standing over her. "Shall we dance, Mrs. Eldridge?"

"I would like that."

Once on the dance floor, she realized it was his height and long arms that made his partners seem so completely enveloped, so safe. It seemed quite natural to lay her head against his shoulder as they swayed to a syrupy song called "Those Little White Lies." She pressed her nose into his jacket comfortably, then jerked back as an odious scent filled her nostrils: Jeffrey smelled of rotten eggs.

Out of the corner of her eye, she could see that her husband had been captured by Bebe Hollowell again, and now Louise could see the woman had a tendency to lead. What was the sense of being a divine dancer if one emasculated one's partner? She found herself loosening her muscles and relaxing more completely into Jeffrey Freeling's arms.

Louise looked into the professor's eyes. "You're quite an operator," she said.

He smiled down at her, as if his rudeness at dinner had only been in fun. "You mean to say, I'm quite a dancer."

"I'm not sure what I mean, as a matter of fact. By the way, it's unfortunate that you don't seem to . . . relate to the Posts. Do you know them well?"

Freeling turned frosty again, and said in a clipped tone, "Mark was a student of mine, and his wife—she was on campus at the same time. Let's just say that some unpleasant things come up sometimes in academia, and that was the case with—them. I shall say no more."

Her mind raced to fill in the gaps. Had Mark been accused of some wrongdoing? Was he guilty? Or could it be that the professor had gotten himself in hot water, dating a student? That probably happened all the time in his little world of academia. After all, Sandy was an attractive little package, thought Louise, one of those "perfect" pretty girls that others envied in high school. She was world-class in sports, an able mountaineer and a fine shot with a rifle, and probably just as adept in bed. In that instant, Louise realized with a guilty start how unkind she was being to a woman who really hadn't asked to be born small, blond, and beautiful.

"I'm sorry I asked," she said to Jeffrey. "It's not my business, and unfortunately, I tend to get too nosy about things in general. Maybe it's because I'm always looking for gardening stories."

He slowed their dancing so that they were merely rocking back and forth in time to the music. "You are a perplexing woman, Louise—but interesting. You know, if you contact me at my office on campus, I'll be happy to talk to you about my work." He grinned diabolically. "All about how I implant foreign genes into plants, as I did with the Sacred Blood iris, and come up with a transgenic plant . . ."

"You mean, a plant with a new gene implanted . . ."

"Yes. In the case of this plant, a red gene from the maize plant was shot into the nucleus of the iris—as well as other genes."

"How do you do it?"

"We start with a segment of the peduncle of the iris . . ."

"Peduncle."

"It's the portion of the stem just below the ovary. We take that piece and culture it, causing it to form a callus, or thickened tissue. The callus is divided up and put in a solution, so that you have this cell suspension of iris, with the possibility of thousands of plants. Then, into this cell suspension, the red gene, and other genes, are inserted. This particular plant has been further engineered both to have a spicy smell and to have a later blooming period than most irises."

"That's produced by other genes?"

"Yes. The one that affects blooming is probably more significant. Now we have an iris that starts flowering with the roses in

65

June, and continues right into July. It is truly superb. Oh, I'll be happy to tell you all the nefarious things I do each day in that laboratory."

"I'd love that."

"Sorry about before—I just didn't feel like being that agreeable at the table, with everyone listening in."

"You seem so cautious about things, Dr. Freeling—"

"Jeffrey, please."

"Jeffrey. Do people really steal each other's work on these projects?"

"I suppose they could. People do steal each other's patented plants. I've heard some growers are pollen thieves—they actually go to someone else's experimental flower beds and snitch pollen, the better to grow things themselves. And I've heard more than one story about a horticulturalist who has stolen patented roses. They sneak into someone's greenhouse, strip the buds from an exquisite patented rose, take them back to their place, graft them onto understock, and grow them themselves."

Louise smiled. "It's a strange world. I see you're more agreeable than you want that world to know."

"Something like that," he answered seriously. "It doesn't pay to wear your heart on your sleeve—or to give away your whole game at the drop of the first card. Life is funny—some people are dealt a very poor hand and deserve to get a better one."

She laughed. Yet she was surprised that this direct-talking professor had suddenly switched to metaphor, as if he were speaking in code, hiding secrets that he longed to reveal. "You mean, put down a few discards and draw a few new ones from the deck."

"Do you play poker?"

"Bill does. I just eavesdrop."

He chose to take even this seriously. "I used to eavesdrop on *life*. These days, I'm disinclined to do so. I want to live it." And he swept her back into the rhythm of the dance.

"Mmm," she said appreciatively, "whatever that means. Maybe that's why you dance so well."

By the time she was escorted back to her seat, she knew why the ladies liked the professor. He had a certain way about him. But he definitely didn't give away his game. If he had always been a bachelor, it had been his choice.

Bill had dutifully danced with each of the women at least once—Bebe, several times. He gave Louise a wry look. "Now I suppose you want me to dance with you after your round with Astaire."

"No, not if you don't want to, dear."

"Good. Then I think I'll just rest my tootsies for tomorrow's hike up Bear Mountain with Janie and Chris and Jeffrey."

"Hike, my foot, Bill. You promised me you would come on the garden tour . . ."

"Oh, yeah. Well, there goes the hike."

"Honey, I'm sorry. I thought I told you that the crew will be small—they could use your help." Suddenly she clutched his sleeve and pointed. "See what I mean—the man's a natural."

The professor was dancing with Jim Cooley's wife. Grace, diminutive and almost childlike in his arms, had assumed the position: head on Freeling's shoulder, eyes closed, body sliding in unison with his when they dipped. "Women don't even have to bother with conversation. It's all movement and music and rhythm."

"Looks kind of lovey-dovey to me."

"It's not that: It's something about the guy—he's not nearly as gruff as he sounded at the table."

"Face it, Louise," said her husband, "you just think he's cute."

The music ended, and everyone adjourned to their separate tables. Louise heard Grace softly thanking her partner for the dance.

The Gasparras had been sitting quietly during the dancing phase of the evening, listening to the music and the conversation. But now they stood uncomfortably at the edge of the room as if they were about to leave. As Professor Freeling was leaving the dance floor, Rod Gasparra stepped in front of him, looking as if he might grab Freeling's lapels. Verbally, he did. "I've heard tonight, Dr. Freeling, that you were one of the ones."

"One of the ones," Freeling repeated archly. "And what on earth do you mean by that?"

Gasparra shook a finger at him. "You're one of the ones that worked on the Iris of the Sacred Blood!"

"Hmh," said Freeling, repositioning his wire-frame glasses on his nose and giving Rod Gasparra a close look. "So that makes me 'one of the ones.' Just what beef do you have with me? My work is in the laboratory, doing research on a plant with a simple genus, *Arabidopsis thaliana,* though my doctoral students and I developed the Sacred Blood iris. We derived its name from the fact that the color of its flowers resembles arterial blood. Tell me exactly why this impinges upon you."

"I am a grower. And I did years of work on a red iris. Work that was stolen."

"*I* see what's at stake: your purported 'ownership' of the Sacred Blood iris. Oh, come on, Gasparra, you're not really going to accuse me—"

"But you must have been in on it!"

Freeling was much taller than Gasparra; this, together with his beard, gave him a greater masculine presence. Looming over the other man, he said, "I came here for a weekend's relaxation, and certainly not to get into an imbroglio with a stranger." He arched an eyebrow ominously and jabbed a finger into Gasparra's chest. "You well know, sir, that there is such a thing as forensic *botany*. PCR and RFLP analyses not only help catch rapists and killers, they can also be used to prove that we did not use your plant in our experimental work. Therefore, if I were you, I would take those charges to the proper authorities, and stop exhibiting this penchant for street fighting. After all, this is a country hotel. You might have brought a few manners with you."

"You insulting . . ." spat out Gasparra, and pulled back a muscular arm with fisted hand ready to strike. Only his wife Dorothy's strong hands on his shoulder stopped him from following through. Gradually, she eased him off to a corner of the veranda, where she quietly calmed him down. Louise was glad trouble had been avoided. She knew that growers were strong from hours of painstaking hand labor in their gardens—and she would hate to see Gasparra's temper put to the test.

Freeling turned around and surveyed the rest of the guests, apparently surprised they were listening, though it was impossible to ignore the loud exchange. For some reason, he now appeared to Louise not a stuffy academic, but an almost rakish figure. Barbara Seymour had risen slowly from her chair, the candlelight flickering under her chin but leaving her face in darkness.

The professor put out a large, graceful hand. "No, Miss Seymour, don't trouble yourself. This can be taken care of in another way, in another place." His gaze passed over each one of them as he said, "And now I bid you all a very good night. I'll see you tomorrow morning. I hope someone besides me wants to climb Bear Mountain. I hear it has a challenging pitch on the north side." Without waiting for replies, he rapidly departed the veranda.

"That's one way to ruin a good time," complained Bebe Hollowell, giving the Gasparras a disgusted look. With a damper thrown on the party mood, the crowd began breaking up. Louise noted that the red nasturtiums in the mauve bouquets were wilting. Their perfect round petals now drooped onto the floorboards like Dalí's melting watches.

Bill yawned. "It's time for an old fogy like me to go to my bachelor's bed anyway. As one who just flew in from Europe, I'm bushed."

Louise gave her husband a nostalgic glance, missing him already. "You're right, darling. Tomorrow we have a million things to do." To Janie she said, "Come on, roommate, let's go to bed."

Nora remained seated. "I think I'll stay here and have a quiet smoke."

Chris gave her an inquiring look. "Are you sure, Mom?"

"Don't worry—I'll be along very soon," she answered.

It had been an interesting evening of questions without answers, strains between people that were not obvious at first, and warnings of possible trouble to come. Louise hoped that she could at least get a good night's sleep, to quiet her overactive mind and rest her tired body.

She threw a last glance at Nora, a lonely figure sitting at the table, smoking. She sat erect, obviously wide-awake—the flame in the hurricane lamp diminishing faster than she was. Suddenly Louise was quite sure the woman was waiting for the return of Jeffrey Freeling. With the way they were dancing, it would be no surprise if the assignation had been planned right there on that sexually charged dance floor. Yet there was more than one woman who would have given Jeffrey her heart tonight—based on his magnificent dancing alone.

Chapter Seven

Louise woke up with a start. She realized she should be sleeping, but instead she was crumpled into a fetal position, as if defending herself against the demons of the night. Her shoulders felt as if they were encased in steel. Seeking comfort, she reached out to touch Bill, but her hand came upon a soft thigh, and not her husband's flat, hard hip. And then she remembered where she was: in a country hotel, on a country weekend, sleeping in a high, antique bed next to her daughter.

She rolled over and looked at her watch, straightening her body. Its illuminated dial read two A.M. She knew there was more than one reason she was wide-awake after less than two hours of sleep: too much riding in a car, no warm, familiar husband beside her, and a gathering worry in her mind about what was going on at Litchfield Falls Inn. The thought of getting up when the night had hardly begun was dispiriting, rather like being the only person left on the entire planet. Without the soothing presence of another living human—without Bill.

Yet she desperately needed to stretch her muscles. Moving carefully to the edge of the high bed so as not to wake Janie, she slid down until her feet touched the wide floorboards. A few seconds' search and her feet had located her slippers. She put on her robe and quietly unlocked the door. But the darkness in the hallway unsettled her. It was as black as a tomb. Her eyes wide with trepidation, she considered crawling back into the safety of the bed. Until something inside her—that little voice that cried "Coward!" and more than once had driven her into deep trouble—made her continue out into the unlit hall.

Wouldn't a hotel have hall lights burning during the night? She couldn't even see the banister that encircled the upper hall or the precipitous twenty-foot drop beyond it. She caught her breath and went forward, edging her way along the inside wall of the hall. She became intimately acquainted with the inn's fine carpentry as she ran her fingers silently over each recessed doorway. Finally she reached the little bay with the window bench. Quietly, she sat down and only then began to relax, her increased wakefulness making her more ready to handle the isolation of the hotel at two in the morning.

She half-closed her eyes and went into her miniexercise regime, extending her arms and twirling them in little circular motions. Next, she concentrated on neck stretches; this would prepare her for the challenge of spending six more hours in a bed not her own.

Tonight, even Puny the pillow hadn't been comfort enough, for she was worrying. Worrying about Barbara Seymour, about Rod Gasparra, and about her friend Nora. Broodingly, she reviewed the ten hours since they'd arrived at the inn. The gradual getting-acquainted. First the newlywed Posts, then the grumpy Gasparras. The Cooleys—or at least Jim; she had hardly exchanged a word with Grace. Frank and Fiona Storm, solid citizens. The interesting Jeffrey Freeling. And just peripherally, the contentious Bebe Hollowell. She had exchanged no words at all with Barbara's niece Stephanie, or her husband Neil, and hardly more than "hello" with their hostess.

That baby-faced Neil Landry was a bad apple, she thought. But how bad? Maybe tomorrow, if she had time, she'd investigate. Just a little.

One more stretch, and she would be ready to go back to bed.

Then a door opened quietly. And then another. Louise had been focusing on her sore neck and her thoughts. Now, her eyes popped open wide and she strained to see. The darkness thwarted her. She could hear, though, hear *and* smell a faint rush, as if someone had slipped by and left behind the faintest fragrance. Was it a woman, or was that a man's aftershave? Now Louise thought she heard yet another door open—and another. This was becoming ridiculous. Were all the guests from the upstairs bedrooms going to congregate out here? Surely she was imagining things.

Then a little sound, far down the hall—a door closing again, perhaps. She was sure this time. And then a rather loud thump that made her catch her breath, and a gentle creaking that told her someone was creeping down the stairs. Trembling slightly, she put a hand on either side of the bench, prepared to run, if necessary, from whatever was out there in the dark.

For a few moments, there was complete silence. Her heartbeat slowed and her body felt more under control. Then, not more than twenty feet away: a yearning moan, a lover's moan.

Were two people embracing, perhaps thrusting their bodies together and making one out of two, in mankind's eternal desire for procreation? In the *hall*? Surely not. And yet these were explicit noises, with a sense of movement. Next came muffled, low-pitched murmurs. And then silence again.

Her eyes fought against the dark, adjusting until she thought she could see two heads faintly silhouetted in a window at one end of the hall. Heads bent toward each other in fervent conversation. Then, a movement of one, the other coming forward to meet it, a hand following to grasp the other person's shoulder.

With a shock, she realized it was the silhouette of two men embracing.

Then the shapes disappeared. Had they seen her there?

Louise sat frozen on the window seat. Things had happened here tonight, but what, she didn't know. It reminded her of the Restoration comedies she had read in an English class at Northwestern—ribald comedies where lovers hid behind screens and darted in and out of bedrooms for assignations.

Of course, she thought, Nora! She must be among this midnight traffic: the most romantic woman she knew—a woman unencumbered with middle-class hang-ups about sex. But it was at least two hours ago that Nora had been seated at that table, perchance awaiting a lover. Had it taken her this long to connect? And it was not Nora, but two men who had shared a passionate moment together at the window, and were probably together now in one of the rooms. Had just the two of them made all that noise?

As quietly as she could, she returned to her and Janie's bedroom and closed the soundproof door. Louise felt the lump in the bed. The girl slept the tranquil sleep of the confirmed heroine, who this past day had helped save an old woman from grief. As she moved past the bed, her foot noisily bumped a chair and Janie emitted a tiny, quick snort, then resumed the normal cadenced breathing of deep sleep.

Louise went to the windows and shoved aside the heavy draperies for an instant. As she suspected, it was raining out there in the almost moonless night. Bad news, perhaps, for tomorrow's location shoots for *Gardening with Nature*. It wasn't a heavy rain, but it was creating a kind of mist in the air that obscured the Georgian lines of the mansion and the neat white outbuildings beyond it, turning them into ghostlike apparitions. A shudder went through her, and she pulled the draperies closed.

Her nerves were so jangled that she knew she would be awake for hours, rethinking what she had seen—and heard. The sound of romantic lovemaking—or raw passion. The sound of someone fleeing.

As Louise lay back in the antique bed, she suddenly wondered: Had other people been eavesdropping in the night? Had others been awake, hidden under cover of the New England darkness?

Make Yourself a Romantic Garden But Think Twice About Planting "Love-Lies-Bleeding"

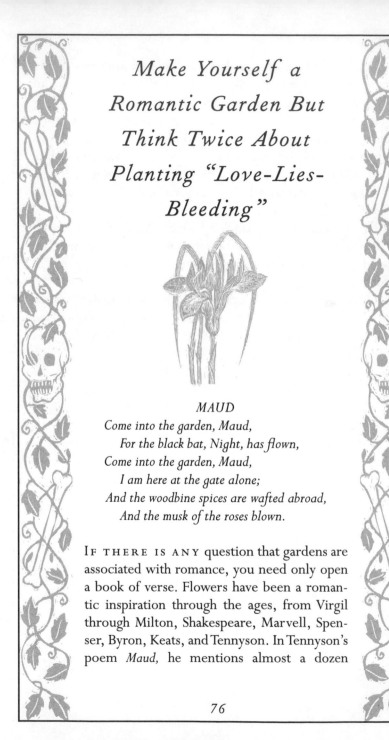

MAUD

Come into the garden, Maud,
For the black bat, Night, has flown,
Come into the garden, Maud,
I am here at the gate alone;
And the woodbine spices are wafted abroad,
And the musk of the roses blown.

IF THERE IS ANY question that gardens are associated with romance, you need only open a book of verse. Flowers have been a romantic inspiration through the ages, from Virgil through Milton, Shakespeare, Marvell, Spenser, Byron, Keats, and Tennyson. In Tennyson's poem *Maud,* he mentions almost a dozen

flowers, and the rose, many times. The flowers talk to him, and he likens his beloved to the "queen rose of the rosebud garden of girls." It is clear from the start of the poem that though he captures the sight, the sound, the touch, and the smell of the garden, what moves him most is the fragrance.

That is what you should do, too, when you plan a romantic garden—appeal to all the senses, but especially the olfactory sense. The aroma of this garden should distinguish it from all others, for the scent of flowers and trees is romance itself—just as evocative as the perfume a woman wears. A perfume for which some flower, of course, laid down its life.

But there is something more important than just fragrant plants: You need a feeling of being swept away. How do you achieve this? Do it with bold plantings, roses or not. With water. With a courtyard—but since few of us have a courtyard available, we may have to improvise. With secret places for lovers to meet and sit.

The garden will have two strong elements: the plantings and the structural fixtures, from which there are many to choose. Water, in the form of a pool or waterfall, is probably the most dramatic. A nine-foot-long bridge evocative of Monet's Giverney can now be purchased by gardeners and placed over that water in your backyard—and what is more sentimental than that? Classical-style statues can be a conspicuous romantic element, such as the ones showing fig-leafed but otherwise

naked lovers with arms intertwined. Do not suffer a Victorian swoon if you have no court-yard; few of us do. But you can improvise. Build yourself a couple of fragmentary open-work brick walls: they need not, in fact *should* not, be perfect. They will create the illusion of an old courtyard. Then smother the walls with roses, tulips, and recurved lilies, and you'll bring ancient Persia right into your own yard.

In the name of romance, more than one gardener has facetiously brought an actual bed to the garden and planted it with flowers. In one case, a gardener contrived an entire out-door bedroom with wicker furniture, the fo-cal point being the "waterbed," which housed flat-growing miniature lilies. Pillows were fashioned of peat moss. Morning glories grew out of men's bedroom slippers, and hanging plants festooned the bedroom walls, which were actually brick garden walls.

If you're not this adventurous, you can add a gazebo to the yard—it's another classic prop of romantic gardens. If you don't have teen-agers to worry about, tuck it into a corner for complete privacy. And never forget the im-pact of a garden pillar or two, swarming with flowers. Pillars cannot be recommended too often, for they evoke not only romance, classi-cism, poetry, but also a bygone era when lovers were not quite so reticent to speak of their emotions as they are today.

Among the fragrant trees you might choose are magnolia, crabapple, black locust, pear, *Viburnum sieboldii,* sweet birch, Siberian

pea tree, and *Catalpa speciosa*. Perfume-rich vines could include hop vine, moonflower, sweet pea, honeysuckle, and wisteria. Among the shrubs with distinctive fragrance: sage, barberry, allspice, blue mist, spirea, butterfly bush, sweet fern, Scotch broom, daphne, eucalyptus, lilac, snowball, many viburnums, and witch hazel.

There are hundreds of fragrant flowers, among them Tennyson's favorite, the rose. Its frilly, voluptuous blooms, if selected for fragrance, cannot be equaled. An example: the magenta, many-petaled Bourbon, *Rosa* 'Mme. Isaac Pereire.' Hyacinth, narcissus, nicotiana, lily of the valley, and certain hybrid lilies—notably Oriental and Madonna—also have an intense perfume.

Assemble flowers in big, graceful drifts rather than in a hodgepodge that looks as if you visited a nursery on bargain day. A sweep of pale pink astilbe, combined with a wave of the grass *Miscanthus sinensis,* is unforgettable. Even a mass of prosaic lamb's-ears (*Stachys byzantina*) will create a stunning gray-and-pink picture when combined with some lyrical, swaying grasses and the pink climber, *Rosa* 'New Dawn.' Don't go just by names. That means that love-lies-bleeding, or *Amaranthus caudatus,* won't have a place in this garden. Though it has the proper nomenclature, this is a garish annual with flowers that are red, chenille-like spikes. It belongs in a garden labeled "eccentric," not romantic. Love-in-a-mist (*Nigella damascena*) is much prettier. It produces a handsome drift of pastel flowers on feathery foliage, but is hardly bold enough to make a romantic statement.

White is one of the most effective colors in the garden, and shows up especially well at night, when romance is easier to come by and all other colors retreat into the dark. Float a few lit candles in your little water garden, highlighting the beauty of arrowhead, papyrus, lotus, and white water lilies such as *Nymphaea* 'Gonnere.' The stage is set for almost anything!

As for shape, remember that flowers are like people: Some shapes are more memorable than others. The iris is classic, as are the sweet pea, the Oriental poppy, the lily, and the large and sensuous hibiscus. The unusual double red *Clematis viticella* 'Purpurea Plena Elegans' lives up to its name. Other eye-catching plants are the single white *Clematis* 'Marie Boisselot' and *Humulus japonica* 'Variegatus,' the variegated hop vine with leaves in green, pink, and white.

The list goes on and on. Choose the plants carefully for this romantic place, and maybe the flowers will speak to you, as they did to Tennyson:

> *The red rose cries, "She is near, she is near";*
> *And the white rose weeps, "She is late";*
> *The larkspur listens, "I hear, I hear";*
> *And the lily whispers, "I wait."*

Chapter Eight

HER HUSBAND'S SOFT, OFF-KEY singing finally woke her up. She realized he'd been at it for some time. "Wake up, wake up, you sleepyhead . . ."

Bill was leaning over her bed smiling, one hand tenderly shaking her shoulder, the other caressing her cheek. "Sleepless night, huh?"

She nodded.

"Janie's dressed and gone. It's time for you to get up if you don't want your television crew to think you're a slugabed."

"Okay, darling." Because of her silk charmeuse gown, she could slide easily off the high bed and into Bill's arms. He gave her a long, healing hug, realizing how exhausted she was. Then he released her, and she stumbled onward into the bathroom. While she slowly washed and dressed, he read her snippets from the local paper. Just as well, since she was too sleepy to tell him about last night's adventure.

When they reached the dining room, everyone was at breakfast. They looked uniformly fresh, like choirboys and -girls. How could they all look like that? Louise knew some of them *had* to have been the night wanderers on the second floor of the mansion. She looked sharply at the men, trying in vain to observe sexual tension in the air. Only Jim Cooley referred to nighttime activity; she could hear him at the neighboring table, making some crack about "thumps in the night."

Nora, in pale rose culottes and top, seemed as lovely and composed as ever. And not as if she had been up all night. Yet her expression was preoccupied. Had Jeffrey ever shown up? Or was Louise wrong about the woman's predatory intentions?

A glance at her own reflection in a large antique mirror on the opposite wall made clear that she was the only one who had suffered from these nocturnal capers. Even after applying her makeup, she looked ravaged. Thinking along the same lines as an undertaker bent on making the corpse look good, she had put on a sporty dress in a flattering peach shade, with a touch of matching eye shadow. Bill, on the other hand, alerted that this weekend was casual except for a couple of dinners, was handsome and relaxed, and wearing his most historic, worn-out tennis shirt in faded navy blue. He loved being away from the sartorial strictures of the State Department and its buttoned-up-tight social scene.

It took her two cups of the Litchfield Falls Inn's robust coffee to wake up, and two more to snap her into working condition. They had eaten in the dining room because the rain made the veranda uncomfortably cool and damp; Louise was glad for its dry comfort.

"Why is it raining?" she muttered uselessly to Bill and Nora.

"It's just a front passing through, darling," said her husband, patting her hand. He was always anxious to keep her spirits up before she had to go to work.

"A little rain won't stop your work, will it?" asked Nora.

Louise shook her head. "Unless it's a hurricane, the show will go on. Marty Corbin certainly wouldn't want us to blow a weekend's work over a few raindrops." Her temperamental WTBA-TV producer always labored under a skimpy budget. Each location shoot cut heavily into it. That was why only the cameraman, Doug, was flying in from Washington, and the rest would be a pickup crew from New York. Yet, she reflected, the very strength of her program was visiting private and public gardens throughout the country. A frown passed over her face. The show could use more funding so they didn't always have to cut corners. Today, to save money, they would be without Marty, who had made the show the success it was. Big, dark-haired, and dark-eyed, his creativity and massive energy kept things at a high pitch. A shoot with Marty was like a good party, with everyone at their well-spoken best, full of body English and charm, but disciplined, and with no time for true party frivolity. With this modus operandi, he pulled from Louise and Doug and all of the crew their very best work.

But today, she and Doug would be running things themselves. Although Marty had expressed full confidence in them, the increased responsibility made her nervous. Her lack of sleep didn't help much, and from the looks of it, they would start out with a "garden in the rain," as the old song said. Just keeping herself from looking like a drowned rat would require a major effort: umbrellas borrowed from the inn, slickers, constantly hovering under shelters in between taping segments. And then, she thought drearily, there would be a problem with the flowers: Too much rain was going to play havoc with iris!

On the other hand, if the raindrops stopped and the skies stayed gray, Doug would rejoice: a "shooter's" sky, he would call it. Perfect weather for outdoor camera work, everything flat and uniformly lit, with maybe just a little battery-powered light pumped in as she did her walk-and-talks through the gardens.

Her spirits revived a bit when Barbara Seymour, walking slowly with what appeared to be stiff muscles, joined them at their table for coffee. She was not in costume this morning, just a faded but neat denim dress with a cameo brooch pinned at the throat. This encounter was just what Louise needed to get better acquainted with the woman. Barbara gave them a brief history of the inn, how her father had inherited it in a decrepit state and begun an enormous renovation. Louise, feeling more alert now, listened to the woman's story and thought she recognized the plot: Single daughter of loving couple devotes life to father after mother dies. What a shame to live such a narrow life, thought Louise: Even in her mid-seventies, Barbara Seymour had a vitality that exceeded that of many younger persons. But she had funneled it all into this mansion.

And now her relatives were putting the bite on her to give it up for development. What a payoff for a life of sacrifice!

They had a pleasant exchange that included a recap of the Eldridges' peripatetic history. "Yes," Louise confirmed with a grin, "we've lived in seven houses—and six different cities around the world. Foreign Service people move a lot. And I have the credentials to prove it: Just give me a house, any house—I can pack it up in a day."

Then, because she felt so comfortable and because she suffered from terminal curiosity, Louise couldn't resist asking the question that was burning in her mind. "Barbara, did I hear that you might turn this inn over to the Connecticut Trust?"

Louise saw Bill roll his eyes heavenward: She knew how

much he hated it when she stuck her nose into other people's business. It was a CIA reflex, since he was always wary of questions himself. And yet, thought Louise defensively, he would be as curious as she was if he had been listening to the conversation at Barbara's table last night, instead of dancing.

The elderly woman gave a nervous laugh. "You probably overheard our little postdinner family discussion. I wanted to turn it over to the state. I do not think my father would have liked this beautiful land becoming a housing project—even if it was tasteful. But my niece and nephew apparently don't agree with me about this." She gave Louise a weary look. "It's hard to balance these things, you know. It turns out that it's a perfect place for a development, if there must be development . . ."

"But if that's not what you want . . ."

"It isn't. But maybe that's what I *should* want. After all, as Jim says, you have to look at the general good of the community of Litchfield, which has to develop *somewhere,* apparently. Maybe I'm being selfish. After all, I'm old, set in my ways . . ."

Louise was appalled at the change in the woman, from the moment she'd stood victoriously at the top of the stairs yesterday, to now. Impetuously, she reached out and squeezed Barbara's thin, blue-veined hand. "You are older, but for heaven's sake, you're not that old—not old enough to take yourself out of the game of life." She groaned inwardly, appalled at herself for using such a cliché-ridden metaphor. Perhaps Jeffrey Freeling's flagrant use of them last night had infected her.

A little smile flickered on Barbara's face. "The game of life. That's kind of—"

"Corny," finished Louise.

"Well, yes, corny. But, Louise Eldridge, I can see you at ninety, still fighting the good fight." She smiled. "There *I* go, using a tired metaphor myself. But truly, I've always been a fighter, too, until this."

"Don't give up so easily, Miss Seymour."

As they left the table, Bill's face broke into a wide grin. "Why didn't you polish it off by telling her it's not over 'til the fat lady sings?"

"Really," she chided, giving her husband a gentle poke in the side, elated when he jumped a little, "you want me to mix metaphors? I was going to tell her not to leave the ring until the bell rang in the last round—but I restrained myself."

When they went into the lobby, Louise saw that the garden-tour crowd included only Frank and Fiona Storm, Grace Cooley, and Bebe Hollowell—plus, of course, her own clique, Bill and Nora.

The climbers, with lunches in their backpacks, also congregated in the lobby, preparing to leave for the hour-long trip to Bear Mountain. Janie and Chris were to ride in the inn's van with Jeffrey Freeling and Jim Cooley. The Posts had already departed, electing to go separately in their Bentley. The Gasparras also were driving alone. Freeling stood off to the side, handsome in his lederhosen and hiking boots, but looking uncomfortable. Could it be that he didn't like the lineup of his fellow travelers to the mountain?

As the two groups dispersed, Louise watched the young dining room manager approach Janie. He slid a worldly glance down her daughter's body, and Louise realized he was nowhere near as ingenuous as he appeared, and probably not as young, either. He gently pressed Janie's arm and said, "Now you take it easy on that mountain." He gave her a toothy smile. "You know what I was telling you last night—it's a pretty tough climb. Nontechnical, they say, but dangerous just the same." He looked out the inn's huge doors into the downpour. "It's even more so today, because those rocks near the top are going to be very slippery. Once you're on the summit, everybody climbs this ancient pile of rocks left over from some cabin—it's kind of like the climbers who stick another flag in the ground once they reach the top of Everest. But you'd better not do that today."

Janie looked about ten years old, wearing shorts and hiking boots, her long blond hair in practical pigtails. It was as if she were talking to her big brother. "Gee, thanks, Teddy, for the warning," she said.

"Yeah, thanks a lot," echoed Chris, putting a proprietary arm around Janie's shoulders and giving Teddy a brisk smile—and a glance that took in his black-and-white staff attire. "But don't you worry about it—I'll take good care of her."

"What am I going to be—a grip?" said Bill.

Louise grinned. "Exactly, because you're going to help Doug do the setups in the rooms, and the outside segments as well. You'll carry stuff, hold stuff, help set up light stands, steady the reflectors—things like that. He'll have about four portable TV lights, all on stands."

"I knew there was some reason you invited me on this trip."

"First, we have to check out downtown Litchfield," she said, propelling him toward the road. Litchfield's "downtown" was only a mile from the inn—a nice stroll. They got their first look at it when they stopped to pick up Nora and Bill's reserved tour tickets at the courthouse.

It was perfect: a model village out of someone's imagination. In the center was a flawless village green, emerald-colored and weedless, with a small white information kiosk tucked under huge trees. On one side was a church that Louise had heard was one of the most photographed churches in the United States: The First Congregational Church of Litchfield. It glistened white even on this gloomy day, its spire looming above sugar maples and pines far into the sky as a symbol of earlier Connecticut residents' enormous piety. Flanking the green on the other side was a prim line of shops, with two other historic churches and a county courthouse sandwiched between them.

Three elderly, fancy-hatted Litchfield women parceled out tickets for the garden tour. They sat at the foot of the courthouse steps, as if they were putting the full power of the county behind their worthy project—and it *was* worthy, with proceeds of the tour going to Connecticut Junior Republic, a home for boys. They carefully checked Bill's and Nora's names off the list, and nodded acknowledgment to Louise with more familiarity than she would have expected. "Oh, we recognize Louise Eldridge—you're part of that television crowd," said one, sniffing a bit. She was a tall, gaunt woman, with parchment skin drawn tightly over her face. "Of course, here in Litchfield we are quite used to you photographers."

"Oh, are you?" said Louise cheerfully. "Good." She turned to her companions and quietly murmured, "Doug has to get some footage of these three ladies before the day is over. It'll make a great B roll for the lead-in to the segment."

Bill and Nora looked perplexed, so she explained. "The primary interview with the talent—that's me—is called the A roll. B roll is the pictures we use with the voice-overs."

Bill nodded at Nora. "That perfectly clear?"

Nora looked uncertain. "Not perfectly."

"I'll explain more later," Louise told them.

Erected above the women and their card table was a tiny tent. For the hats, Louise realized: The hats were the things to be protected from the prevailing weather, for they were high-crowned and intricate, their droopy silk flowers showing their age. She wondered if they could be part of the village's historical preservation efforts. Hats from the past? She was beginning to know Litchfield, and she bet that they preserved *everything,* just like Louise's tightfisted grandmother had back on her farm in Illinois. Old lumber, dented pails a half-century old, used nails, falling-down buildings, broken furniture: all things made for man's use that must be carefully repaired and *continued* to be used—lest God think man was wasting His goods. As she discreetly glanced at these pleasant, firm-jawed women, she could picture them living two hundred years ago. *These gals would have been the social and moral conscience of the village,* thought Louise, *and a pretty tough one, at that.*

As if reading her mind, the woman who had spoken to her before said, "I bet we look like ancient relics to you." Her faded blue eyes held a dangerous twinkle.

"Oh, my, *no,*" said Louise, caught off balance.

The woman gave a big, hearty chuckle, and the droopy flowers of her hat shook like a garden in the wind. "Well, we are, and so are our hats. We're actually blood relatives of old Litchfield families. And we'll be glad to pose for you when you come back to take our pictures." Still chuckling, she reached out a skeletal hand and gave Louise's hand a hard little squeeze.

As they continued down the street, Louise said, "Now how the dickens did they know we'd come back to take *their* pictures? Did she hear me?"

Bill said, "They know all about what's picturesque—because *they're* picturesque. Probably've been photographed as much as the Navajos out in Arizona. Native people, Connecticut-style."

Louise cast a long look at the two blocks of upscale shops radiating from the courthouse. They included several boutique restaurants, the boutique woman's wear store, followed by the boutique deli, the upscale bookshop, drugstore, and antiques store. Louise realized that ordinary businesses such as hardware stores or repair shops had been driven from the area to make way for tourist-oriented enterprises.

Wandering around a corner they found another village delight—the post office. It was lodged in a charming old white Federal building, and its windows were filled with huge flowering and tropical plants. Louise thought ruefully of the tan postal station she took her packages to in northern Virginia: Its home-liness and grime discouraged would-be postal customers.

Litchfield had to be one of the most idyllic little communi-ties in the United States. It appeared to be buffered from the evils and problems that beset most places. No wonder she was attracted to it: *You could come here,* she thought, *and hide from the real world forever.*

It was only a short walk to the first house on the garden tour, where they met Doug and the rest of the TV crew near a big white van. Doug stopped busily unpacking equipment to come over and embrace Louise like an old friend. She introduced him and the others to Bill and Nora, and with amiable, quick glances, the New York contingent checked Louise out. She gave them an enthusiastic hello. Then, one of her fingers went up and touched the skin under her eyes in a reflexive female gesture.

"It's okay, Louise," said Doug, slipping an arm around her shoulders and walking her a ways down the sidewalk. He reached over and straightened a piece of her long brown hair. "You don't look that bad. You look wonderful, in fact."

Cameramen, on occasion, were known to stretch the truth, especially if it meant reassuring the talent. Doug was about her age, and the same height as she was. As she looked at him she saw real sympathy and affection in his friendly, luxuriously bearded face. Along with Marty, this was the man who had helped make her a Saturday TV personality, who made her look good week after week. He ranked right up there with her fa-vorite people, like Bill and Janie—and Marty, of course. "You can tell, can't you, Doug—I was up late last night. I hope my cover-up masks the circles under my eyes." Her hand strayed to her face again.

"Babe," he said, stretching out the "a" sound, "you look great. Terrific dress."

She looked down and gave the skirt of the peach cotton creation a little pull. "You're right—the dress will help a lot. It's a color that even a dead cat would look good in."

He grinned. "So that's why you bought it. You'll look good today, Louise, even if you are coming off a bender." He looked down the street at the idyllic village center. "But how could you find anything to do in this place? It doesn't look like it has much life in it."

"It wasn't that, Doug—it was just insomnia."

Unlike the tourists who lined up in front of the house with their umbrellas opened to protect them from the residual raindrops, the crew was allowed to photograph the inside of the house. The photo ban for the general public was a necessity, Louise had heard, for the owners of these beautiful two-hundred-year-old houses didn't know who was in that line out there. Some visitors could be burglars who would use a photo record of the place to help them decide what to steal in a break-in.

Today, her crew would tape inside only one house, and in three of the gardens. A hip-roofed carriage house was the first stop. Much more elegant as a fine residence than as the horse-and-carriage storage place it had been centuries before, the home was surrounded with informal gardens that Louise was a little disappointed to see contained only standard plants. But next they visited a two-hundred-year-old home in Early Federal style. Louise had heard that through the years the various residents had insisted on gilding the lily, adding to and embellishing these homes with one feature after another—railings, additions, redesigned windows. However, authenticity was the goal of this homeowner, and inside, all the furniture, the paintings, even the assorted vases and other objets d'art were appropriate to the period. With great care, the crew (including Bill) set up lights and reflectors in the downstairs rooms. The lights blazed in Louise's eyes as she launched into a prepared spiel about the Early American decor and low-ceilinged construction. Finally they moved to the yard, where the homeowners had planted only flowers and shrubs that were used in that era. A massive display of plume poppy, with its intricate curvy leaves, and masses of later-blooming *Clematis paniculata* adorned the gardens. Old-fashioned phlox flourished near the little outbuildings and in clumps around the old stone fences and ledges.

This was the first time Bill had been with her on location, and he had been plunged into the action. As she did her walk-and-talk through the garden, Doug walked backward in front of her and recorded it with his Steadicam, while her husband the grip guided him with one hand on his shoulder so he wouldn't lose his footing or step in a hole. Finally they ended at the ancient garage with a carefully restored stone wall that Louise coveted at first sight. She had seen it before in the many photos the associate producer brought back when he did a site survey in Litchfield. But the reality was so much better.

During a break, Bill sidled up to her. "This is kind of fun. But now I know why this job obsesses you: Everything has to be perfect—the lights, the camerawork, the script dovetailing with the action . . ."

She grinned. "Doing the right thing, and saying the right thing, at the right time—that's my job, and it is a bit of a trick."

He squeezed her arm. "Honey, twenty-one years as a Foreign Service wife gave you the perfect training."

"Didn't it, though?" She thought, not without some bitterness, of all the years of trailing her State Department husband to overseas posts and acting the part of the perfect woman. She frowned. Was she just doing more of the same in her new career as a TV garden-show host? But all TV people—even the ones who seemed like impresarios and off-the-cuff commentators—

actually worked with the bread and butter of television production: a script. True off-the-cuff moments were few and far between. Marty, the associate producer, Louise, Doug, and Rachel, the scriptwriter, had worked on this program for weeks.

Louise consulted her notes now, rumpled pages of dialogue she had studied carefully, to refresh herself on the next segment to be taped. The next house, apparently, had one of the best gardens. It was more majestic, High Federal style, its mansard roof soaring above the white clapboard walls and ringed with an intricate guard railing. Louise doubted the guard railing had been there when the house was built.

The gardens here followed the perimeter of the yard—comfortable, familiar plantings, but done with style. Tall, majestic stands of lilies, daisies, hollyhock, astilbe, phlox, mullein, and the giant, bulbous purple balls of allium. But Doug's eye was caught by something not in the script: the wonderful wide *allée* beyond the house lined with tall columnar oaks that bespoke a European influence. The cameraman said, "This will be great: Look how the light is hitting those trees. Bill, come over and help me again." Doug skillfully kept Louise in frame as she strode down the long lane. "Good," he declared when they were finished. "We'll see how that flies."

Louise had been so focused on the shoot that she hardly noticed it was lunchtime. They were only two blocks from the town green. The New Yorkers were wise to all the best restaurants within a two-hour radius of the city: They grabbed Doug to go to lunch at a small, chic place called the West Street Grill. Though the new crew members were like old friends now and anxious to schmooze with her, Louise declined to join them. Somehow, a comfy outdoor restaurant she had noticed, the Aspen Garden, seemed a better choice for their group: Bill, Grace, the Storms, and two smokers—Nora and Bebe Hollowell. The Aspen Garden had big umbrellas to keep off the mists, and Louise liked sitting and watching people walk by. The locals hurried to work, while the tourists, relaxed and slow-gaited, realized the world was their apple—for the moment, anyway.

Louise's gaze turned from the menu to the group seated at the large round table. Bebe wasn't her favorite person, but no doubt it was her turn to hear all about the late Ernie Hollowell. And she wanted to find out more about Grace, who was apparently a real garden aficionado. The young woman had gone into raptures over the tour and pulled a little red notebook from her skirt pocket at every new stop, writing as furiously as a botanist compiling the enormous garden reference, *Hortus,* on a tight deadline. Louise had exchanged just enough words with her to find out what she was writing, but she was intrigued.

"The gardens are simply *delightful,* so evocative of the period," Grace effused. Louise was impressed with her ardor: She had started out with it in the morning, and it had grown as the day wore on. "They've taken nature and improved upon it, in the gentlest, kindest ways—with a bed of tall old-fashioned flowers standing against an old wall, with one magnificent geranium set in an ancient concrete urn on an old stone terrace. And I hope you didn't miss the smokebush growing out of that rock wall." Grace was leaning over Bebe to direct her comments to Louise, clutching the notebook full of flowery script.

Grace looked flowerlike herself, Louise thought, in a pale lavender lawn dress with patch pockets, her eyes feverishly bright. "They pay so much attention to the older flowers. The *Macleaya*, especially, is a work of art! They make the gardens so historically in touch with the beautiful houses."

A contrary look came over Bebe's face, and sure enough, she

had to counter Grace's statement. "I saw some brand-new varieties of flowers at all three houses."

"Oh, yes . . . but at least they're trying," said Grace, retreating a little, and Louise saw that she was used to retreating: Here was a woman unsure of her own opinions. "One always adds a few newcomers to a garden, or at least I think . . ." She took a sip of tea, and Louise saw her slip a couple of pills in her mouth and swallow them along with the hot liquid. At least one of them looked like echinacea, an herbal remedy to ward off colds that had gained popularity lately. In Grace's case, she might have hoped it could protect her from maladies of other kinds, such as verbal attacks.

"I agree with that," chimed in Louise. Grace's enthusiasm, as delicate as a dessert soufflé, had been studiously ignored by Frank and Fiona Storm, and Louise sensed something that she hadn't picked up yesterday: They didn't approve of this childish woman. Grace looked relieved when Nora asked whether she, too, wrote poetry. Soon, the two of them were deep into the world of verse, and it turned out Nora knew the New York poet from whom Grace took classes.

As Grace happily clasped a fellow poet to her bosom, Louise had ample opportunity to listen to Bebe's forlorn tale. She had heard little snatches of it the previous evening. The poor, deceased Ernie had been a rich farmer, elderly enough to be Bebe's father. A genial old "cuss," as she called him, he was given to wearing bib overalls and hanging around the general store. Everyone adored him for his daily supply of down-home jokes and generous contributions to folks in trouble. So when he had the temerity to die, people felt a keen loss and cast suspicious looks at Bebe. "He died in bed—heart attack. And for no particular reason except that he died by *himself,*" complained Bebe, "the town's coroner was called in. From then on, the rumors spread. . . ."

"Rumors of what?" asked Louise, fearing she could guess the answer.

"That *I* gave him something to induce a heart attack. That in other words I *murdered* my husband." The green eyes blazed into Louise, who shrank back a little but nevertheless reeled off the obvious question.

"Why?"

"Because he had no history of heart problems."

"Was there any evidence of . . . murder?"

"None, that's just it—but apparently there are some things a person can do, that leave no trace . . . things like oleander, for instance."

"Yes," Louise murmured, "unfortunately I've heard of things like that."

"But where would I ever get *oleander?*" the woman said in a whiny voice.

Where indeed, thought Louise. She stared at the enormous tuna salad sandwich the waitress had just set down in front of her: It was big enough to feed a starving truck driver. Then she looked at Bebe. Of the two, it was preferable to continue giving her attention to Bebe rather than risk choking to death on this puffy-rolled monstrosity. So Louise sipped her tea and picked at the fail-safe french fries while she plied Bebe with more questions—although it was more like turning on a tap than "plying."

Louise had always been good with people like Bebe, people on the edge of hysteria. She helped soften the *idées fixes* that colored their entire conversation. But not with Bebe: This woman held on to her *"idée"* like a dog with a bone. Only her brother, apparently, believed she had no part in her husband's death. "And sometimes he has doubts," she lamented.

Nora was claimed in conversation by Frank Storm, leaving Grace to sip her soup quietly. But Bebe must have sensed she was wearing Louise out, for she turned suddenly to Grace, leaving Louise to munch her french fries.

It was a polite question, as if Bebe were trying to change her approach to the timorous Grace. "Do you have enough room for a garden in Brooklyn?"

The younger woman brushed a damp piece of rosy-colored hair away from her forehead and looked grateful: It seemed safe to answer. "Oh, yes. It's small, but it's lovely. I have just installed what I call my 'romance' garden. Actually, I get ideas from roaming through the New York Botanical Garden —that's in the Bronx." A little shadow passed across her eager face. "In fact, my husband thinks I spend too much time in the garden—though it's just a little over an hour, no trouble, just two train transfers from our house in Park Slope. Jim wants me to do other, more useful things, I guess."

"So what did you do to your yard?" encouraged Bebe, hanging on Grace's words as the younger woman described digging up most of her and Jim's tiny yard and transforming it with a small waterfall, herb garden, and "romance" garden.

"Precious," said Bebe. " 'Romance,' that means 'love.' Tell me what's in the love garden." The older woman was trying: She had made a giant step toward becoming a good listener.

Grace, who had a tendency to talk with her thin hands, described knots in the air. "Love-in-a-mist—the blue variety, love-lies-bleeding, of course, and the usual romantic flowers—roses, phlox, delphinium, big puffs of baby's breath. The yard is only twenty by fifty, but I had to have rosemary"—her huge eyes pleaded for Bebe's understanding—"for remembrance, you know?"

"Oh, yes," said Bebe.

"As well as little patches of comfrey, rue, lavender, and chervil . . ."

"How lovely," said Bebe, in a shaky voice. "It makes me want to weep."

This apparently touched Grace, for she reached out and put her hand on Bebe's. "I know you're crying because you have lost Ernie, the man you loved."

97

At that moment, Grace broke through Bebe's crust and sealed her fate. She was Bebe's companion from then on.

Nora sidled up to Louise and said, "There's a kind young woman. She doesn't know what an obligation she has taken on. But she'll find out."

Chapter Nine

THE AFTERNOON WEATHER CLEARED
up, but the air was still filled with moisture.
The temperature soared into the nineties,
making Louise feel like a pudding in a
steamer. Their final destinations, before the
much-anticipated visit to Wild Flower Farm,
were two historic houses, one the birthplace
of Harriet Beecher Stowe. Courtesy of the
tour guide, they had another immersion in the
history of staunch Connecticut citizens with
consciences and the courage to speak them.
Though the Beechers themselves had lived in

a Greek Revival–style house, another house had now replaced it: a seventeenth-century saltbox in rusty red tones that seemed to Louise a true reflection of Yankee austerity and honesty. The second house was a simple, elegant colonial, but with profuse gardens: a patio garden—surely, a modern turn of events, thought Louise—and a kitchen garden in the style of a *potager,* with separate beds for herbs, others for squashes, still others for a flurry of tall annuals, cosmos, and baby's breath, and in the circular center bed an elegant sculpture of an enormous beehive.

By the time they reached this last house, Louise's body felt leaden, and she wondered if she would have the stamina to make it through the rest of the shooting; her lack of sleep was beginning to tell. She was the first to respond favorably when someone suggested a tea break. They began the walk back to the green, and when they wandered by the Congregational Church again, this time they went for a look around. Inside were neat walled pews which enclosed each family—for better concentration while praying, Louise imagined, thinking of the devout settlers. She felt a pang, an unaccustomed desire to go back to a time when people were truly and unashamedly dedicated in their faith, and didn't have to make jokes or wage societal battles, one way or the other, about religion. And yet she knew things weren't that simple, even two centuries ago.

Nora had been true to form and found a man to monopolize during the afternoon portion of the tour. The noble-looking Frank Storm seemed to enjoy her company, and Fiona seemed to enjoy it equally, swinging along with them in her fashionable white sharkskin slacks and top. It was interesting that Nora could relate so well to the staunch believer, Fiona, while Louise had failed so miserably. She was beginning to wonder if she were wearing her politics too publicly, like a flashing neon sign on her forehead that said, "Hidebound, knee-jerk liberal: Conservatives beware."

Ah, but even Nora was running into trouble with the

Storms, Louise discovered as she fell in stride with the trio. Frank was gently chastising Nora about being a woman alone. "Remember the words of Rumi," he said.

"I'm afraid I don't know Rumi," said Nora.

"Oh, you should. He was a thirteenth-century poet, a kind of mystic. He said, *'It is dangerous to let other men have intimate connections with the women in your care. Cotton and fire sparks, those are, together. Difficult, almost impossible, to quench.'* " Unaccountably, Frank had grown deadly serious: Did he disapprove of a woman of Nora's beauty going off on a weekend without her husband?

Nora was walking between Frank and Fiona. Now she slipped an arm in each of theirs to make a threesome. "I'm sure, with you around, Frank, I will be completely safe from sparks." Louise wondered, however, if there was something to fear from the electric combination of Nora and Jeffrey Freeling; she was glad Jeffrey had chosen to go climbing instead of coming on this garden tour, for it was proving to have its own charged moments.

Crossing the green again, they went into the deli. As predicted, Bebe and Grace had become inseparable, and their emerging friendship continued as they chose to sit together at one end of a long, group table. Louise and Bill sat next to them with the crew. Nora and the Storms sat at a second table.

"So at last we're off to see the Sacred Blood iris," said Doug. "I'm glad the drizzle has stopped, or you'd be slogging through the iris fields just like that time in Wilmington when the Winterthur grounds were soggy as a sponge."

Louise looked out the window at the slightly brighter skies above Litchfield. "I hope it will be perfect. Just wait until you see this new flower—I hear it's magnificent."

"Magnificent?" Doug's eyes shone mischievously, and she knew she was in for a hard time. "Maybe so, but Sacred *Blood?* Are they kidding with that name? Are they dedicating the proceeds to the church, or something? I'm a Catholic"—he

wagged his head playfully—"especially when things get rough. I can tell you that name's sacrilegious, and I'd *hate* to tell you what my pious old grandma would think. Man, they're talking about the Sacred Blood of Jesus, right out of that picture Granny has over her bed, with the crown of thorns and the exposed heart with little droplets going down Jesus's chest . . ."

"How you do go on," Louise told the cameraman, and patted his hand. "It's just a plant name, Doug."

Bill chimed in. "I couldn't agree with you more, my good man. The name's definitely irreverent. Does Rome know about this, Louise?"

Louise shot her husband a wry look. "I'm amazed at your concern, Bill, especially since you haven't practiced your religion since I met you twenty-two years ago."

Grace piped up boldly from the end of the table in her childish voice. "I can't wait to see it: It is the most authentic bright red iris ever grown—that's where the name came from. The color of fresh blood." Louise knew this information had been published in scores of garden magazines, in addition to Jeffrey Freeling's mentioning it last night during his dispute with the Gasparras. And Grace was certainly abreast of all the new developments in the field.

Louise told them, "I heard it took hundreds of thousands of dollars to develop. Lots of money spent, and probably lots of money to be earned, selling such a beautiful flower."

Bebe leaned her elbows on the table and clutched her iced tea in both hands. "I would just *love* to go and pick a huge bouquet of them, and put them on my husband's grave."

"Oh, dear, *no,*" protested Grace.

"What's the matter—you don't think graves should have flowers?" asked Bebe, her tone a little sharp.

Grace answered gently. "It's not that. It's just that I don't believe in picking flowers. Each one of them is God's creation." She laughed, closing her eyes self-consciously, as if when she did that, people would not be looking at her. Ironically, this only emphasized her beauty—the luminous skin, the finely sculpted face, the pale, long lashes. "Some things I truly believe in. Over my dead *body* would I have a picked bouquet in my house. It disturbs the unity of God, earth, nature, and man."

"Oh, for *heaven's* sake," said Bebe, "that sounds so off the wall—is that New Age?"

"I'm sorry you don't like it," said Grace, chin firm—for once. "I just don't happen to pick flowers and let them die—it's unnatural." She smiled radiantly, her defenses down after a pleasant, social afternoon. "I even wrote a poem about it."

"Really? A poem?" asked Bebe.

"Yes. I keep the poems I write—and other snatches of verse—in here," and she produced her little, rumpled red notebook from her pocket. In a soft voice, she recited:

> " 'The pulse of life in the iris red
> Is the passion that makes my blood flow fast.
> Oh pick it not, this perfect flower,
> For, like desire, we must make it last.' "

She looked around the group, seeking approval.

"Far out," said Doug, stroking his ample beard. He directed a good-natured smile toward Grace: "This woman is a poet, that's for sure. And it even rhymes—I *like* that in a poem."

The Storms, listening from the next table, seemed to be a trifle disgusted with this latest speech. Louise could understand that Grace's poetry did little to add to the success of Higher Directions.

"I like it very much," Nora called from the neighboring table.

Encouraged, Grace said, "I was telling Nora about Coleridge. He was one of the many poets who wrote about or used the symbolism of the flower." She riffled through the notebook again. "Ah, here it is: This was written after he read the German Romantic poet Novalis' writings about the 'blue flower'. . ." She searched out Nora's face. Her fellow poet nodded encouragement. Grace read.

> " 'If a man could pass through Paradise in a Dream,
> and have a Flower presented to him as a pledge that
> his Soul had really been there, and found that Flower
> in his hand when he awoke—Aye! and what
> then?' "

She looked around again. "Isn't that lovely and mysterious?"

It was hard to read Bebe at first, hard to see the anger in the woman in her sleeveless tank top, shorts, and New Spirit walking shoes. But this young woman was treading on all of Bebe's gut feelings about graves and death. "Well, Grace, you've got a problem."

"A problem?"

"Yes, because somebody *picked* that flower Coleridge was carrying through Paradise, didn't they, now?"

"Oh, but I didn't mean—"

Bebe went on relentlessly, green eyes flashing an unkind look at Nora as she did. "You and Nora may be the intellectuals, the English majors, the poets, who spout off about all these books about German Romanticism and nonsense like the 'blue flower.' What does 'blue flower' stand for, anyway, some secret sex symbol? You may be the one who has to jot all those garden notes and poetry down in your little notebook all the time . . ."

Grace, sitting opposite Bebe, was almost visibly wilting, as her lawn dress had already done, her joyous nature attacked frontally by her companion.

". . . but as far as I'm concerned, it's ninety percent pure foolishness. Foolishness comes in many forms. There's this intellectual stuff you're talking about. There's the town gossip where I live—it's all the same." Bebe's face was red and perspiring, her voice even hoarser and louder than usual. "Oh, yes, our town is like a bad joke—the people are like the kids who followed the Pied Piper. They follow and believe anyone—anyone, even old biddies!—who tell them some juicy story in a convincing way."

Whether Grace thought she still possessed the woman's friendship, or whether she herself was fed up and ready to strike back at the older woman, Louise didn't know. The pale blue eyes were guileless, the hair with the now-sagging tortoiseshell clip flopping in her face, giving her a faintly mad appearance. But Grace threw out the next remark in an innocent voice, like a grown-up who had not yet learned all the rules of politic speech. "Bebe, you've gone back to talking about your husband's death. There's something to be said for keeping your own counsel on some of these personal matters—at least I try to do that. Don't you think you're complaining too much? Why, surely people will think that a person who is innocent would not have to be constantly complaining—"

The rest happened in a flash. Bebe rose from the bench, shoving it and its other occupants mightily back from the table so that they had to grapple quickly with it to keep it from tipping over. She stood there, a large, apoplectic presence, with her hands knotted into fists. The still-seated Grace cringed before her. "You *twit!*" she bellowed, bringing the young man and woman behind the food counter hurrying over. "You over-*romanticized* little twit, who doesn't know diddly-squat about life, to say nothing of gardening . . . who are you to accuse me of killing my darling Ernie? How *dare* you?"

The Storms had a strange reaction to the outburst. At first, they seemed to enjoy someone telling off Jim Cooley's wife, but then they swiftly amended their expressions when they realized there was every indication that Bebe was going to do physical harm to the younger woman.

At Bebe's first loud words, Bill, who had been talking to the crew, had slid off his seat and hurried over to the woman. Now, he stood between her and Grace, his voice low, like someone trying to talk a terrorist into giving up his gun. "Bebe, maybe we'd better save this conversation for later. I know you're upset, but—"

"It's all right," said Bebe, shoving her way past him. "I've said my piece." She fumbled inside her purse, extracted some cash, and gave it to Bill, who was patiently following her. "Pay my share, will you, while I go out and have a smoke? I need something to soothe my nerves."

Nora realized how far things had deteriorated and stepped up to take her turn at monitoring Bebe. She put her arm companionably through Bebe's, turned her calm gray eyes upon her, and said, "I'll go with you, since I'm a smoker, too."

Louise looked at Grace. The woman's hair and dress were messy, her blue eyes as blank as an empty TV screen. Her only link with reality at that moment was the little notebook she clutched in her hand. But was there any reality in that notebook?

Her heart stirred by pity, Louise took a step toward her, but the young woman flinched and turned away, too crushed to accept solace.

Chapter Ten

THE BESPECTACLED YOUNG MAN had been following them all day, aiming his Nikon at Louise and Doug, as Doug aimed his camcorder at Louise. Tom Carrigan was with *The Litchfield Hills Sentinel,* doing a story on her visit to Litchfield County and the program she was shooting for *Gardening with Nature.* In between shoots, he would sidle up to Louise and ask her questions about her show, which she would answer politely but distractedly. Given a choice, she preferred to be left alone to concentrate on the script during breaks.

It wasn't until they were at Wild Flower Farm, three miles out of town, that Louise gave young Carrigan a good look. He was a narrow-shouldered, academic-looking fellow with a calm, intelligent face. Suddenly she felt like a cat contemplating the demolition of a mouse. Because she was going to use the press this time—instead of the usual pattern of the press using *her*.

They had reached the garden path lined with Sacred Blood iris, and she dismissed the reporter from her mind for the moment. Now Louise realized what all the excitement was about: The flowers were the most stunning she had ever seen. She had to work hard to maintain some measure of professional detachment in the presence of Doug and the crew. After taking her first look at their exquisite red forms, she was afraid she would babble something like, "I *adore* these gorgeous beauties!" Instead, she somehow stuck to the script. The translucent red blossoms seemed to glow, like the red of an Art Deco vase from the hand of a master, and they stood out all the more on a day that was still shrouded in mist. The glaucous, swordlike foliage complemented the red, only making their beauty more irresistible. And they exuded a faint, spicy, incredibly desirable smell.

Once she had recovered from her horticultural swoon, Louise became aware that this was one of the botanical discoveries of the decade. And Wild Flower Farm was going to make a killing—eventually. Their price was fifty dollars per plant, and the nursery would be paid a royalty for each plant sold by another nursery, *in perpetuity!* But Wild Flower Farm had already *spent* several hundred thousand dollars bankrolling the research at NYU that had produced this wonder, and it would take some time to recoup this cost before the profits began to roll in.

With the iris segment completed, Louise and the crew made their way to the next setup at the farm's popular Moon Garden. Looking up, she saw the reporter had fallen into step with her on the wide path.

"Nice piece of equipment," she said, noting the Nikon with

telephoto lens slung around his neck. "That camera makes you a . . ."

"Photojournalist," Carrigan finished with a smile, pinching his glasses up from where they had slid down on his nose. "It suits the budget of a small paper to have reporters take their own pictures."

"I should have guessed that." As they walked, they talked about how her program's popularity had spread to several hundred PBS stations throughout the country. He jotted down everything she said. Suddenly she plucked his sleeve. "Let's sit here for a minute," she said, directing him to an aged teakwood bench at the edge of the path.

She called out to Doug, "I'm stopping here, just for a moment or two."

Doug nodded. "No problem. I'll give you a heads-up when we're ready for you."

Once seated, she got right to it: "I have information that might make a story—a big story." Big for a paper the size of *The Litchfield Hills Sentinel,* anyway. Then she told Carrigan about Barbara Seymour's desire to turn the Litchfield Falls Inn over to the Connecticut Trust. "With its thirty acres and that waterfall, it has to be one of the prize properties around here."

"*The* prize property. There are millionaires who would give a good chunk of their fortune for that site. Tell me all about it."

Louise felt only a few brief pricks of guilt at babbling someone else's business to a reporter, but her great desire to make Barbara Seymour safe soon overcame these twinges.

"Does her family go for this?" asked the reporter. "I'd heard that the family wanted a bigtime development there— especially her niece's husband, who's a builder from downstate. Word here is he's a little overextended, needs a bailout."

Neil Landry: He was known even at this tiny, but growing, county newspaper. But then, Louise reflected, the size of the newspaper has nothing to do with a given reporter's capacity to amass knowledge—or suspicions—about the larger world.

Carrigan, for instance, wearing a dress shirt and tie on a steamy day in the face of all the other men's casual sports shirts, and choosing a Nikon as his camera, looked like an overachiever in the category of Woodward and Bernstein. At any moment he would surely be driving down to Manhattan to knock on the editorial doors of *The New York Times* or *Newsday,* seeking a job. He needed a big break. Probably much bigger than the story she was giving him, Louise thought wryly, but what the hell.

"The only way to get this story is to call Barbara Seymour herself," she told him. "She's the owner, and she's the one who will make the decision. I hear she wants the property to stay undeveloped."

"Well, that's what the town wants, but she's owned it for so many years that none of the local covenants could stop her if she wanted to build four or five hundred homes on the place."

"Ah," said Louise, "five hundred homes. Definitely talk to Miss Seymour. I think you'll find that's as far from her thoughts as traveling to the moon."

Louise and Bill arrived back from the long day's shoot two hours after the rest of the crowd. That left little time to find Barbara Seymour. Louise had wanted to prepare the inn's pro-prietress for Tom Carrigan's phone call before she became busy with afternoon tea.

While Bill joined the group lounging on the veranda, Louise detoured into the kitchen annex. It was a recent add-on to the inn, its counters, sinks, ovens, and refrigerators gleaming steel, its huge Aga stoves deep blue enamel. On one counter were steel pans with majestic racks of lamb resting on them, waiting to be roasted. Teddy Horton bustled about, assembling tea things, his cowlick visible even from a distance; its unruly aspect seemed to be the last thing he was concerned about. Completely focused on cutting lemons into narrow wedges, he still took a moment to give Louise a cheery greeting. Barbara was standing near the big ovens, looking weary. A trail of whitish-yellow hair had escaped from her sumptuous bun and was lying, sweaty, on her wrinkled cheek. She was examining a tray the pastry chef had just removed from the oven: miniature tarts with English custard and raspberries.

"Yum," said Louise. "I can hardly wait to try one of those." From their expressions, she could tell she was intruding at a busy time, but she had no choice. "Um, Barbara, can I talk to you for a second? It's important."

Trying to disguise any minor exasperation she might have felt, Barbara led Louise to a kitchen garden tucked behind a four-foot-high Connecticut rock wall. Here, raised beds held herbs of many kinds, while others contained squashes, broccoli, beans, and kohlrabi. Barbara sank gratefully into a cushioned lawn chair and beckoned Louise to the one by its side.

"How delightful," Louise said, looking around. But Barbara seemed truly exhausted, so she hurried to deliver her message about her meeting with Tom Carrigan.

"You discussed the disposition of the *inn?*" she repeated incredulously. The woman's proud shoulders seemed to droop visibly.

"I—I was scared for you, Miss Seymour."

"I know why you did it, Louise," the older woman said in a wan voice. "It must be as plain as the nose on your face. Anyone could see that stair rod had been loosened, for the whole world knows how well we maintain this place."

"I don't think everyone thought that," said Louise.

Barbara made no attempt to straighten herself in the chair. Instead, she closed her eyes, and for a moment Louise thought she might be falling asleep. But then she spoke. "Louise, you are keen of eye and of mind. And I like you. It appalls me that someone might have wished me harm. But I suspected immediately that Neil Landry had given way to his darker nature—for I always knew he had one. And you figured it out soon after."

The blue eyes opened and suddenly crinkled in a smile. "You're a very practical problem solver, and I think this Tom Carrigan might be just the solution to the problem at hand."

"The story could go in Sunday's paper if you're willing to talk to him. Oh, I'm so glad you can forgive me for being nosy."

"I'll do it, Louise. I'm not ready to go out just yet." And then little frown lines formed in the noble forehead, like cirrus clouds passing overhead and putting the weather's future in doubt. "The only problem that remains is darling Stephanie. You don't know her yet, but she is a worthy young woman—too worthy to be linked with a man who would attempt to harm someone."

Louise didn't know what to say. Barbara stretched out a hand and touched Louise's arm, her eyes half closed. "Now leave me, my dear. I'm finding it very comfortable here: just the place to rest my legs and take forty winks."

"Should I—tell the staff that you're here?"

"If you don't mind terribly, just tell Teddy. Then everything will be all right." She opened her eyes. "You see, I can trust Teddy with everything, Louise. He's proved himself. He's become like one of my own."

Louise's pulse quickened. "But your heirs are—"

"My heirs are Stephanie and Jim. But I've provided for Teddy, too, although they don't need to know that—that's just between the two of us." The tired eyes closed again, and Louise went to tell Teddy where Barbara was.

When she found the young man, the staff had completed tea preparations, and he was on the phone. "Tom Carrigan?" he said. "Hi, Tom—yeah, I remember you. Just a minute, I'll get Miss Seymour for you." He gave Louise a curious glance as he rested the phone on the counter, and she felt a little like an intruder. Had he guessed that Barbara Seymour spilled her business to Louise?

But true to form, he gave her a disarming smile and said, "Mrs. Eldridge, I have a feeling *you* know where Miss Seymour is—don't you?"

Louise had barely joined the group on the veranda when the hikers filed in, their faces strangely taut. They discarded their backpacks on the wide-board floor, slumping into available seats or leaning against pillars.

Janie came straight over to her mother and her slim body melted against Louise's, almost as it had when she was a tiny baby. "Ma," she murmured against Louise's shoulder, "you won't believe it." She said no more, deferring to someone older to speak for the group.

The group included Mark and Sandy Post, Janie and Chris, Rod and Dorothy Gasparra, Jim Cooley. But no Jeffrey Freeling.

"What's the matter?" asked Bill curtly. "And where's Jeffrey?"

Jim Cooley was the one to speak. Always the leader. "Bad news, Bill. Dr. Freeling had a fall from the summit of Bear Mountain. He's dead."

"My God, man, when?"

"About three hours ago. We were climbing up the north face—I was pretty close behind him. It was misty when it happened, so no one could see exactly what went wrong. He reached the summit first, and then he seemed to lose his footing. He fell, oh, I'd guess a hundred feet or more. After that, we all scrambled down. Someone on the trail had a cell phone and called the State Police. They questioned all of us, then drove us out to the trailhead." He heaved a big sigh and let his head sag in his hands.

Chris approached Cooley, as if he wanted to help the man in some way. "Mr. Cooley's pretty bad off, Mr. Eldridge. He was the one who nearly saved Dr. Freeling."

Cooley maintained his bent posture and shook his head sadly. Louise thought he looked like a collapsed version of Rodin's statue, *The Thinker*.

Chris continued, "As soon as we found him, Jim—I mean Mr. Cooley—gave him mouth-to-mouth, and pounded his chest."

"He started breathing," said Janie, "and then he stopped again." Her eyes filled with tears and she couldn't continue. Louise tightened her grip around the girl's waist.

"Jim did his best," said Rod Gasparra diffidently, his eyes tormented.

"He did—he tried and tried," added Mark Post. "They both did: first Jim, then Sandy . . . they're both CPR experts." Sandy sat limply in one of the chairs, her eyes closed. She appeared to be on the verge of total collapse. As Mark spoke, Jim looked at Sandy closely, a crease in his brow showing his concern about the effects of all this on the young woman.

Barbara Seymour, Teddy, Elizabeth, and the other members of the inn staff had gathered on the veranda, and the story had to be told again.

"I am so very sorry for all of us," said Barbara, with a worried look in her eyes. "By the way, where's Stephanie, and where's Neil? Were they hiking, too?"

Teddy bent his cowlicked head comfortingly over his employer and said, "Don't worry, Miss Seymour, it's all right—*they're* all right. Remember: They went antiquing out in the country. They're really all right."

Barbara seemed to feel better after hearing that, and clasped Teddy's hand in hers. "A horrible accident, but not the first life those mountains have claimed . . ." Then, recovering herself, she disengaged her hand, drew herself up tall, and said firmly, "We will still serve tea in half an hour, for those who feel up to it. That will give you a chance to freshen up. Tea will help all of us cope. Then we will delay dinner for an hour." She turned away, and then had another thought. "And dinner—you must feel no obligation to dress for dinner, of course."

Louise was listening intently to the story told by the shocked hikers. Only gradually did she see how debilitating the news was to each one of them, in very different ways. Mark hauled a cigarette out of his pocket and lit up nervously, but remembered to put a supportive hand on his wife's shoulder, for Sandy was letting the tears fall now. The Gasparras, not much for conversation at the best of times, tried to make suitable small talk about Jeffrey. But Louise thought such sociability seemed unnatural, coming from them. Grace hid behind her dark glasses, and then disappeared like a nervous fawn down a stairway to the lawn. Bebe had to be helped to her feet by Bill, and was grateful to be escorted to her room. "What a nice man he was," the widow kept mumbling. "All the nice men seem to die."

The Storms stood to one side. They were like figures carved of stone. These were people who had obviously experienced death before. Frank Storm moved to where Jim Cooley was sitting, huddled and exhausted, and put a sympathetic hand on his friend's shoulder. Jim looked up and the two men exchanged a long glance that to Louise seemed to say, "I feel what you feel."

As others stood in clusters and continued to talk about the death, Nora sat alone and stared at the hills, visible in the far distance between the groves of pine and hardwood trees. She neither spoke nor was spoken to, almost as if she were conducting a brief, private memorial for Jeffrey.

Bill hovered near Chris and Janie, with Teddy hanging on the edge of the group. Louise saw her husband's arm around their daughter now, and realized he was anxious about how she would handle her first brush with death. No, not her first: her second. Louise had forgotten the mulch murder, the results of which Janie saw firsthand—the severed body parts, the blood . . .

Teddy approached Janie and asked, "I sure hope you're all

right." She gave him a compassionate smile and enfolded him in the conversation, causing Chris to glower at the man who was stepping so nervily into his territory. Teddy seemed to flourish under the spell of Janie's approval, and Louise saw that he was indeed an interesting-looking young man—could he be a man with a future in Janie's life?

Like a father to the rescue, Bill had gone into a little monologue aimed at soothing nerves and relieving guilt: "It is shocking. The world has lost a man who was a leader in the field of plant genetics. But, Janie, terrible accidents happen sometimes. It isn't anything that could be helped or prevented—there's nothing you could have done . . ."

Janie gave him an impatient look. "Unless, of course, we'd all stayed in town and just gone on the garden tour. Look, Dad, I know all that. I'm perfectly all right, even if you think I'm not. So please stop hovering." She turned her back on the solicitous men and grabbed Louise's arm. "Ma, come on, let's go upstairs. I have something important to tell you."

The Sci-Fi Future of Gardening: Genetic Engineering and Tissue Culture

GARDENERS MAY NOT KNOW it, but many of the plants, trees, vines, and bushes that they buy were created in a test tube. The sci-fi future of gardening is here, as millions of the plants we use are grown through **tissue culture** and new plants are designer models created by **genetic engineering**. Tissue culture creates masses of **clones**, while genetic manipulation of plants creates what are called **transgenic plants** or **transformants**. And this isn't quite as spooky as it sounds. Tissue culture, at least, is user-friendly, and something the curious gardener can try in the family kitchen.

Gardeners through the millennia have found many simple ways to propagate and hybridize plants to create new genetic varieties: sticking a tree branch in the ground and letting it root; dividing rhizomes, roots, and bulbs; and cross-pollinating. Today, these methods are still popular. But now, instead of laboriously growing fields full of experimental, cross-pollinated plants, the scientist can take a gene gun, shoot a desirable gene into a host plant, and grow the experimental baby plants that result in a petri dish four inches in diameter.

These new technologies have quietly revolutionized the growing of farm and ornamental plants. Scientists and plant breeders create disease-resistant farm crops that save millions in pesticide costs and bolster the business of growing food for the planet. They identify and then mass-produce plants that help cure cancer and other diseases. Their "clean" stock opens the way for the worldwide exchange of plants, and raises hopes that endangered species can be saved. Last but not least, they create designer plants with such pizzazz that backyard gardeners are snapping them up like Beanie Babies.

Tissue culture, also called micropropagation, is based on the fact that plant cells can replicate themselves. Breeders start with a small amount of plant material—anything from a piece of root, stem, leaf, or bud to a single cell. When this is placed in a nutrient medium, it grows and proliferates, creating plantlets that are clones of the original plant. As these, too, are multiplied, up to a million new plants can be generated within one year from a tiny piece of the original plant.

Genetic engineering can involve one of three things: 1) shooting additional genes into the nucleus of a host plant; 2) altering a plant's genetic makeup with chemicals or radiation; or 3) fusing together the protoplasts of two different plants. Any of the three processes results in a brand-new plant. But to create a transformant may take years of painstaking work.

The popularity of these methods is growing, and more and more plants and trees are created and/or propagated in that smallest of all greenhouses, the test tube. More than 250 million plants emerge every year from seventy-five enormous micropropagation labs in the U.S. Countless genetic projects are going on around the country and the world at universities, botanic gardens, and private laboratories.

Though tissue culture is associated with *mass-production* of plants, and genetic engineering with the *creation* of plants, both can produce eye-boggling beauties. Tissue culture produces them by accident—when occasionally the genes in a cloned plant go haywire. Genetic engineering does it on purpose, forcing the issue by adding genes to alter the plant's DNA.

The payoffs of tissue culture and genetic engineering are many, for agriculture as well as the ornamental-plant business:

- "Clean" plants, trees, and vines, free of bacteria, fungi, and viruses. Unlike plants raised in soil, they can be shipped anywhere in the world. This has created a worldwide plant exchange not possible before tissue culture came into its own in the past quarter century.

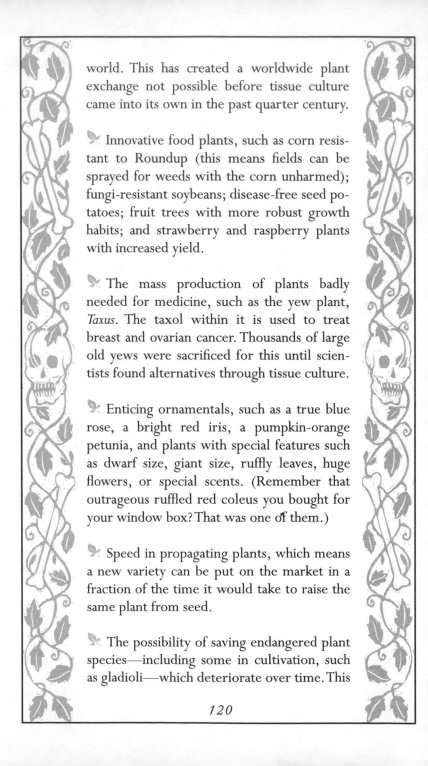 Innovative food plants, such as corn resistant to Roundup (this means fields can be sprayed for weeds with the corn unharmed); fungi-resistant soybeans; disease-free seed potatoes; fruit trees with more robust growth habits; and strawberry and raspberry plants with increased yield.

The mass production of plants badly needed for medicine, such as the yew plant, *Taxus*. The taxol within it is used to treat breast and ovarian cancer. Thousands of large old yews were sacrificed for this until scientists found alternatives through tissue culture.

Enticing ornamentals, such as a true blue rose, a bright red iris, a pumpkin-orange petunia, and plants with special features such as dwarf size, giant size, ruffly leaves, huge flowers, or special scents. (Remember that outrageous ruffled red coleus you bought for your window box? That was one of them.)

Speed in propagating plants, which means a new variety can be put on the market in a fraction of the time it would take to raise the same plant from seed.

The possibility of saving endangered plant species—including some in cultivation, such as gladioli—which deteriorate over time. This

work is being done in this country and abroad. However, tissue culture is expensive, and breeders and growers do not do this unless there is an economic return.

The cost of a tissue-cultured plant is high, and therefore only practical when there is a large market for it. Then the price drops precipitously, as it did with the Boston fern, which is hard to propagate and would have been an expensive purchase years ago, before it became an early subject of tissue culture. (Take fern runner tips, throw them in the blender, and macerate. Place them in a Murashige and Skoog medium, the famous formula discovered to aid tissue culture. Wait only a short time before multiple shootlets emerge from each little piece. Mature plants are ready in a year.)

Orchids started being tissue cultured around 1950, and they were transformed from a rich man's plant into one that can be afforded by any supermarket shopper. (Take one meristem, place it in a liquid culture, create a protocorm cluster, divide the plantlets, and grow in separate test tubes.)

As nursery growers prepare thousands of new baby plants in these sterile conditions, they find "accidents"—some happy, some not. All clones don't resemble their parents. A **somaclonal variation** usually ends up in the trash can, but if it has distinctive beauty, it will become the next subject of tissue culture and end up as the hot new variety in next year's garden catalogue.

The *genetic* development of a new plant can take years, and the process is not without its critics. *Pomatoes, indeed,* they sniff, viewing the potato-and-tomato-bearing plant that resulted after the fusion of the protoplasts of a tomato plant and a potato plant. They think tissue culture and genetic manipulation of plants may have detrimental effects later on.

What does the home gardener have at stake in this? Certainly the opportunity to buy many new and interesting plants, and maybe more. Some people have spent a lifetime in the garden and no longer feel like double-digging. Tissue culture, a world of miniatures, is definitely for them. They will work with tiny little plants, lightweight flasks, test tubes, and solutions, without stooping. The price is manageable, and so is the math, although one does have to measure those nutrient solutions, for each plant has a different "recipe" for propagation. And no need for an autoclave: A pressure cooker will suffice. Imagine the joy of raising a little forest of baby orchids in one's own kitchen. (Gardeners who want to try tissue culture themselves should read *Plants from Test Tubes*, by Lydiane Kyte and John Kleyn; third edition, Timber Press: Portland, Oregon, 1996.)

Chapter Eleven

JANIE, STILL WEARING HER mountain shorts and boots and a rugged T-shirt, was sitting forward in the overstuffed chair, one hand twirling a pigtail and the other gesturing for emphasis in case her mother didn't get it. "Look, I'm trying to tell you, anyone could have killed him. *I* could have killed him. *Chris* could have killed him. But what I think is that either Rod Gasparra or Mark Post killed him."

"Janie, if somebody shoved him, someone else would have seen it."

"That's just it. When did the rain clear in town?"

"About noon. But it was misty after that."

"Exactly. Misty. It was as misty as that gorilla movie up there! Nobody could see anybody else very well, unless they were ten feet away. It was beautiful—swampy ravines and terrific forests—enormous hemlocks, mostly, and sycamores"—she extended her arms to either side as far as they would go— "*wider* than that, trees that must be hundreds of years old. Then we got near the summit and people began taking separate paths, and *nobody* could tell what was happening, because it was hard enough just to keep your footing on those slippery roots and rocks. Teddy Horton was right. *He* knew what we were in for—it was as if those rocks were covered with a thin sheet of ice." The girl's gaze moved to the window, full of the late afternoon sun's rays. She might have been thinking about the homespun young man who gave them such sage advice. "I don't think Chris respects Teddy for what he is."

"And what's that?"

The blue eyes narrowed. "He's one cool dude, Ma. And smart. Even if he isn't a pretty boy."

Intrigued by the girl's comment, Louise nevertheless forced herself to remain on the business at hand. "Janie, who's investigating this accident?"

"The Canaan station of the State Police. They had lots of cops around, looking at the place." She threw up her hands. "But what can they find? After all, a shove is a shove: It doesn't leave any fingerprints."

Louise stood up and smoothed her skirt. "Are you telling me you're convinced Jeffrey Freeling was pushed off that mountain?"

"That's what I'm telling you." The girl, suddenly tired, collapsed back in the chair.

"Why do you think it was Rod Gasparra, or Mark Post?"

Janie leaned forward again. "Here's the skinny: On the way up, and it was a long way up, about six miles"—she gave a long sigh——"Chris and I moved back and forth among the people and learned all sorts of things. First, Gasparra: Just like we all thought last night when he nearly punched out Jeffrey on the veranda, the guy has a grudge. His wife told me. Said someone stole all their work on a red iris and turned it into the Sacred Blood iris. Dorothy said they came here to get 'satisfaction.' She's nice enough, Ma——she's a real trouper on the trail. But with a chip on her shoulder a mile high, just like her husband. I guess they think Jeffrey was partly responsible for stealing their——patent, or whatever you call it."

"And Mark and Sandy Post, what did you learn about the Posts?"

"Lots," said Janie. She sat back, crossed her leg over one knee, waggled the booted foot, and pointed a know-it-all finger at her parent. "I meet her on the trail and fall into step and do sympathetic listener. I guess you already figured this: Sandy Post is pretty rich——old Connecticut money. Every summer when she was a kid she went to Switzerland and did mountain climbing. She's spent lots of time training on the Olympic biathlon team the past few years——she fit in college courses where she could, and just recently got her B.A. Then she decided to settle down and do the thing girls are supposed to do——get married."

"To her old beau from NYU," said Louise, nodding.

Janie found another relaxation pose——by plopping her legs up over the fat arm of the chair. Louise bit back a reprimand along the lines of *"Get your sweaty legs off the arm of that yellow chair."* The girl said, "The trouble with the old beau, Mark, is that he is a fraud. He's in trouble and someone's probably going to repossess that poop-marked Bentley any day, if it isn't in Sandy's name. Someone's about to sue Mark, she told me, for stealing a software program he is selling for big bucks. She, of course, believes in him: thinks he's innocent of all wrongdoing. I don't know why she married Mark, but maybe I can find out by the time we leave for home. Maybe it's sex: She *touches* him all the time—but for some reason he doesn't respond. He doesn't seem to be on her wavelength. Even came on to me for a while, as if flirting were part of his daily exercise program. But so *phony*! For a guy who just got married, he's totally weird. He doesn't seem as—*you* know . . ."

"Passionate?"

"Horny. Like, not nearly as horny as Sandy is."

Louise's jaw dropped. She was appalled by one element of her daughter's vocabulary. "Did you *have* to say '*like*'?"

Janie grinned. "Ma, don't worry about it. Everybody uses 'like' these days. It's cooler if I talk like that—it's appropriate to my age, even if it doesn't sound so good coming out of the mouth of someone as old as Sandy." Sandy, at twenty-eight, was over the hill in Janie's eyes.

"Anyway," her daughter continued, "back to my point. I think maybe it's because Mark has taken the nerdy MBA route. She even teases him that he can't have out-of-body sexual experiences like she can, because he's an uptight MBA." Janie arched a dark eyebrow. "For 'out-of-body,' read—"

"Oh, I *get* it, for heaven's sake. Is that supposed to be *funny*?"

Janie cocked her head. "*I* thought that was funny, in a kind of crude way. She's pretty smart, Ma: Don't be fooled by the way she talks. Now Mark, he's a very *status* kind of person. Succeed-at-all-costs kind of philosophy. So anyway, I finally weaseled the story about NYU out of her. Guess what! Jeffrey Freeling broke the university rules and dated her a few times; then he chilled out and dropped her." The girl threw up both hands, as if imparting headline news.

"Mark and Sandy were kind of together back then, but he was still pretty upset. Then, Mark cheated on Jeffrey's science exam so he could graduate on time, only Sandy thinks he was forced into it by someone else. He did some stupid thing like breaking into Jeffrey's office and copying the final. He got caught and thrown out of NYU. What's more, Jeffrey apparently saw to it that he didn't get into the MBA program of his choice—which you can be sure was Harvard." She grinned. "Had to take what he could get at some state university."

"That's good background checking, Janie."

Janie accepted the praise with a flourish of one hand. "Thanks. You can see there was plenty of reason for the sneaky Mark to do the deed. And yet it was funny . . . there was Sandy telling me all this —I think she needed a cathartic —while . . ."

"Maybe catharsis."

"Whatever. While she was tactfully spilling her guts, I filled in all the gaps of the story myself."

"You mean, some of what you just told me was guesses?"

"Well . . . I'm just telling you this is more or *less* what happened among the three of them. It was kind of a veiled conversation. Very typical, Ma, of certain kinds of women; rich, protected women, who can't call a spade a spade, but have to go through all these hoops, using, uh, you know—"

"Euphemisms?"

"Whatever. Well, that's Sandy for you. So, while Sandy and I are doing our woman-to-woman, blonde-to-blonde thing, Mark was, like, sucking up to Jeffrey. It was as if he were trying to make up for the past. And I remember a minute there, when we saw them together—maybe she even got a shot of it with her expensive little camera—they looked like the best of buddies, Jeffrey all red-haired and fresh-cheeked and happy, and Mark all eager-beaver. Then Sandy did the same thing, trying to make peace with the professor, maybe. Later on, she helped Jim Cooley try to resuscitate him: She's really good at CPR." She shook her head, and Louise saw that the reality of the death was beginning to sink in.

"It's going to be hard, darling." Louise was silent a moment, her mind spinning. "Now, if they were acting like the best of buddies, why would you ever suspect Mark?"

Janie shook her tousled head. "Dunno, Ma. Weird chemistry everywhere, weird chemistry ever since we got here, right? I just think Mark is not all that he seems to be. He was *straining* to be a good buddy to Jeffrey. Maybe he needed a reference letter from him to stay out of jail."

"Did you tell the police what you thought?"

"Naw," said Janie. "Chris and I talked it over and decided they wouldn't believe us. But what I did do was give a meaningful look to the chief investigator as we left in the car."

Louise smiled. "It probably made the man's day. Sure he didn't think you were flirting with him?"

"I looked really *hard* at him and sent him a mental message: *This dumb accident is no accident.*"

"What did he do?"

"You're right: He gave me a big smile. Thought I was coming on to him." She directed a cool glance at her mother. "So, as usual, Ma, it's you and me—and Chris and Dad, of course—solving this thing, if it's ever to be solved. Which this time I seriously doubt. Rocks, after all, do not talk. They don't hold onto DNA very well, either."

She swung her legs down, flounced to her feet, and stomped toward the bathroom for a shower. At the door, she turned back to her mother, smiled, and said, "Only time for one bath before tea, and I smell a lot worse than you."

Tea at the inn was a grave, depressing affair. It was served on the veranda, now dry enough for occupancy. The tall pines and willows surrounding the huge Georgian mansion registered their mournful tenor complaints as a strong afternoon breeze whipped through them and blew away some of the mugginess that had followed the rain. The primordial hum from the trees quite suited the sad occasion, Louise thought.

There was little conversation, but guests gratefully and rather greedily partook of the fresh pastries and tea, as if determined to manifest some sign of life in the face of death. Despite

Janie's suspicions, no one showed any signs of guilt. There was only sorrow and regret over the death of the professor. Some had showered and changed, while others, like Bebe Hollowell, Grace Cooley, and Louise herself, were in the same rumpled clothes they had been wearing all day. Louise imagined that the two had drained the strength from each other by saying cruel things that may have been true, but were too hurtful and should never have been verbalized.

Stephanie and Neil Landry had just returned from a journey to antiques shops in nearby towns. They came out on the veranda and self-consciously offered their condolences to the rest, as if by being absent at the time of the tragic announcement, they had not shouldered their proper responsibilities. Stephanie still looked fresh in her bright shirt, shorts, sandals, and big trendy hairdo. Neil was casual, in a well-cut jacket, chinos, and white leather sports shoes. Louise noticed that he acted bolder than he had last night at dinner, when Jim Cooley's quiet authority had somewhat quashed him.

A pang of fear ran through her: Was Sunday's newspaper going to be in time to safeguard Barbara Seymour? Whether or not it was foul play, Freeling's death struck uncomfortably close to home—and the tension that seemed to haunt the inn this weekend. She only hoped Tom Carrigan's story did what she hoped it would. As if reading her mind, Landry slowly turned and looked at her with narrowed, suspicious eyes. It was discouraging to Louise that she couldn't seem to disguise her disapproval of people—or even her minor philosophical disagreements, as had been the case with Fiona last evening. She would have to learn how to put on a better face for the world. After all, sometimes the occasion demanded it. Bill, of course, had always said she would make a terrible spy and a rotten poker player, because she wore her emotions on her face.

After all that had happened today, Neil Landry was an outrage: Louise wasn't about to sit here and engage in a staring contest with him. Anyway, she needed some rest before dinner, and she was sure others must feel the same way. Nora still sat apart from everyone in a haze of depression. Grace looked exhausted, either because of the verbal slashing from Bebe, or because of Freeling's accident—probably both. She was involved in a tense conversation with Jim, and appeared to be pleading with him about something.

There was no doubt about Bebe Hollowell's feelings: She loudly proclaimed them. "This day has been way too much for me, folks. I've a headache that just won't go away. I don't feel well at all."

Stephanie interposed, "Why don't you rest, and someone will bring dinner to your room? Then maybe you can join us later for dessert and coffee."

Bebe heaved an important sigh; she delighted in every attention. "Oh, would you do that? I would so like to call it a day and try to forget everything—that disastrous garden tour, and that poor man's death." She accepted the slim Stephanie's help rising from her chair. "So tragic, these deaths," she sobbed, as she slowly left the veranda.

Jim Cooley, in fresh slacks and shirt, looked around at the group. "Grace doesn't feel well, either," he announced.

"It's just that I have a raging headache," Grace explained quietly.

Jim gave his wife an unreadable look. He seemed to be curbing whatever criticism he might want to offer. "I suppose we all might feel poorly at this juncture," he continued, "but it would be good if the rest of us could return for Barbara's superb meal."

Of course, thought Louise: Loyalty above all, and in this case, Louise agreed with him. It was loyalty to their plucky hostess, Barbara Seymour. Jim took Grace's thin hand. "Dear, suppose we arrange to have your dinner sent up to you, too?"

Grace gently separated her hand from his and thanked him, then left the veranda. Frank intercepted both Grace and Bebe in the sunroom and escorted them into the interior of the inn. Jim

Cooley half rose, looking after his wife with real concern, then sank back in the chair, apparently thinking the better of going with her. The rest of the guests lingered, finding comfort in each other's presence.

Louise, Bill, Janie, and Chris sat together with little left to say to each other. They listened to the murmur of the wind in the huge pines. "That beautiful sound," said Bill idly. "It's coming from second-growth trees."

"Second-growth—really?" said Louise.

"Yes. Don't be deceived by their size. All of Litchfield Hills' virgin forests were taken down; these hills were made bare once. This is second-growth forest."

Janie jumped impatiently from her chair. "Dad, I can't believe you're talking about trees when someone really neat has fallen off a cliff." Her voice was filled with disgust. She reached a hand out and pulled Chris to his feet. "Come on, Chris, let's go swimming."

Louise gave Bill a wan look. "I hope Janie's going to be all right with this. I don't know about you, but I'm wiped out—I have to go lie down." He went with her to her bedroom suite, and they sat together on the edge of the bed.

He put an arm around her. "This has been a hard day for you."

"It's just too much, Bill." She pressed her head against his shoulder, and, not finding that enough, clasped both arms around him. He turned and shoved her long hair back with one hand, found her lips, and gently kissed her. Then he lifted her onto the bed, and they made love slowly, drawn closer in this act of creation by the knowledge that one of their companions had lost his life today.

At dinner, Louise noted the sober mood that prevailed; the absence of Grace and especially Bebe also made the crowd quieter. Even the faint curtain of mist in the air outside the veranda seemed to enclose them in a kind of quiet gloom. Louise had put on a fresh dress but hadn't bothered with makeup. Nora looked like a woman out of the Old Testament, in her black caftan and sandals. There was little joy to be found, except among the outside dinner guests, who knew nothing yet of the death. And then there were the flowers, robust, patriotic-colored bouquets of red geranium, blue delphinium, and white daisy, that flew in the face of emotions like sadness and mourning. Obviously, they were prepared before the staff learned of the accident. Or was Barbara Seymour doing her best to restore a sense of normalcy to the inn?

Louise also noticed that young Teddy found many excuses to pass their table, which was probably what started all the trouble. And Louise didn't need trouble, after her nearly sleepless night, performing all day in front of the camera, and returning to the inn to deal with the trauma of Jeffrey's accident. But trouble it would be, when they all finished their appetizers and Janie, looking more grown-up than usual in a calf-length, sleeveless, pale green print dress, impetuously got up from her seat next to Louise. She crossed the veranda and caught up with Teddy, guiding him down the porch stairs with a firm hand. Louise could only see their heads. Her daughter was talking rapidly to the young man, hurrying, as if she wanted to get back before the next course was served. He bent down to listen, his cowlick cunning as ever, his eyes alight with interest.

Their little conversation created waves. The red-haired waitress, for one, seemed infuriated that Teddy was conversing with a guest. She flounced by and stared down at the pair, nearly spilling her tray when she bumped into a chair. Chris reacted in a similar jealous fashion. Blond and handsome in his best clothes, he stared indignantly at the two of them for a while. Then he excused himself and stalked over, descended the stairs, and joined them. Louise could see from their gestures that Chris didn't want Janie to divulge more to the young maître d'hôtel. But when he tried to pull her away, Janie coldly removed his hand from her arm.

At this juncture, Mark Post appeared from somewhere on the lawn, where he had apparently gone to smoke. He came up the steps past the young people, shooting them a surprised look. Janie and Chris returned to the table, Teddy resumed his maître d' responsibilities, and Louise incorrectly assumed that peace had been restored.

"What was that all about?" Louise asked her daughter.

Janie's eyes shone with excitement. "I told Teddy what Chris and I suspected about Jeffrey's death—that it was no accident. That Mark or—"

"Now, wait, Janie," she interrupted, "I think you and Chris are going too far."

The girl waggled her legs like an accordion under her fancy print skirt, and said, "No way are we wrong."

Louise moved a hand over and gently pressed upon her daughter's legs to stop the wiggling. "Darling," she whispered, "I know you're nervous, but don't do that."

Janie pushed her mother's hand away. "Aw, c'mon, Ma, don't obsess. You just wait—time will tell whether Chris and I are right. In the meantime, it's good to have Teddy in this with us." She cast a wary glance at Chris sitting on the other side of her. "Except Chris doesn't think so."

Suddenly, Mark Post rose from his table on the edge of the veranda, came over, and crouched down between Janie and Chris. His thin face was dark red, his mouth twisted angrily. Janie's blue eyes widened.

"What a couple of losers *you* two are."

Louise, alarmed, leaned in so she could hear. Even from where she sat, she could smell his tobacco breath. For some reason, he'd been smoking up a storm.

"I just overheard you talking to that young hick who runs the dining room. And I heard my name mentioned, and then something about how I probably shoved Freeling off the top of that mountain today. Now, are you kids crazy or something? Did you ever hear of slander? You're *slandering* me, and I'll be damned if I know why. Sandy told me just now that she spilled the story of what happened at NYU five years ago. Well, talking about that could be slanderous, too, because, you know, none of that was ever proved: I pleaded nolo contendere for some very good reasons . . ."

The candlelight falling on his sharp features gave him a malevolent look, rather like a thin gargoyle sculpted in stone grimacing at the world. "I'm not about to explain this whole thing, because you wouldn't even understand it—you're too damned wet behind the ears. I'm just telling you that you'd better not talk like that about me again or I could sue you. Do you hear that? *Sue* you: a real grown-up concept you'd better learn right now before you shoot your mouths off again."

Done with his warning, he stood erect. As if Chris would take the lead in this, Mark gave him an encouraging little hit on the shoulder and said, "Get that, buddy?" Then, as an afterthought, he leaned over and hoarsely whispered in Chris's ear, "Don't be a fuckin' *loser*." He strode back to his own table with the grace of an athlete, but Louise noticed his wife took no notice of him and simply kept up her own conversation.

"Well, well," said Louise.

"Don't say 'I told you so,' Ma, although you did. It's okay. We'll just be more careful how we go about things next time." Janie put her hands in her lap and clasped them together.

"Who, you and Teddy and Chris?"

Janie cast a regretful glance at Teddy. "Not tonight. Teddy has a date, unfortunately. But we'll get together with him again tomorrow. See, he's not so trusting as you, Ma. He agrees that Jeffrey could have been shoved." She flashed a quick look at her mother, and then turned her attention to her rack of lamb.

It was apparent that no one had the heart to make it a late evening, although Janie and Chris, only slightly subdued by

Mark's angry outburst, drifted off together as soon as dinner was finished. Their whispered exchanges practically telegraphed their intentions, and Louise looked at Bill in dismay. "They're still snooping, I can tell. Why can't they just play a quiet game of Scrabble in the library and then go to bed?"

"Dream on, Louise. Just who did you think you were dealing with? Talk about 'her mother's daughter.' " Still looking at his wife, he cocked his head toward the door and then turned to include Nora. "Come on—let's all get out of here and go for a walk."

When they left the veranda, they passed Jim Cooley, perched on the veranda rail with the remaining guests of the inn clustered around him like moths to a flame. Jim was playing the hero again, engaging them in a warm conversation, obviously trying to soothe their frayed nerves so that they could leave Litchfield Falls Inn tomorrow with happy, not morose, feelings.

With Nora loosely holding one of Bill's arms and Louise the other, they sauntered up one of the winding paths through the wooded hills. The cloud-harassed sun had set somewhere beyond the trees, and there was little light left. Louise glanced at Nora as her neighbor trudged slowly along. "This must be sad for you, walking here," said Louise. "Isn't this the way . . ."

"Yes. We're retracing the path that Jeffrey and I took yesterday afternoon. It takes one to a very deep, magnificent pool. It's beautiful." There was a catch in her voice. "As for Jeffrey, I don't believe I've ever met a nicer man . . ."

"Better not dwell on it, Nora," said Bill. "What you have to remember is that it was one of those terrible accidents that sometimes happen to people."

"Bill, our daughter doesn't think it was just a terrible accident," said Louise. She stopped when she saw the look Nora shot her.

"Janie doesn't think *what?*" demanded Nora.

"Oh, well, Chris will be telling you, anyway—though heaven

knows I don't want to upset you. I don't want to upset anyone more than they've already been upset. Chris and Janie believe Jeffrey was pushed off that mountain."

Nora stopped in the middle of the path, pulling the others to a halt with her. "Tell me that isn't so," she whispered. "It's what I have feared the most, and what has been intruding more and more on my subconscious." Louise saw in the woman's gray eyes the kind of dreamlike look that had been there when she predicted danger and death in the past.

And Nora had always been right.

"Who did it?" she demanded suddenly.

"Oh, Nora, please," said Louise. "They suspect Mark Post or Rod Gasparra, but it's merely suspicion. Apparently both Mark and Rod had some sort of grudge against Jeffrey. But there's nothing there, or the police would know about it."

"Would they?" Nora asked.

Bill, ever practical, grabbed their arms again and hustled them forward. "Friends, do you realize how useless it is to speculate like this? Let's just go for our walk. We can sleep on it and talk about it tomorrow morning. Agreed?"

"Agreed," Louise echoed. "I'm sorry I brought it up."

With Nora as the guide, they took one of the three flower-lined paths that led to the falls. It was the middle path that emerged where the twenty-five-foot-high waterfall plunged into a pool and rushed on across a tumble of rocks to become a lively downhill stream.

The path turned, and they walked alongside a pristine pool so deep they could not see its bottom. It was fed by the constant flow of water from the falls above, which broke the mirrored surface with a pleasant chattering sound. The last rays of the sun peeked through the woods and caught the edges of the iron-gray rock, highlighting ferns and other bog plants tucked into the moist rocky crevasses by both nature's hand and the hand of the inn's groundskeeper.

Momentarily, this beauty distracted their eyes from seeing

what was so obvious, and so much more important than the plants and the flowers and the sound of falling water and the motion of small birds as they darted about, catching tiny bugs on the pool's surface.

It was the broken body lying at the edge of the deep pit, partly in and partly out of the water. The body in its wet lavender dress, thin and pathetic. Slim arms flung over a head cocked grotesquely back on the neck and resting below the surface. Wide-spaced blue eyes still open and staring up into a dusky sky. Rosy-colored strands of hair swaying in the cool water, like so many pale, slithering snakes.

The body of Grace Cooley, a broken flower lying at the foot of the falls.

Chapter Twelve

"IT LOOKS LIKE A suicide," said Sergeant Ed Drucker.

"Suicide," said Louise. She sat opposite him, legs crossed at the ankles in a most lady-like fashion, her hands placed serenely in her lap. "I suppose *murder* is something that never happens in Litchfield."

He chuckled. "You think nobody ever gets killed around here?"

"I would have believed that when I first came here. Maybe it's because this place is so beautiful, so . . . well-painted. Even the oldest barns and outbuildings, carefully preserved, cherished. I jumped to the conclusion that people would be just as careful with preserving lives. But all of a sudden everything appears much darker——" She stopped.

"Darker?"

"Yes," Her hands twisted together for comfort. "Darker, and more dangerous. Two of us are dead, and another one survived an accident meant to do serious harm. Suppose someone has killed, and wants to kill again?"

Drucker chuckled again, longer this time. She noticed that he had a groove on his forehead above the dark shock of hair pushed down by his gray felt trooper's hat. He was a big man, probably six foot six, with an innocent-looking, boyish face, and laugh lines that fanned out from his eyes and down the sides of his cheeks. Women, probably his mother and later his wife, had told this man how special he was. He was unself-consciously assertive, but with an affectionate regard for his fellow human beings. And yet his dark, searching eyes told her how tough he was: Those eyes had scoped her out from the moment the two of them had sat down to talk.

"You have some imagination, all right, Mrs. Eldridge," he told her. "Anyway, there's fifteen more of you to go. You don't think someone's trying to mow down the whole bunch?"

She gave him a sheepish smile. "Maybe not everyone. But two are dead, and who knows what might happen next?"

"Well, to answer your previous question, we have had murders in and around Litchfield, but don't get the wrong impression. This is a quiet, law-abiding village. The people here do lots of good works, and are very generous in funding things like the boys' home and a home for recovering alcoholics. But there is occasional violence. Why, we had a nasty little murder just last year. A son of a prominent local businessman shot the son of another longtime resident. The young fellow parked his pickup on a side street, walked up to the other man, and shot him clean through the head."

"Why?"

"Drug deal gone wrong."

Louise shook her head. "Well, at least he didn't kill someone on the town green: That would be more than anyone could bear." To have that picture-perfect New England scene bloodied was unthinkable.

"Yep. We also have the occasional domestic killing. Back a few years ago, there was a whole crime wave up-county. We had a killing, a run of burglaries, and a couple of house burnings in a short span of time, all by one individual. When we caught this individual, the county's crime wave disappeared into thin air." Sergeant Drucker smiled calmly at her.

He must think this idle conversation would have an effect on her, perhaps win her over. He had asked her for this private meeting in the mansion library, so of course he was calling the shots. But what he didn't understand was how determined she was not to get involved. Or not any more than she already was.

"So, Mrs. Eldridge, suicide's hard for you to believe? Me, too. It's hard to believe people will actually destroy themselves. Indicates a lack of faith in the future, don't you think?"

Louise didn't answer, staring out the many-paned window at the tall pines fronting the mansion. *Yes,* she told herself, *it would indicate that Grace had no faith in poetry, or in the beauty of nature which she claimed to love so dearly, or in God* . . . Tears came to her eyes and she wiped them away with the back of her hand, since she had no handkerchief.

Suddenly, she felt a softness against her bare legs, and realized Hargrave the library cat had come over to get a pat—or was it to give comfort? Where have you been keeping yourself, old boy, Louise wondered. She reached down and stroked his soft, round head, and immediately felt better.

When she tried to turn her attention back to the trooper, however, Hargrave would have no part of it. The instant she stopped petting him, he began weaving back and forth around her legs, bunting each time so there was no possibility of ignoring him. She suspected the animal was trying to tell her something. Probably hungry, and figured Louise for a soft touch. She was; she would rustle him up some food as soon as she and this policeman finished talking.

Then she looked up, and caught Sergeant Drucker in the act. He was unashamedly staring at her, his eyes crinkling with his smile. Drucker's eyes were his weapon, sometimes twinkling, sometimes sad as a puppy's. The man was trying to pry opinions out of her much as he would pry sardines from a can: gently, one by one.

But why, since she had known Grace Cooley for the space of only one day? As head of the state's western district major crime squad, he had been called in by Litchfield's resident trooper to investigate the death. The state troopers' barracks were a half-mile from the inn, so the response time was fast. Yellow police tape was hurriedly strung up around a large section of the property, including the mansion itself.

The fifteen guests and the staff members had waited dispiritedly in the sunroom until Drucker's officers plucked them, one by one, and took them into an office for separate interviews. Louise had been impressed. The troopers were taking no chances, even if this did appear to be suicide. If it turned out otherwise, they were assuring that no evidence was disturbed. By ten, the interviews were over, and Louise expected that she would be free to go like the others. That was when Drucker, after a polite word with Bill, had called her into the library.

"I need you for a few more minutes," he had told her.

"I hope it's just a few," she had said, with a limp smile she had hoped would evoke pity.

So now she sat here with everything under control, even her tears. There was no way she was going to be caught in the emotional maelstrom of grieving for Jeffrey or Grace. Two people, virtual strangers, dashed to pieces on Connecticut's rocks. It was bad enough that death had reared up again in her path; this time she intended to shun it.

But it was hard. The lump in her throat was palpable as she remembered the last time she saw them: Jeffrey, the dashing sportsman in loden shorts and hiking boots, rucksack on his back, the light of adventure in his green eyes. Not even disdaining a 2,300-foot peak because he loved climbing so much. And the night before, dancing with zest and grace, talking spiritedly about his work with plants.

And Grace, the earnest learner, who brought the delight of a child to the garden tour today, even overcoming her shyness to recite her floral poems. She had seemed emotionally wasted after her row with Bebe. Contending with a raging headache, and the terrible news of Jeffrey's fall, she had to be escorted off to bed, again like a child.

Louise silently choked back more tears, and reached her hand out to her friend, the cat. None of it was her business, she firmly reminded herself, even if she had made a bond with both Jeffrey and Grace in the short time she had known them. The dynamic scientist. The romantic gardener.

She sat stoically, staring at the fireplace, and felt herself sinking into a quiet depression. The room was dark and this, perhaps, was why the bookcases and the marble busts loomed so ominously. Near the fireplace, a dried bouquet made of silver-coined money plant and lavender statice was in perfect harmony with the gloomy surroundings.

Cold hearth, dead flowers: Louise shuddered. But then an orange spark caught her eye—a sign of life in a dead room. She sat forward and took a closer look. The hearth was not cold. Wisps of smoke emerged from a few still-glowing embers that squirmed like a tiny nest of restless orange worms.

Wasn't it remarkable, she thought, that with all these terrible distractions, the staff had remembered to make a fire tonight?

Drucker's dark eyes were still pinned on her, as if he were trying to force his way through the shell she had built around herself.

"I expect something of you, Mrs. Eldridge."

"You do? What?"

He gave her a semblance of a smile, as if he could see right through her, even if he couldn't get to her. "I bet you can figure as well as I can. When I heard about a dead woman at the foot of Litchfield Falls, I had just barely digested the report that came in on that professor's death up at Bear Mountain. I bet you don't know how treacherous that little mountain is, with a fifteen-foot pile of stones on top of the summit that everybody thinks they have to scramble up. Maybe he lost his balance up there, who knows? Now you"—and he leaned forward and rested his hands on his knees—"probably have the same kinds of thoughts running through *your* head—thinking the deaths of two of the inn's guests within hours of each other is too strange to be a total coincidence. Then I heard about Barbara Seymour's tumble down the stairs. Though you might not know this, that lady might have died or at least become an invalid from that fall. She has bones like porcelain."

"It was just a miracle that Chris and Janie were able to break her fall," Louise said faintly.

"As for what I want, I have to confess that I've heard about you, or read about you, can't remember which came first. The garden lady who's solved crimes."

Snapped back to attention, she gave him a dour look. Did he really think she was going to be flattered by being identified like that?

"Sergeant Drucker, please—I don't want to get involved."

He scratched his fulsome head of dark hair, puzzled. "Ma'am, does a smart lady like you think you're not already involved? You're all involved: your husband and your daughter, and your friend and your friend's son. So is every guest at Litchfield Falls Inn—at least until we make a determination of cause of death. And you can be of special help."

"How?"

He leaned back and retrieved a small notepad from his shirt

pocket, resting it on his knee. This move evoked the memory of her Fairfax police detective friend Mike Geraghty so strongly that she could almost overlay the image of Geraghty's big body, cheery Irish face, and bright, marblelike blue eyes onto Sergeant Drucker's more prosaic countenance. "First of all, I want you to know I go by the book. Though this case looks like a cut-and-dried suicide, I preserved the scene and we're going to great lengths not to miss any evidence that may be lying about. And our inquiries will not stop until we're completely satisfied there was no foul play. Though the Freeling death is not in our jurisdiction, it is possibly related to this case, and so our inquiries will also extend in that direction, as well as touch on Miss Seymour's fall, if necessary. Three potential crimes, you might say. Now, you and your family have had a kind of a catbird seat this weekend at the inn—I figured *you,* particularly, know everything about everybody."

Louise was quiet and he continued with his speech, shaking a big finger for emphasis: "Pure and simple, Mrs. Eldridge. I want you to help us rule out murder in the death of Grace Cooley. And if you have anything to offer on Barbara Seymour's accident or Jeffrey Freeling's fall, well, that would be gravy."

Seeing her eyebrows come down in a frown, he hastened to add: "Believe me, I hold your skills in high regard, or I wouldn't be trying to enlist your aid. I'd like you to run through some of the things you've seen, things you've heard—or overheard. Anything that helps us get a better handle on the relationships between the people around here."

Satisfied that he had made his point, he scooped up his little notepad, leaned his arms on his sturdy legs, and turned his penetrating gaze upon her. "Now, let's take the most recent event first. The husband, James Cooley, is not a suspect in Grace Cooley's death—he wasn't out of sight of the others since the time she left the veranda about five P.M. That sharply reduces the odds that it was foul play: You and I both know that the spouse is the likeliest candidate in a situation like this. What we're looking at—and I know these people were strangers to you—is *connections*. What associations, not immediately apparent, there were between the guests."

Louise looked at the sergeant and saw in him what she saw in herself: a puzzle solver. He had tweaked at her and finally broken her shell, her firm resolve not to become involved in the investigation of these deaths. They were both driven by a desire to know what happened, how it happened, and why. And most important, they needed to know who could have committed murder.

She held up a hand casually, feeling as if it were a white flag of surrender. "Okay, I'll help. Connections. Sure. I have lots of things I can tell you about connections."

He smiled broadly. "That's what I'd heard. You probably have a complete vitae on the whole bunch of 'em by now."

"Oh? From whom did you hear that?"

He was embarrassed. "Actually, I made a call to Fairfax County. I, uh, didn't want to enlist your help without checkin' a little closer. Talked to a Detective Geraghty."

"I know him well."

"Yep, he said that, too. And he said if anyone can smell a skunk in the woodpile, it's you." He smiled encouragingly. "He thinks very highly of you."

"Doesn't think I did it, does he?"

"Oh, no, ma'am, absolutely not."

Once, the Fairfax police *had* put her on the list of suspects, in the death of Madeleine Doering. She guessed Sergeant Drucker hadn't delved *that* deeply during his background check. "And how is Detective Geraghty?"

"Oh, he sends you his best." Drucker's mundane features broke into a big grin, and she couldn't resist smiling back. Flipping over a page in the little notepad and extricating a pen from his pocket, he said, "Let's just go through the list, shall we? Better still, let's walk and talk."

"Sure—I've been doing that all day. What's a little more?"

"I want to take you to the Cooleys' room. There's something there that you might be able to decipher for me. Poetry. Not exactly my specialty."

She sighed. "All right, Sergeant Drucker. And then I suppose you'll want to hear about the bumps and thumps in the night."

His eyes lit up. "Would I ever."

The words were penned in a round, neat hand. The dots for the "i's" were tiny, neat circles. They were written on a sheet of paper about nine inches long by six inches wide that was torn off a desk pad imprinted with the name of the Litchfield Falls Inn. Only in the fourth line was there disorder, as if the author was confused.

"Is it supposed to be a suicide note?" asked Louise.

"Read it and see what you think. I think it's possible."

Sergeant Drucker and Louise were in the Cooleys' bedroom suite, which Louise noted was much larger than the others: special family privilege, no doubt. A suite tucked around the corner at the end of the hallway, it was done in pale rose and green. An empty vase stood on the bedside table. Louise could imagine Grace removing the bouquet from her bedroom, since she was philosophically opposed to cut flowers.

The faint residue of Grace's perfume was still in the air, a light French variety that Louise recognized as *L'Air du Temps*. The bed was made, but the pink-and-green quilt that covered it bore the faint impression of a body, and someone had lain their head on the ruffled pillow sham. It gave Louise an eerie feeling: Grace's imprint, there on the bed. On the nearby desk was a pen, with its cap off, lying on the sheet of ivory paper.

Louise could visualize Grace, distracted, probably holding her head in her hand since it was aching, sitting at the desk and composing the lines.

She automatically reached out to touch the note. The sergeant said, "Please don't. Just read it."

Bending over, she read aloud:

> " 'It is all gone now, since last we kissed
> Our precious flowers, our love in the mist
> My love lies bleeding, near the Iris Red
> And my pulsing heart is pleading—' "

The words trailed off; Grace could not think of a phrase to complete her poem. "Dear God," Louise whispered, as a wave of coldness ran through her body.

"What is it?" asked Sergeant Drucker.

Was this the point at which Grace, so unsure of herself, so frail and nervous, the poet and erstwhile student whose only expertise was gardening and a certain capacity to write—was this the point where she gave it up, left this room, walked the trail up to the falls, and jumped to her death?

"So, what do you think?" coaxed the sergeant. "This poem could be a definitive piece of evidence."

She forced her eyes away from the paper and slowly wandered around the large room, trying to feel the vibrations of the delicate and poetic Grace. She paused to stare out the large windows that afforded a superb view of the distant hills. What tipped Grace over the edge, made her unable to go on with her life?

Finally she answered him. "It's so dark, so morose. And the references to 'our love in the mist,' and the 'Iris Red,' which I'm sure refers to the Sacred Blood iris—"

"Sacred blood?" His eyes widened.

"Plant nomenclature is a bit strange," Louise said matter-of-factly. "The question to ask, Sergeant Drucker, is whether this is the way a woman talks to her husband in a suicide poem. I think it is, if all is lost between them. I'd be very curious to know exactly what the status of the Cooley marriage was."

She circled back to the desk and read the unfinished verse again. "Yes—it definitely says there's been a parting of the ways. What did Jim tell you? That is, if you're at liberty to share that with me."

Drucker's eyes scanned the room as he spoke. "He maintains she was very down in the dumps lately. She apparently suffered from depression—went to a psychiatrist once a week. Took antidepressants on occasion."

Louise's mind perversely called up a picture of a happy young woman enthusing over old-fashioned garden flowers. Yet each new fact supported suicide. Ongoing depression. The need for antidepressants. She tried to force herself to acknowledge the increasing possibility that two people leaped or fell to their deaths today, without benefit of evildoers to help them.

"I did see her taking pills at every stopping place today. But they looked like aspirin to me—aspirin and echinacea."

"Take a look at the bottles." Using a handkerchief to keep from contaminating any fingerprints with his own, he opened the drawer of the bedside table and pointed to a series of bottles. "Here's her medicine. Let's see, Prozac—well, that's pretty strong. Saint-John's-wort: She'd used most of the bottle. Echinacea."

Louise understood it now, and it made sense. Grace believed in natural remedies, medicines from flowers. She doubted that the woman had depended on Prozac to get through life, so much as she did the natural herb, Saint-John's-wort, a popular remedy for depression.

"And here's a little plastic Baggie," said Drucker. "It looks like aspirin, and"—he held it up to the light with the same handkerchief and peered at the impression on the pills—"it is aspirin. But Mr. Cooley said when they were in the room together before coming down for tea, she took one of those Prozacs. Who knows? The autopsy will tell us just what and how much medication she consumed before going up to the falls."

Louise stared at the Baggie. It was the one from which

she had seen Grace removing pills. Surely, popping aspirin wasn't that bad, was it? It was from a plant, too—she'd read that somewhere.

Drucker continued: "Mr. Cooley also mentioned something else. They apparently couldn't have children, in spite of lots of special efforts—" His face reddened. "You know, temperature-taking, etcetera."

"Well, that's enough to drive some people over the edge. The trying and failing, that is."

"That's what they did: They tried and failed. So as a substitute, she spent a lot of time gardening—or so he says."

"Yes, she told us at length about her garden. She was immersed in it."

"He called it an obsession, which he finally had to try to 'curb,' as he put it. She took to writing poems about it—well, that poem in the room was just one of them, I guess."

"So you're saying there was strain in the marriage, created by depression, obsessive behavior, and maybe the lack of children. I bet Frank and Fiona Storm could tell us more about it."

"They probably could, if they chose to—but they have been the soul of propriety, especially as private family matters go. Mr. Cooley admitted to me that he told his wife he wanted her to get her feet on the ground. But he came off sounding pretty protective of her. Not like somebody who was going to ditch her for not producing an heir for him, or for being a flighty garden fanatic."

Louise turned toward him so quickly that he flinched. "*Flighty* garden fanatic. Well, I'm one too, you know, Sergeant Drucker. In fact, that's how I make a living. I work at being what you would call a flighty garden fanatic every day of my life. That's why I felt a certain empathy with Grace. She was *passionate* about gardening—not flighty."

The sergeant's face was crimson. "Ma'am, I apologize. I was just talking from Mr. Cooley's point of view. He's the one who considered her fanatical—not me."

"Of course," said Louise, not quite exonerating him. He was just another person who viewed gardening as a kooky pursuit, not one of America's major industries. "Now, Sergeant, let's not get hung up on that. Did you find Grace's notebook?"

"She had a notebook?"

"Yes. It was like a teenager's diary. She wrote in it constantly—a little red leather looseleaf notebook about three by five inches big. She noted everything she saw on the tour, put in poetic quotes she liked, things like that. You must have found it."

"Most likely someone has already checked it into evidence. I'll find out."

After a moment, she added, "In fact, I'd say that notebook is another definitive piece of evidence. Grace put her heart into her writing. We garden fanatics do that, you know." She smiled kindly at him; every man deserved a second chance.

Drucker gave her a wary look and changed the subject. "So what do you think of what Mr. Cooley said?"

"Well, in Grace I saw a person who was very happy and delighted one moment, then floundering in a deep emotional trough the next. Very sensitive to everything, but of course, all of us were devastated to hear that one of our fellow guests, uh, fell off the mountain."

"Believe it or not, we've had more than one do that over the years."

"This accident was a shock to everybody at the inn. Yet Grace barely knew Jeffrey. What was almost as traumatic, I'd guess, was the terrible fight she had today with Bebe Hollowell. Why, the woman was about to punch Grace in the nose. Grace said some tactless things and hurt Bebe's feelings. Then Bebe lashed right back at Grace."

"How'd she do that?"

"It was rather silly at first. Bebe said she'd like to put some of that new red iris on her husband's grave. Ernie Hollowell—he recently died, you know—"

"She told me all about it."

"And Grace told her she didn't believe in picking flowers, *period*. That, of course seemed to denigrate Bebe's desire to beautify Ernie's burial spot, and Bebe just blew her top. Then Grace made matters worse by suggesting that Bebe's constant talking about Ernie's death made her appear guilty of something."

"Huh," said the sergeant. "So that's what happened. Mrs. Hollowell didn't give me details. But she does seem to be suffering from guilt."

"I haven't talked to her since we found Grace."

"Never seen the likes of it. She's with a trooper now, who's trying to calm her down. No wonder she's upset. There's nothing like having someone die after you've just had a fight with them. And then there's her lack of alibi."

"Oh?"

"Yes. Mrs. Hollowell was up in her room, like Mrs. Cooley, from teatime on. There was only one other person out of sight near the time of Mrs. Cooley's fall."

Louise had a dim memory of someone excusing herself directly after dinner, pleading exhaustion.

"Fiona."

"Yes. Fiona Storm."

She looked at him. "There were about seventeen people staying in this house, weren't there?"

"Yes, not counting Barbara Seymour and her staff."

"You almost need a chart to keep track of people's comings and goings, and of all the strange events of the past day or so. The odd behavior people had toward each other. The disagreements and fights. The bumps and thumps . . ."

"Oh, yes—you mentioned them. Now, this was last night?"

"Last night, very late—actually about two in the morning. And the other sounds . . ." She sighed; she was going to have to tell him about the love moan.

"What other sounds?"

"As if some of the guests had sneaked out of their rooms and were tiptoeing around the upstairs hall in the dark. And there was a kind of moaning, as if someone were . . . making love."

Drucker looked at her incredulously.

"I'm only telling you how it sounded. I couldn't see much of anything because all the lights were out—someone must have thrown the circuit breaker. I heard doors opening and closing, but I'm not sure how many, and someone went down the front stairs—I know that for sure, because the stairs squeaked. And, as I said, somebody was moaning, as if . . ."

"As if they were enjoying themselves, huh?"

She laughed nervously. "It's a wonder we didn't hear a ghost playing the pianoforte in the living room! And then, there were the two men I saw in silhouette, in front of the hall window. They appeared to be—hugging each other. That's all."

The sergeant's eyebrows shot up in surprise. *That's right, Sergeant Drucker,* she thought, *add homosexuality to this perplexing set of deaths and you really have a mess.*

"Was that before or after the, uh, moaning?"

"Just after."

His brow had creased into a formidable set of wrinkles. "You're right, Mrs. Eldridge. We'll have to reconstruct the whole weekend. This is going to be something to try to sort out."

Reconstructing the Garden: Don't Deconstruct Yourself While You're At It

SOME THINGS, LIKE DIAMONDS, may be forever, but gardens are not. Seemingly solid, earthy, and unchanging, they need constant care. They must have a yearly freshening up, and on occasion, bigger changes. Here are some important tips:

🌿 This comes from a botanical garden director, who warns that renowned gardens didn't get that way without a lot of work. Although it may sound strange to you, make your motto, "Maximum manure, and maximum disturbance of plants." Most of the plants in botanical showplaces have been lifted each year and rich new soil tucked under their tushes and around their sides.

🌿 Many backyard gardeners have deconstructed themselves in the process of reconstructing their gardens—for instance, after deciding to do a complete garden overhaul in the space of one weekend.

🌿 If you have too much garden, downsize, and put in plants that "pay rent."

Do these seem to be warring ideas—treating our gardens like ICU patients to make them prosper, and in doing so putting ourselves into intensive care? The answer, as usual, is to compromise. You can have a near-prizewinning garden without destroying your back. It requires a sensible garden plan; a rational schedule to do the work; the right kind of tools; physical training; and a Tom Sawyer approach to getting others to help you.

Yes, you should train for the gardening season, just as any athlete would train for arduous physical activity. As long as you avoid ruining yourself, gardening is very good for you: You will use up as many calories as you would taking a brisk walk, or playing a round of golf. Don't go overboard—follow a work schedule and don't dig for longer than you can handle. Start out slowly and harden yourself as you would a seedling, by first working in the shade, then going out gradually to face the sun. Dress sensibly, and carry a big water bottle. One woman, known for overgardening and ending up in bed on a heating pad, keeps a cell phone in her jeans. Her husband calls from work and warns her after three or four hours that it's time to quit for the day.

Needless to say, this gardener has tools that help her avoid self-destruction: easy-to-use high-quality pruners and tree loppers; a sharp shovel and hoe; and a set of three or four sturdy cart wheelbarrows. Their size makes it impossible to carry a lazy man's heavy load, which is her natural tendency. Several carts make it easy to sort garden materials and collect spent dirt.

The first step is to sit down with your garden map and study it. You don't have one, with plants marked with their full names? Make one. Even a crude one will do fine. After you use it for your latest garden renewal, tape it to your refrigerator door in summer— what better use could a refrigerator door have? As you acquire new plants, you can quickly jot down their name and location. In fall, put this valuable resource tool into your looseleaf garden notebook. No notebook? It is a place to keep your garden's history, and should include an informal diary of what happened in your planting patches all year, what succeeded, what failed. It can hold the list of annual tasks to be done, empty seed packets, seed-starting calendars, garden snapshots, and articles about plants.

Look at the big picture and then zero in on the particulars. First, study the microclimate of your yard. Is it changing? Microclimate includes wind, sun, shade, and water supply. Since deer are invading even the White House

grounds and seem to make all our yards their playgrounds, your analysis should include a system for deer-proofing your precious plants. Don't be content to just let things happen naturally. Remember, the very definition of a gardener should be "one who tinkers with nature." Don't be afraid to make changes in the microclimate that could benefit plants and trees for decades ahead. This might mean "limbing up" big branches of a tree to open a view; planting a row of trees for wind control; erecting a high screening fence against the deer; felling a tree completely, or moving it to another site; and creating hills and swales in the land purely for aesthetics, or for water dispersion and control.

Try to save this heavy-duty work for when there are helpers around—neighbors, friends, family. They'll have a special feeling for you if they've helped you rope, tie, and haul a two-hundred-pound cedar tree to a new location in your yard. If we're talking gargantuan tree, hire a landscaping company; it is worthwhile, for mature trees add enormously to your property's value. If you wield a ruthless pruning scissors, you can delay moving trees and bushes for years. Get a book and learn how to prune, not by snipping off the tips of limbs, but by removing them at the base, and leaving the collar. Do it regularly; do it to flowering trees after they bloom.

Strangely enough, once they have a hole in their landscape, some people seem to think they must fill it with a big plant. This reflects a Camus-like, existential view of life, and ignores a delicate truth: Gardens should be permitted to *grow*—to develop over time. Your home garden is not expected to look finished on a day-to-day basis. The idea of "becoming" perfect should be valued by gardeners, as well as the idea of "being" perfect. Therefore, when you think replacement plants, think smaller.

Once you've created an enormous bare spot by ripping out a huge shrub, try landscapers' tricks to fill it. Use self-seeding plants, like *Coreopsis* 'Moonbeam,' white cosmos, snapdragons, or ground covers. A jazzy, newer variety is the dazzling chartreuse-leaved sweet potato vine, *Ipomoea batatas* 'Margarita.'

When dividing plants, you don't always have to do it the hard way. Bearded iris and peonies are among the plants that can be divided by the overhead "ax-murder" technique. That means chopping straight down from above the plant and lopping off a root section at the edge of the plant. Also, do not move specimens that are nicely filling their spaces. Enjoy, and don't consider changes until plants grow far beyond their boundaries or die out in the middle.

You may be getting to the stage in life where you feel older than you did last year. After all, immortality doesn't go on forever—or did Yogi Berra say that? You look at your wonderful but needy garden with the jaundiced eye of a Gerstner of IBM. You begin to scream inwardly, *Downsize, you fool!* It's easy: Just put in woody shrubs, variegated foliage plants, small evergreens, ornamental grasses,

peonies, hostas, and ground covers such as ferns. Pros say they're the kind of plants that "pay rent." That is, they provide maximum visual glory with a minimum of effort. They are perfect choices for the downsizing gardener.

Chapter Thirteen

BILL SAT ON THE veranda, staring at an unusual sight. The tall hemlocks at the edge of the forest, backlit by the moon, cast huge shadows onto the lawn that looked for all the world like prostrate worshipers to a pagan god. He let his imagination run loose. *If this were a horror movie,* he thought, *the worshipers would rise up from the lawn and come and get me; a Disney movie, and they'd get up and do a spirited dance together.*

But there was little joy in his fantasy, for he could not share it with his wife. He stole a look at Louise. She sat ramrod-straight beside him, stress emanating from her like a high-tension tower. He had a sudden feeling that if he touched her, he'd be electrocuted. No, she was not approachable right now. In fact, he didn't like the way things were going at all in the pretty hills of Connecticut. What was supposed to be a relaxing weekend for his family and friends had been anything but. And Louise looked ruined. Usually, she was sensitive to the fact that as a TV garden-show host she was a public figure, if only a minor one. Her summer dress was fresh and attractive, but her long brown hair was messy, and she hadn't put on any new makeup since she'd washed it off in the shower they'd taken together late this afternoon. Deep circles cut under her eyes, heightening the vacant expression in them. Yet he could hardly tell his forty-three-year-old wife to go to the ladies' room and put on a little makeup.

Louise was now mixed up in the deaths of two strangers—attracted like a bear to a honey tree by anything resembling a mystery. One death appeared to be an accident, one a suicide—but who knew for sure? Certainly not that Boy Scout of a state trooper, Drucker, who'd had the chutzpah to drag Louise in on the investigation. Yet Drucker had cleverly issued the same invitation to them all, as Bill had discovered from talking to Janie and Chris and Nora. The trooper told each one of them that he needed any scrap of information they had, and that they should hustle it right over to him—even phone him at night—if they thought of anything.

Bill felt sorry for the guy. He had come upon an assortment of fifteen out-of-towners, practically strangers to one another, and needed to find out—quickly—about any hidden relationships, grudges, or alliances that might exist among them. And Drucker didn't want anyone to leave Litchfield until the preliminary investigation was completed, around noon tomorrow—which was fine with Bill since their plane reservations from New York back to Washington were not until tomorrow evening.

It made him uncomfortable, though, that Louise was the one Drucker'd singled out to take to the Cooley bedroom and show the evidence. What especially annoyed him was that Drucker had called Detective Geraghty in Virginia to vet Louise before essentially signing her up as an extra detective. He would have to keep an eagle eye on his wife, because he knew from past experience how impetuous she could be. Geraghty's imprimatur would encourage her to God knows what kind of lengths to "help the investigation"!

Now Louise, Nora, and Bill sat at a table on the nearly empty veranda with a brandy nightcap provided by Barbara's staff. Off to one side, Sergeant Drucker was just concluding a conversation with the local reporter Louise had befriended today. His wife had apparently spilled the beans about Barbara Seymour's plan to turn the mansion over to the Connecticut Trust. Then the young reporter had heard about Grace's accident and probably ditched his Saturday night date to hustle over to the inn. He looked over at them briefly, and Bill could see a hunter's gleam in his eye.

Through talking to the reporter, Drucker and his men solemnly gathered up their notes and prepared to go, leaving one trooper stationed inside the mansion tonight. An unhappy-looking Jim Cooley came out to speak with the sergeant then, and from the fragments of conversation he could hear, Bill guessed Cooley wanted to go to the morgue where his wife's body had been taken.

He looked at Louise. She had heard the exchange, too.

"I suppose it would be a comfort to him," he said, shrugging his shoulders. "Maybe he wants to find out the exact cause of death. She may have OD'd on Prozac and then staggered up that hill and jumped."

"Maybe," said Louise, her eyes staring right through him. Then she seemed to come to her senses. She looked at him again, only this time she saw him and gave him a little smile, like a token gift to a friend. Her shoulders relaxed about a millimeter. "I'm exhausted—are you?"

"Certainly am. Why don't we say good night to the veranda at the friendly old Litchfield Falls Inn and hike off to bed?"

"Just a minute—I'm thinking."

Nora was sitting across the table observing Louise, and she nodded in a knowing way. "Her detective juices are flowing. Don't disturb her." Bill drew back as if Nora had struck him. *Since when can't I talk to my own wife?*

Nora was beginning to get on his nerves. She had been down in the dumps ever since they heard about Jeffrey's fall, and seeing Grace in that pool at the base of the falls had made her mood even darker. He wished she could find some little thing to be happy about. Maybe it would be less annoying if she hadn't worn that black mourning outfit for a guy she'd known for ten hours total.

"So—what are you thinking about?" he asked Louise. He sat back carefully in his chair, trying not to feel left out, desperately wanting to become a member of her club.

Without answering him, she turned to Nora. "Would you have guessed Grace was suicidal?"

"I don't know, Louise," Nora said. "Today she acted intoxicated—all excited by the garden tour, I expect. And then just as quickly she was wounded, like a small, vulnerable animal, when Bebe said a cross word to her. That's strange behavior. She could have been near the breaking point, for reasons we don't even know."

"How about this reason: a marriage about to break up?" asked Louise.

"That could explain it," said Nora.

"Yes, sure could," parroted Bill.

Louise touched his arm and said, "Honey, you'll be interested in this, too." These words made him feel better; he sat forward to listen as she pulled out a little pad of paper and read them the poem that Grace had written and left in her bedroom. "I wrote this down as best I could—I think I have it right."

"How would you finish that?" said Bill, his mind instantly clicking into action. "Has to rhyme with 'iris red.' So it's 'dead,' 'fed,' 'head,' 'led,' 'said,' or 'wed.' " He grinned. "Or maybe it's 'abed.' "

Nora inhaled her cigarette and glanced at him disdainfully; his attempts to lighten the mood were not being valued highly. In a sad voice she said, "It sounds like a tragic goodbye to her husband."

"Then Drucker damned well ought to find out what was going on between Jim and Grace," observed Bill, returning to a serious tone. "I could tell that woman was ready to break."

Louise leaned toward him. "We have to remember that there were two people unaccounted for when Grace disappeared from her room."

"Who and who?" he asked.

"Bebe—you remember how Bebe had her dinner sent up, like Grace—and Fiona. Fiona scooted away from the dinner table as soon as she finished her main course. But Sergeant Drucker thinks she wouldn't have had enough time to be involved. And Bebe? She was a wreck this afternoon. Could she have been strong enough to get Grace up to the falls?"

"There's no exact time of death, I suppose," said Bill.

"No. They never can cut it that close." Louise smiled wanly at them. "Only in detective stories, where the murderer breaks the victim's watch during a struggle."

Bill was glad to see even this small bit of levity from his wife. "Or topples over the grandfather clock," he added.

"So let's conclude that Grace is a suicide, at least for the moment. What about Janie and Chris's theory about Jeffrey's being pushed? They've shared it with that Teddy Horton . . ."

"And inadvertently with Mark Post," he added.

"Is it worth thinking about?" she asked.

"Maybe, maybe not," said Bill pontifically. "We have to re-member to keep our minds open." He looked at the two women guiltily. Since they had done him the honor of including him in the conversation, he wished he could have offered some-thing pithier. "Maybe" and "maybe not" were not the brightest things he'd ever said.

They all fell silent for a moment, and then Nora said, "Louise, promise me something." The woman's large gray eyes focused in on Louise like a laser. Bill had a wild desire to wave his hand between the two women's faces and break the connection.

"Of course," said Louise.

"I realize this place will be swarming with police again in the morning," said Nora. "But be careful, please—I beg you."

Oh, oh. It was Nora's sense of impending danger again. At this late point in the evening it bugged the hell out of him. Bill knew about her extrasensory powers, but it was the first time he had seen this oraclelike woman coming out with one of her prophecies.

He shoved his chair back roughly and crossed his legs. "Aw, c'mon, Nora," he said, "you're not telling us you sense di-saster again. Do we really believe this?" His words were sharp, because he was feeling nervous, not wanting to be part of this crazy stuff, not wanting Louise to be frightened again. Though God knows at the CIA he had been involved in se-cret scientific studies of this very topic: first, the studies of ultra-low-frequency ground communication with American submarines—a venture attempted in rural Wisconsin that failed miserably. And then, the corollary studies of ESP to see if men in airplanes could communicate with those same nuclear-equipped subs: This again was a super-secret, but eyebrow-raising, failure. Even the memory of it was embarrassing. He recollected how the U.S. secret services—army, navy, and CIA—resuscitated these efforts over and over in the '70s be-cause of repeated rumors back then of the Soviets' success sending thought messages through space and water.

It was crazy then, he thought, and it was crazy now. As a young CIA officer at that time, he had suspected that the Soviets were putting the Americans on; but no one wanted to believe a low-ranking employee who had barely blown in from Harvard.

Right now, all that didn't matter. He was in trouble. His facetious remarks had been bad enough, but the perceived insult was over the top. He could see that a distinct tremble had developed in Nora's sensuous, pink bottom lip; she was going to cry. Here was their attractive neighbor, a woman Bill liked very much, one of the most composed women he knew, about to shatter into tears.

"Nora, look, I'm *sorry*—I didn't mean to insult you. It's just that I'm not sure it does Louise any good—"

"—to be warned her life is in danger?" Nora said the words in such a low voice that he could hardly hear them.

"You think her life is in danger?" he repeated, feeling foolish.

Nora sat back in her chair, much as she had the evening before, as if she were closing Louise and Bill out, physically and spiritually. A picture of Athena popped into his mind, often described in *The Odyssey* as the gray-eyed goddess who directed the affairs of men. Whimsically, he imagined Nora as their very own gray-eyed goddess.

But the goddess was pissed off right now. She turned her back to them with quiet deliberation, and for the first time in his life he understood fully the term, "turning a cold shoulder." The smoke from her cigarette floated around her like a filmy mantle as she stared into the shadows of the night.

"I believe you, Nora," said Louise in a tight voice. "And I will take care." She grabbed Bill's hand. "Walk me up to my room, will you? Nora wants to be alone. But I surely don't."

She hurried him through the downstairs rooms. His banishment was to be swift. Without turning her head to him, she hissed between clenched teeth, "Did you have to fight with Nora? Surely, Bill, you can deal with that woman by now—she means only good."

165

"Sorry, honey. But all that mumbo-jumbo ESP stuff . . ."

"That comes *straight* from her inner, poetic self. Don't you understand?"

Understand Nora? He wasn't sure he understood his own wife.

Softly, he muttered, "What you have to remember is that I've been there, done that . . ."

"What did you say?" Her voice was sharp. "What do I have to remember *this* time?"

"Oh, nothing important."

She was sitting cross-legged on the bed, her pink charmeuse nightie riding up around her thighs, but she barely noticed it. The little pad of paper on her lap was illuminated only by the dim millefiori bedside lamp, the antique shade made of the pieces of glass left at the day's end in the shop of some ancient glassblower. It cast a multicolored glow on her pad: cute but impractical, since she had to squint to see what she had written.

Scribbled on the pad was Grace's unfinished quatrain. How had Grace intended to finish it? Granted, Louise and her husband and her friend Nora had agreed that Grace was the suicidal type. And yet Louise couldn't quite lay the matter to rest, or get this poem off her mind. She knew if she could find the right words, she would be able to tell whether Grace had jumped or had been forced over those falls.

> *"It is all gone now, since last we kissed*
> *Our precious flowers, our love in the mist*
> *My love lies bleeding, near the Iris Red*
> *And my pulsing heart is pleading—"*

" 'For I will be dead'?" she muttered to herself. " 'Until I am dead'? 'Why should I not be dead'? No, that's not right." Bill's rhyming words also led nowhere.

Louise pressed the pencil against her lip. Bill. The thought of him made her guilty. She had been snappish with him this evening, over Nora. She thought philandering, not ESP, would be the issue that caused a flare-up with Nora.

ESP, indeed. Even Louise was skeptical. She knew in her heart when she was in trouble—she didn't need Nora's special powers to detect it. Only once had her friend pulled out of the blue a forecast of impending danger. The other times had been as predictable as a CNN weather map predicting a big storm. She thought, *Snoop into the affairs of dangerous men, and of course I'm going to be in danger.*

She would have to apologize to her husband first thing in the morning.

With that resolved, she turned her attention back to the quatrain. Grace appeared to have been a clever although not brilliant rhymester. Louise herself did not write poetry. She had in fact gone to great pains to avoid doing it her whole life, from grade school right through college creative-writing classes.

The lump on the right side of the bed moved, accompanied by the relocation of a mass of long yellow hair. Janie's muffled voice said, "Aren't you ever going to stop mumbling and go to sleep?"

"In a minute, darling."

"You could at least quit talking to yourself."

"Yes, darling, I'll do that." Louise looked at the door that led to the hall, and it came to her in a flash: If she could sort out what happened in that hall last night, everything else would fall in place—she wouldn't even have to decipher Grace's rhyme.

Without wanting to be, she was drawn to that door. The attraction was as strong as if she were a character in a Poe horror tale. Then, the millefiori lamp suddenly went black, and she had no choice. She put her feet on the floor and fumbled around until they found her mules. Then, in a kind of impromptu blind-man's buff game, she stretched out her hands to find the over-stuffed chair, picked up her robe, and put it on. She silently moved to the door.

The hallway was a pit of darkness. In a shock of understanding, Louise realized that the lights had been deliberately shut off both last night and tonight. But why again tonight? The only explanation was that someone at the Litchfield Falls Inn intended to perpetrate a crime in the rich, velvety darkness. . . .

She had released herself from the safety of her room and now felt as if she were adrift in a black sea. She took a few steps into the hall. What drew her there was the knowledge that the answers were there, among the occupants of this vast upstairs floor.

Like one of the lower, invertebrate animals, Louise slunk along the wall, making her way again to the relative safety of the bench under the windows. Her fingers found the highly pol-ished ancient pine seat, and she sat down carefully, ducking so that her silhouette was not outlined against the window. She had seen the moon bright in the sky earlier—yet clouds had moved in and now stood in the way of any light reaching into this dark hallway.

After a few minutes, she began to hear the little noises again, as she had last night. Clicks of doors quietly shutting, the spooky sense of footsteps back and forth. A low murmur of voices at the far end of the corridor, and tonight, in the deep gloom, only a suggestion of movement by the window at the end of the hall. Then a thrill of terror surged through her like an electric current, as a big body crowded in next to her and arms encircled her. "Oh!" she started to cry out. A strong hand was clamped over her mouth. With every fiber of strength she pos-sessed, Louise tried to pull away and failed. Then there was a loud whisper in her ear. "Shut up and listen."

She had been overpowered so completely that until that moment she had been sure it had to be a man. But now there was the rich, feminine voice and the odor of perfume on the body next to hers. Nora? No. Bebe.

Louise shook her head vigorously, freeing it for a moment from the smothering hand. "For God's *sake,* Bebe," she hissed, and then the hand clamped onto her mouth again, tighter this time.

"I *told* you, listen, don't talk! Half the people in this inn are wandering around this hall, but I'm only interested in you. If you promise not to yell, I'll take my hand away. Promise?"

Louise nodded her head sharply, up and down. The hand was slowly drawn away, but Bebe continued to hold her in her vise-like grip.

"Why are you doing this?" Louise whispered angrily.

The other woman talked directly in her ear. "I'm warning you, Louise. I'll let you go in a minute. I know you're the one working with the police. I want you to know all about me, because I'm the only one without an alibi for when Grace . . . went over those falls."

"How do you know that?"

"I figured it out from talking to the others. So now I'm afraid they might charge me. How do I *know* what they'll do to me?"

"Bebe, I don't think they will. Why would they?"

"The same reason they did in my husband's death: I'm *around,* and I don't have an alibi, like the rest of you. So, Louise, I want you to know I didn't do it. And I want you to call my brother—he's in Mattson. He knows I'm not a murderer. He's the only one that will vouch for me. Him and a bunch of old folks."

Louise had dealt with strange people before, but she guessed Bebe was one of the strangest. "Now tell me, just what on earth have old folks got to do with this?"

"I teach dancing at the old folks' home in Mattson. They love me, Louise. I come once a week and teach them everything—the waltz, the fox-trot, even the tango. I'm a volunteer, and they love me! They'll speak for me. The ones that can, though some of them don't make much sense—too senile. Them and my brother. The rest of the town thinks I did it."

"The sheriff still thinks—"

"*Yes*," she rasped, and Louise felt the noise rebound through her ear canals. "He has tests still out at some lab, trying to prove I murdered Ernie. When he hears about what happened down here in Litchfield, who knows what they'll do . . ." The woman was crying. Finally she removed her grip from around Louise and sat back on the bench.

Louise exhaled in relief, then rubbed her arms where the woman had held her. She was perplexed. Was this a ruse to cover up her guilt in another murder, or was the woman simply half crazy over the thought of being falsely suspected for a second time?

Bebe snuffled.

"Shhh," said Louise, "listen." They could sense, more than hear, the presence of other people.

Bebe leaned over and whispered in her ear. "There's bad things going on around here, Louise."

"Oh, God, do I need you to tell me that, too?" She scrambled to her feet. "I'm going to bed. There must be a good night's sleep left in this weekend for me. I suggest you do the same."

But fear was catching. On her way back to her room, the sense of something evil in this dark old hall began to take hold of Louise's mind. By the time she reached the door, she was clammy with sweat and nearly running. She clawed the door open, and closed and locked it behind her. Then she leaned against it, exhaling a great breath, as if she hadn't dared to breathe for several minutes. Bebe was no phantom in the night—she was a flesh-and-blood person, or Louise wouldn't still feel the pain of her unwelcome embrace. But who else was out there?

More than anything else, those bumps in the night convinced Louise that murder had been committed in Litchfield County. Last night was like the prelude, and tonight, the reprise.

Chapter Fourteen

Louise dove into the deep end of the rocky pool and came up shivering. A dozen vigorous strokes brought her back to where Bill and Nora were still inching their bodies into the shallow end. She could see the goose bumps on their upper legs. "Very cold," she said, "but you'll *love* it once you get in."

"That's what people like you always say," grumbled Bill. He liked his pools or oceans warm, preferring the Pacific to the Atlantic, a hot springs pool to the YMCA's. There was no sun this morning, and a faint drizzle of rain was coming down, reducing the water temperature below his comfort level. It hadn't deterred Janie and Chris: They were already diving and playing together like two porpoises, delighted with this pool adjacent to the river. It was another natural cavity in the land, like the watery pit at the base of the falls where Grace had been found dead.

Finally, Bill and Nora immersed themselves and swam enough to at least warm up. It was time to call their clandestine meeting to order. After all, who would bother them, in an isolated pool near the river's bend, in a drizzle, at eight in the morning?

"This better be fast," said Bill, shivering. "I'm turning blue."

"Then let's decide what to do," said Louise. "First, concerning Jeffrey. Any ideas?"

Janie raised a dripping finger. She looked at the woods surrounding them, possibly fearing that Mark Post would pop from behind a tree. "Just remember what I said about certain suspicious dudes." She splashed Chris and the two of them dove off in a wild race to the edge of the pool.

"I have sources," said Bill, and Louise recognized this as an understatement. He could use the resources of both the State Department and the CIA. "I'll check on Mark and Sandy Post. Mark, I gather, is the one with a possible grudge against Jeffrey. Tom Paschen will know Sandy's dad, since he's big in politics." Louise had never even thought of reaching back into Washington and asking their friend Paschen, the President's chief of staff, for help. He had played a part in Louise and Bill's investigations before. A strange, uptight sort of man, he always was helpful when they needed him. "The police will be running a check on the Gasparras," Bill continued. "Maybe I'll run a separate one, just for luck."

"Good," said Louise. "As long as you're doing that, why don't you include Bebe Hollowell and Neil Landry." She had not told them about her encounter with Bebe in the hall last night; she would rather leave it out for now, in fairness to Bebe. She said this much: "We know that Bebe despised Grace by the end of that garden tour. And Neil—we're pretty sure of what he did to Barbara Seymour."

Bill plunged himself up and down in the water a few times for warmth, then hugged himself. "Okay, Louise, let's see if I have this straight: We're trying to find out if Jeffrey's death was murder or an accident; whether Grace's death was murder or suicide; and whether or not Neil Landry engineered Barbara's fall. That's it, huh?"

"Yes, darling," she said airily, making little bicycle exercise motions with her legs in the water.

"That's a lot of things to look into," he said. "I thought we had pretty much agreed Grace self-destructed—"

"Bill, really, what a way to put it. We did. But we might as well check everybody out while we're checking. So many things have happened. They might be connected. And if they aren't involved in one thing, they might be involved in another."

"Oh, for Pete's sake," said Bill glumly, "is there anyone here we consider innocent, except possibly me?"

"Not until we prove them so," she said, laughing.

"And the police? You're sure we're not like the circus horse, stepping into the doo-doo . . ."

"No," she said. "We're just doing what Sergeant Drucker asked me to do—remember, he *invited* me into this mess, I didn't just barge my way in."

Bill raised an eyebrow, but he didn't say, "As you usually do." Instead, he said, "All right. We have three assignments, then."

Louise said, "First, let's talk about Grace. Nora, you said she took a class from a New York poet that you knew. Can you call him—or her?"

"Him. Yes." Nora swirled her hands back and forth in the water in large, graceful circles. "I'll do that. At least it might tell us how she was feeling—since poetry is so reflective of one's inner state."

Louise was happy to note that Nora was less sad this morning, and hoped she continued to improve. She said, "And we've taped a *Gardening with Nature* program at the New York Botanical Garden, so for what it's worth, I know the director of horticulture, Paul Warren. Grace talked a lot about visiting there. I'll phone him; he might have something to offer us."

Janie and Chris had returned, out of breath, to listen. Janie said, "How about those Higher Directions people? The Storms, and, for that matter, Jim Cooley himself?"

"Jim Cooley's off the hook," said Bill. "Don't know why we would bother with him."

"But there's Fiona," said Louise, reminding them that she left the dinner table early. "Yet the sergeant insists she didn't have time to do anything. You know who could find out about Cooley and the Storms for us? Charlie Hurd. Why don't I call him?"

"Louise," cautioned Bill.

"Yes?"

"What we have to keep in mind is that Charles Hurd is a cocky, unscrupulous little son of a bitch."

"But Bill, we *need* him." Charlie had catapulted to fame as a result of a political exposé written by someone else. The young reporter, a slight, sharp-nosed blond man with a giant ego and the conscience of a gnat, had taken too much credit for the story, and Louise had known it. But she'd been helpless to stop it, partly because the story was important and partly because a political exposé that big needed a name attached to it—even the wrong one. In the wake of the story, Charlie had been hired on by *The Washington Post*. At least now Louise could extract some repayment from the arrogant young twerp.

Thinking about him, her lip curled in a smile. She could just imagine him hurtling around the nation's capital in his avantgarde sports car in pursuit of the next big story. He probably *dreamed* of exposés at night.

"What's so funny?" asked Bill, teeth chattering.

"Charlie will think this is boring, after the last time."

"Bet he'll be impressed if we find out some of these dead people didn't get dead on their own," muttered Bill.

"God," said Janie plaintively, "*we* bring up Higher Directions, and you have a reporter friend of yours checking on it. So what are Chris and I supposed to do?"

"Let's see . . ." Louise thought about it, still treading water.

"Hurry up, honey," urged Bill. "What can they do? How about checking out staff people—Teddy, for example?"

"Great," said Janie, "we'll talk to Teddy. I bet he sees lots of stuff going on. He might not even realize the significance of something he's picked up just from watching the guests."

"If you're checking him out, I'm doing it with you," said Chris, grabbing Janie's shoulders and threatening to dunk her. She escaped him by diving underwater and the pair started splashing each other again.

Bill turned to Louise and Nora. "Our battle plan is laid. That's about the best we can do, folks. Now, can I get out of this arctic pool before rigor mortis sets in?"

"Sure," said Louise. She nuzzled under the surface in a smooth breaststroke, raising her head long enough to tell them, "I need to do a few more lengths." In the solitude of the velvet-soft water, she stroked firmly across the pool and back a few times, then around its circumference, diving under and surveying the rocky kingdom below. She reveled in the silky sensuality of swimming, the strong unity of muscles working together, and knew the joy of the amphibian.

Leaping out of the pool, Louise had more energy than when she had climbed in. To her dismay, she saw that the sky was glowering with black clouds. More rain might interfere with their return visit to Wild Flower Farm today. Sergeant Drucker had said that they could leave the inn briefly as long as they stayed together and came back for some final questioning around noon.

Bill stood near the pool's edge and handed Louise a beach towel, while Nora waited quietly on a rustic bench nearby. It was an idyllic scene, the red horse barn and dirt road in the background, the hills rising beyond it. As she gave herself a quick rubdown, Louise glanced enviously at Nora's sumptuous figure so visible in her bathing suit; hormone pills, taken to relieve menopausal symptoms, were increasing Nora's curves, though her weight now was on the cusp. Five more pounds and someone might call her chubby. Louise herself was gaunt by comparison, with her long lean legs. She slung on her robe, gathered up her duffel bag, and decided to forget figures. "My gosh, it's almost nine, folks. We don't have much time for detecting before we're off to Wild Flower Farm."

As the three of them left Janie and Chris frolicking in the water and walked quickly up the long hill to the inn, a sense of hopelessness sneaked up on Louise. "I wonder if we can do it."

"Do it?" asked Bill. "Do what—our investigating?"

"Yes. What can we learn on a Sunday morning on a rainy summer weekend when most normal folks are doing things like eating breakfast, reading the newspaper, or going to church? Will we be able to get through to anyone? They're not clucking around, like we are, trying to uncover phantom murderers who probably don't even exist."

Bill shrugged. "Look, maybe we'll get lucky; maybe we won't. Whatever happens, let's agree to meet at noon in the library to compare notes."

Nora caught stride with Louise. So only Louise could hear, she said, "We can only do our best, and keep ourselves tuned in to what's really going on around here."

Sure, thought Louise skeptically. But not at the price of more testy confrontations between Nora and her husband. He refused to take life as seriously as their neighbor did. And yet she couldn't forget: Nora had always been right about her dark predictions of danger in the past. Louise had ignored her before. She had the scars to prove it.

Once back in her and Janie's room, Louise dressed in her favorite, many-pocketed shorts and a plaid sports shirt. She put through a phone call to the Botanical Garden in the Bronx and finally wangled the home phone number of Paul Warren from the reluctant operator by telling her she was with the Connecticut State Police. The director of horticulture must have been doing some of those normal things that people do on Sundays; she left a message for him and said she would call back in one hour. Her tension level grew. She would have to do better than this if she was to help Drucker get to the bottom of these two "accidental" deaths.

Next, Louise called Charlie Hurd, got his answering machine, and started biting a fingernail in frustration. Her message was terse: She told him she needed his help urgently. She heard back from him in ten minutes, and that told her more about Charlie—he was a type A personality who constantly monitored his home messages. Though he was not her favorite person, he couldn't be all bad. He had responded immediately when she said she needed a favor.

"Louise," said Charlie, "what are you into now—anything *I* can get my teeth into?" It was his usual tone, pushy and self-centered.

Sprawled barefoot on the bed with the phone, she plopped her head back on the pillow and tried to relax. This could be a lengthy conversation. "Oh, I don't know—what would you think of double murder and an attempted murder, with two or maybe three perps?"

Charlie sounded disgusted. "Louise, you should remember who you are. *Perps?* That's no language for a housewife and mother to use—"

She'd raised his hackles—good!—while he'd also raised

hers, of course. "Charlie, you're not the only one who can cut a swath through the world using inappropriate gangsta slang."

"At least get it right, Louise. To you it may be 'gangsta' slang, but actually it's 'policespeak.' Cops use it constantly."

"Yeah, I know. Cops. Gangsters. And cocky P.I.'s in detective stories." She sat up on the bed. "I'm not just a housewife anymore. Think of me as an on-camera talent, because that's what I am."

Had she shut him up yet?

"Okay, Louise, point taken. Except I hear they don't pay much at WTBA-TV—like maybe slave wages."

"Maybe," she answered smoothly. "But it's those extra perks—the voice-over jobs. Very, very lucrative."

That was enough—in fact, two "verys" was one too many. She had his attention.

"Seriously, Charlie," she said in a more conciliatory voice, "we have some problems here at Litchfield Falls Inn. I need your excellent, um, investigative skills." There, that would certainly appeal to his ego. Briefly, she ran through the events of the past two days.

"Whew!" he said. "It *could* be a helluva story, Louise. And then, it could be, well, just dull as dishwater." His voice perked up again. "Yet, even an accidental fall off a mountain by an absentminded science prof, plus a tragic leap by a young maiden is good, very good—"

"Matron. Young matron."

"Young matron off a boiling, roiling, rural Connecticut waterfall . . . all *right*! She wasn't a little bit pregnant, was she?"

Down to business at last. "I don't think so, Charlie. So here's what I need, if you can find out fast . . ." She told him about Higher Directions and about Jim Cooley and the Storms. He would get back to Louise as soon as possible, he said.

She closed her eyes and pressed her fingertips to her forehead. Dealing with Charlie had given her a mild headache. He seemed to bring out the worst in her. If she didn't have coffee and food soon, she would perish. She packed her belongings in the space of two minutes, not in the pristine way that Bill would have packed, which would have taken five times as long, but surely good enough for the short trip from New York back to Washington, D.C. Carefully, she retrieved Puny off the bed and tucked it safely in with her clothes. Should the maid decide to clean while they were gone at Wild Flower Farm, Louise didn't want her peerless pillow misplaced among the inn's polyurethane neck-breakers.

She hurried into the hall, remembering with a little shudder her eerie experiences there. Only those fuddy-duddy Seymour ancestors rendered in oil on the wall knew what really had happened.

She stopped in her tracks and sniffed. Breakfast and coffee smells wafted enticingly up to her, but suddenly she remembered she had to tell Sergeant Drucker of last night's adventures. This time she was sure they were not just figments of her imagination. Back in her room, she quickly dialed the number he had given her, listening to her stomach growl.

But Sergeant Drucker was at the morgue. Another trooper took the details. In the end, her little story did not move him—the darkened hall, Bebe's pleas, people moving around, doors opening, whispers.

"So that's it?" he said indifferently. "Sergeant Drucker will be at the inn as soon as he can; *I* think it's safe to wait until you see him to tell him about this."

Fine, Louise thought. She'd wait.

In the lobby Louise found Jim Cooley, looking for all the world as if he were hung over. He had not shaved, and that alone dramatically changed his usual bandbox appearance. Even his smooth, dark blond hair seemed slightly askew in a boyish sort of way, as if a comb had not gone through it at all today. His olive sports shirt matched the color of his hazel eyes, giving him a melancholy, monochromatic appearance.

Her heart went out to him. "Jim." She came over and touched him on the shoulder.

"Hi, Louise."

"Why don't you come with us this morning? We're going to Wild Flower Farm. At least it will be a diversion while you wait . . ."

What was he waiting for? To be dismissed so he could go back to his Brooklyn home, alone, just a few hours away?

As if reading her mind, he said, "They're finishing the autopsy; it got delayed last night." A grim smile. "People insist on getting their sleep." A long sigh. "Maybe I will go with you—it would take my mind off things for an hour or so. And it would be a fitting tribute to Grace."

"She must have loved Wild Flower Farm." Louise could feel her eyes dampening as she thought of Grace, lost in the beauty of the gardens yesterday.

"She visited there several times with Barbara, and she did love it, of course. I'll check in with Drucker and then I'll be ready to go. Thank you, Louise."

She passed her husband, who was sitting in the sunroom talking on his cell phone; he must be completing his own calls. When she arrived in the dining room, most of the others already had settled in to eat. Quickly, she negotiated for her first cup of morning coffee. Barbara Seymour sat at a table with her niece Stephanie, and Louise was appalled at the inn proprietor's appearance: The elderly woman looked somehow shrunken. Barbara must be bereft over the loss of her niece by marriage.

Mark Post was just sitting down at a neighboring table with

his wife Sandy and the omnipresent Widow Hollowell. It was a sober little group, except for Mark. He stood at his chair, gesticulating in the air with a cigarette in his hand, as if to illustrate some point. Sandy had a sour expression on her pretty face; she was obviously not impressed with her new husband's story.

Louise's mind suddenly evoked an image of the two tall men she had seen embracing in Litchfield Falls Inn's dark hallway early Saturday morning.

It was a stretch, and she wouldn't even have thought of it had Janie not mentioned the man's sexual aloofness toward his newlywed wife, a wife who appeared to be increasingly alienated as the weekend wore on. Could those have been the silhouettes of Mark Post and Jeffrey Freeling? Had they become entangled in a love affair that had gone wrong—and that Mark was anxious to conceal now that he had married an heiress?

Was that why Jeffrey had died?

Her eyes alight with excitement, Louise drank down her coffee and charted what to do next. Who at NYU was going to be forthcoming enough to verify or shoot down such a mad tale, which, as she thought about it, grew even madder: Beautiful blond Sandy, apparently tossed between two men, a professor and a senior student. But in reality a cover-up for their homosexual love affair. A love affair that blossomed again at a Connecticut country inn, shortly after the former student's marriage to the girl.

Louise took a good look at Mark. There he was, MBA, entrepreneurial businessman, computer expert, with political connections and available money. But murdering Jeffrey Freeling to permanently get rid of his sexual past? A stretch, indeed.

But she couldn't let go of the idea. She had to find out if Mark was gay. That would help sort this thing out. But what should she do? Go up to Sandy and say, *How's your love life? I hear your husband is a little less than heterosexual?* Frantically, she tried to recall any connection she had at NYU. What she needed right now was a raging gossip who knew the sexual proclivities of people on campus. After all, people did not conduct their love lives in a vacuum. But Louise knew no one who could help her there.

Bill sat down and she leaned forward to touch his arm. "Bill, I've got a theory."

"About what?" he asked warily.

"About Mark Post——"

A shadow fell across them and she looked up, startled. Jim Cooley had suddenly appeared at her side.

"Can I join you now?" he said.

"Of course, Jim." She rubbed her fingers gently against her eyelids, trying to quell her impatience. Now she would have to mentally switch gears again, set aside her exciting new theory about Mark and Jeffrey's past, and concentrate instead on the new widower. Bill was right: There were so many angles, so many things happening around this old inn, that it made it hard to concentrate on anything.

Jim Cooley looked around the room, and for a long moment his gaze rested on the unhappy-looking Sandy Post. Then he turned back to Louise and Bill. "Want to hear the latest?" His voice was deep and morose. "I talked to Sergeant Drucker; he's already busy with his men on the grounds, as they say, 'processing' the scene. He says the coroner found her blood levels of antidepressants very high."

"Did she normally take heavy doses?" asked Louise.

He shook his tired head. "Lord, no, Louise. One made her exceptionally woozy and took all the edge off that needed coming off. Two or more—why, that would have made her not care about anything."

And that, in fact, was what Grace had looked like there in the pool at the bottom of the falls, a woman who no longer cared about anything: her husband, her community, her garden.

A woman who could no longer relate to the planet on which she lived, and sought peace elsewhere.

So, there was one death accounted for. Maybe Louise shouldn't even bother to call back Paul Warren at the botanical garden. What could he tell her, anyway?

How Do You Relate
to Your Planet?
The Garden As Therapy

PEOPLE ARE BEGINNING TO realize the earth's pain. There is no doubt about it when world leaders talk as seriously about global warming as they do about potential war in the Middle East. Closer to home, many others are becoming concerned, and are doing something about it. A growing movement in both therapy and religion focuses on earth-based spirituality and therapeutic healing.

Prestigious organizations such as Harvard, and religious icons such as Catholic bishops and certain priests and ministers, are taking up this issue, in spite of scattered critics intimating earth worship. But the movement is very grounded: At its heart is the belief that mankind is alienated from the earth and needs to return to its bosom. Both the psychologists and the theologians involved maintain that people can no longer "feel"—can no longer give and receive affection. Some cite this vacuum of meaning in people's lives, shopping, frenetic activity, and a constant appetite for scandal as by-products of this condition.

The garden, the earth we touch, the bedrock on which we stand, the birds and animals, are all thought to help reconnect us to Mother Earth. Proponents talk about how mankind must include "land and the nonhuman community" in its concerns and its prayers. Catholic bishops have called for "environmental justice." Citizens of communities threatened with environmental pollution are beginning to consider it a moral matter—not just a Superfund cleanup job.

This concern for the ecology has become a part of the healing arts. Botanic gardens, of course, have long provided training in horticultural therapy, to help the physically and mentally handicapped. But the movement is becoming more widespread. A Harvard-associated institute, as well as several other

---

The earth and its trees appear to be coming to man's rescue in some of these cleanups. A species of poplar tree is now being used experimentally to purge pollution from the soil of nuclear and chemical sites, including the Rocky Flats Plant, Colorado, where warheads made for nuclear bombs left behind plutonium pollution. Poplars are thought to soak up and break down toxic organic compounds in soil.

American colleges, is now teaching "ecopsychology." And child therapists are using actual gardens to help their clients recover from traumatic stress.

Psychotherapy usually focuses on the individual. Ecopsychology is different: It tries to connect patients with their fellow human beings and with their planet.

A client emerging from a session with an ecopsychologist may have some strange homework. Among the possible assignments: Choose a plant or tree or animal near your home, and study it for five minutes each day. Go out in your yard and find out what kind of soil is there, what kind of geological bedrock, what watershed you are in. The natural world, then, becomes part of the cure, and the disturbed person develops what is called an "ecological self," or "holon," something that is a whole in itself, as well as a part of a larger whole.

Ecopsychologists believe that we humans can hear the earth speaking through us. Thus, our individual symptoms of unhappiness are not only indicators of personal or family dysfunction, but signals of trouble in the environment in which we live.

"We feel the pain of the earth," says Sarah Conn, a Harvard lecturer in psychology who teaches ecopsychology at Cambridge Hospital. "The news about environmental degradation is hard to avoid. Anyone who walks, breathes, looks, or listens knows that the air, the water, and the soil are being contaminated and that nonhuman species are disappearing at alarming rates. Yet the great majority of us, in this country and in much of the Western world, seem to be living our lives as if this were not so."

She believes we are so cut off from our connection to the earth that "even though we are bleeding at the roots, we neither understand the problem nor know what we can do about it." One such signal of grief is shopping. Conn calls it a "materialistic disorder" of such importance that she would like to see it catalogued in the psychologists' diagnostic manual. The need to consume, she believes, "is a graphic signal of our culture's disconnection from the earth. Our only current way of hunting and gathering seems to be shopping and accumulating merchandise."

Conn thinks many people are like those unfortunate plants that live in an impoverished monoculture. "The inner emptiness that results from the breakdown of community and the rise of consumerism leads people toward addictive behavior as they attempt to fill that emptiness with products, substances, celebrities, and activities." Thus, there is need for not only growth in human relationships, but identification with the biosphere as a whole. And that can often start with a simple reconnection with the soil or plants.

Children's affinity to nature was written about in the moving story *The Secret Garden,* in which three youngsters grow and heal while restoring a hidden garden landscape. A children's medical center in Massachusetts is breaking new ground by using a specially

designed garden to help children heal from traumatic events. It is a one-acre space filled with trees, small hills, a cave, water ponds, and streams. With their therapist, the young people explore the land. Some areas encourage risk-taking, while others appear as safe havens.

The theory is that sensations help unlock memories. By lying facedown on a mound in the garden, crouching within a "cave" made from an ancient yew tree, or crossing the cold river to explore an island in the middle, the children can unlock memories and feel the things that created their problems.

People over the millennia have known that gardens are good for the soul—although we can't ignore the mixed results for Adam and Eve in the Garden of Eden. Four hundred years before Christ, the Persians brought gardens to perfection. They named these enclosed and irrigated refuges *"pairidaeza,"* or paradise parks. Today's gardeners are just as wise as the Persians. They know full well that a few minutes a day spent weeding or hoeing the garden, or simply stretched out on a couch enjoying its beauty, can be as helpful as a therapy session and as spiritual as a church service. But for the benefit of those who have missed these simple truths, mental health professionals and religious leaders are bringing them into the doctor's office and the church.

Chapter Fifteen

I T   W A S   A   C H A N G E of scenery, and everyone needed it. Even the three-mile ride in the Litchfield Falls Inn van to Wild Flower Farm was a pleasure. For a moment, they could almost forget the sad events that had taken place in the past day.

The beleaguered guests were getting the gold-plated tour of the farm from the horticulturalist himself, a man in his sixties. On the back of his sunburned head he wore an old work hat that had seen plenty of New England weather. He gathered the group together in the begonia greenhouse and patiently explained, probably for the thousandth time, how these lush beauties were propagated by cuttings. As he talked, his gentle hands fondled 'Ninette,' an apricot begonia from the Blackmore and Langdons strain of Bath, England. He was repeating what he had said for the WTBA-TV camera yesterday, so Louise fazed out the words and lost herself in the psychedelic beauty of the flower. She had already resolved to buy a 'Ninette' for her own shady garden.

She soon discovered she wasn't the only one who wasn't paying strict attention. Sandy and Mark Post were standing behind a half-wall, deep in their own conversation. She sidled over and tuned them in, pretending to study the begonias intently.

No, it was not a conversation. It was a quiet squabble. An upper-middle-class squabble. No yelling, crying, waving of arms, tipping over tables, or throwing a few dishes, which could vent some steam and possibly lead to a romantic reconciliation. This one was quiet and venomous, guaranteed to leave them both unhappier than when they started.

Sandy was a vibrant young woman, and Louise was almost embarrassed by the fact that she had read her so well. Sandy was dissatisfied sexually. There was no way to avoid that conclusion.

Louise watched the couple for a moment, and then walked slowly back to the cluster of listeners, so as not to be conspicuous. Their behavior only strengthened Louise's far-out theory about Mark's sexuality. Could Jeffrey Freeling have been his partner?

Even if Sandy Post knew this, a young woman with her background and pride would never divulge the information, probably not even to a close friend—probably not even to Louise's seemingly guileless daughter, Janie, an expert at extracting confidences from people.

As her gaze wandered over the little crowd, Louise saw something even more upsetting than the quarrelsome newlyweds. The Gasparras were missing. She decided instantly to try to find them, ducking out of the huge shed and into a faint Connecticut drizzle.

It took just a few steps for both her clothes and her sneakers to become soaked by the rain. She ignored her damp state, for she wanted to find the Gasparras quickly. Something told her Rod was asking for trouble. The first place she looked was in the building that stood two structures down from the begonia greenhouse, its door ajar. She peeked through the crack. Inside, tables were filled with neatly packaged plants awaiting shipping. And Rod and Dorothy were standing just inside. Practical people, they wore yellow slickers, rain hats, and black-and-yellow rubber shoes; unlike her, they were probably dry as toast. Since Rod had shoved his raincoat aside, Louise could see a bulge in his sports jacket pocket, and wondered half seriously whether he was carrying a handgun. He was talking angrily to a third person, his words spouting out with bitter abandon.

By moving her head closer to the crack, she was able to see the third person: Wild Flower Farm's owner, Fenimore Smith. "My *dear* sir," Smith was saying, in his cultured voice, one aristocratic eyebrow moving upward in apparent shock, "I take umbrage at your attitude . . ."

Louise had met the suave Mr. Smith yesterday. He ran the successful nursery as a hobby, only appearing here on weekends—otherwise busy in New York running a large publishing company. He was a tall man in his fifties with fine features and thick, salt-and-pepper hair. He was wearing a gray translucent slicker over a sweatshirt and chinos. A rakish Tilley canvas hat was set well back on his head. Right now, he had his hands pushed confidently into his coat pockets, and he was rocking back and forth on his deck shoes. His hooded eyes never left Gasparra's face. Yesterday, Louise had felt the effect of those hooded eyes locked on hers: She interpreted it as a power move, New York–style. A Washington mover and shaker, she thought, would not have been quite so "in-your-face." He probably would have smiled a little, flattered a little, put a little spin on his words with the thought that someday he might run for office and would need the Gasparras' vote.

Not Smith. ". . . and I can't fathom what you are charging me with, since of course I have never obtained pollen illegally," said the nursery owner, "any more than I would infringe on another grower's patent, as you seem to be on mine." His nose seemed to elevate a little, and Louise couldn't help feeling a little sorry for the disadvantaged Gasparras, shorter, homelier, and less well-spoken.

Smith was tough native stock, like a wild rose, while Gasparra had been hybridized many times through unions of many nationalities. Ironic, she thought, that while in the plant world the hybridized one was prized above the native one, just the opposite was true in some circles of human beings.

"The development of the Sacred Blood iris is very clearly documented," Smith continued. "We paid almost three hundred thousand dollars for that work. We have records of every step in the genetic-engineering process, including all costs for the research, which were, as I said, enormous. It's true that many others attempted to approach the red quality that was finally achieved through the wonderful work of Dr. Freeling."

He took a step closer to Gasparra and his wife. "I talked to him only yesterday morning, and he mentioned your charges, Mr. Gasparra, and said he told you there was recourse for you if you think we've stolen one of your irises for our research. But to come here, the very day after that great scientist died!" Smith slammed his palm down on the plain board table piled with plants. "Jeffrey was a man of impeccable honesty—God rest his soul. What a terrible accident it was that took his life. I couldn't believe it when I heard it."

The mention of Freeling's accident gave her a chill, for Louise realized how easy it would have been for an angry individual like Rod Gasparra to shove Jeffrey off that mountain. After all, he had a twisted motive: revenge for fancied misdeeds on the part of the professor. And people with twisted motives sometimes did strange things. Maybe he had killed Jeffrey Freeling yesterday, and intended to complete his vengeance by killing Fenimore Smith today.

Smith made clear what Louise had always suspected. Gasparra didn't have much of a case. At any rate, DNA tests could prove the matter, one way or another—so why would Freeling and Smith take a chance on stealing someone else's plant material?

But Gasparra wasn't finished. "My wife and I," he said, "we're the ones who spent years creating the bright red iris—genuine field-grown plants, not some fancy magic out of a laboratory. And then, someone came and stole our work from under our noses!"

"That's true," said Dorothy, in a strained voice.

"Improbable, my dear people. You were working with an iris *similar,* but not identical, to the Sacred Blood iris. My dear man, if you know iris, you know how profligate they are." And he rolled his eyes, as if talking of a wanton woman.

"But now you will sell it for fifty dollars a plant, and receive royalties from anyone else who sells it!" Gasparra cried, desperation creeping into his voice.

Through the crack Louise could see Fenimore Smith advancing on Rod Gasparra. "Listen, Mr. Gasparra, or whatever your name is, you've got to prove it, you know, not just make the argument. Whatever your product, it was not the Sacred Blood iris. And furthermore, if you disbelieve me as you apparently disbelieved Dr. Freeling, then go see my lawyers. They're in Manhattan. Be assured, however, you will pay the court costs when you lose." Louise could see Smith rummaging in his shirt pocket for a pencil and a scrap of paper; he was so confident, even arrogant, that he didn't sense the danger in the man standing so near to him. "Here, I'll even write their name down for you . . ."

At this, Gasparra's temper exploded. "Why, you prissy son

of a——" He shoved Smith just as his wife Dorothy tried to intervene.

"Rod, oh no, please—that's enough!" she cried, but Rod was busy now, rummaging in his layers of coats and jackets and elbowing her rudely away. Metal glinted in the dim light. He *was* carrying a weapon.

Louise realized she had to act, and act now. She grabbed the shed door and slammed it open with a loud bang. Rod Gasparra froze with his clutched hand halfway out of his pocket. Louise strode over to Smith, nodding in a friendly fashion at the Gasparras on the way. "Hello, Fenimore," she called jovially, as if she had just blown in out of the rain. "What a day! Too bad the weather isn't better for your summer tea. I'm glad it wasn't quite as dreary yesterday. It'll make for a better show when it's aired on television."

She chattered on for a bit, then turned to acknowledge the Gasparras' presence, taking special care to include them in the conversational group. She noted with relief that Rod had lowered his hand to his side. "Dorothy, Rod—is Mr. Smith giving you a special tour? Isn't it wonderful here? It must be particularly interesting for fellow growers like yourselves to see how this place operates."

Smith lifted a quizzical eyebrow, at a loss to know whether Louise was aware of what was going on. He was looking at Gasparra with a different expression, she noticed. Wary now, not believing he was totally safe even yet. Taking a cue from her, the nursery owner said, "Perhaps all of you would like to rejoin the tour, for alas, I must return to Manhattan tonight. Big meeting coming up tomorrow morning."

"Let's do that," encouraged Louise, but Rod Gasparra didn't move. He stared from under his heavy, dark brows at Fenimore Smith. "You were going to write a name down for me," he muttered. "Why don't you do that now."

"Be happy to," said Smith. He rummaged again, and this time

came up with a slip of paper on which he wrote a few words. He handed it to Gasparra. "And good luck to you. I mean that in the fairest way, Mr. Gasparra." He turned to Dorothy and reached out his hand to her. Reflexively, hers came out to shake his. "It was nice to meet you, Mrs. Gasparra."

Louise smiled benevolently. She avoided eye contact with the Wild Flower Farm owner, but she and Dorothy exchanged a quick look. Then the three of them left the shed.

Once outside, Louise took a deep breath and continued her charade. "I bet we'll find the others in the Moon Garden. They're serving tea there, under a tent." In the distance, she could see the inn guests clustered near the all-white garden, now overflowing with white delphinium, achillea, phlox, and daisy. She wished she had been here in May, when the garden was overlayered with the white panicles of the wisteria. The Gasparras, with a rather beaten look about them, trudged across the wet meadow to join the group.

Louise went her own way, down a separate garden path, for she needed a moment by herself to think things out. Rod Gasparra didn't act like a killer back there in the potting shed. Blustery, frustrated, yes. His vanity injured by losing the recognition that would be given to the creator of a bright red iris. But Louise had been able to stop the downward spiral that could have led to violence. If she hadn't done so, probably the competent Dorothy would have. All in all, she was inclined to cross him off the list of those who might have done harm to Jeffrey Freeling. In Gasparra's eyes, Fenimore Smith was the offensive SOB who was reaping the harvest, earning the acclaim of horticulturists and making the big profits. It was obviously not the aloof scientist, Jeffrey Freeling. So why would he have killed Jeffrey?

That still left Mark Post. Could he have killed Jeffrey— either because of some homosexual love affair, or as retaliation for the shame Mark endured when he was thrown out of NYU five years ago?

The rain was beginning to encroach on her. Louise hurried from underneath the dripping branches of an English beech and past a gloomy stand of rhododendrons as tall as a small house. Then she slowed her pace despite the rain, bewitched by a pleasant, open path lined with flower beds. As she turned a corner, she met Jim Cooley. He, too, was avoiding the company of others.

"Hello, Louise," he said wearily. Jim brought out a motherly instinct in her, although she didn't know why, for the man, along with Frank Storm, ran three of the toughest schools in the country. "Tell me something," he pleaded.

"Of course. What?"

His voice was monotone, driven flat with depression over his wife's death. "You've solved crimes before. Just how do you do it?"

"I don't have any special tricks. Mostly it was just by being there. Being there, I mean, at a time when some evidence showed up."

A short silence as they wandered down the path. Jim's unhappy eyes were trained on the ground straight ahead, as if he dared not view the wider world lest he be hurt again. "Grace's death appears to be of her own volition. But suppose it's not—suppose it turns out to be something else? You could help find that out, couldn't you?"

The man obviously did not know she was already helping the police. But nevertheless, his query made her feel odd, for a combination of reasons. It *was* a rather intrusive request. The weather—close and breathless and damp. And the surfeit of emotion created by one crisis after another. She was beginning to feel like a character caught in a soap opera. Indeed, this weekend had the right mix for one of the daytime dramas—suspicious deaths, sorrowing survivors, an emotional widow, angry and possibly crooked businesspeople, and warring lovers. Perhaps not enough sex, though, to get those needed Nielsen ratings.

With her feet and sweater now dripping water and her body cooling—soon to face the shivers and shakes—the only sur- cease was a cup of hot tea and something sweet to go with it. It was time to head for the refreshments tent, not to talk about murder versus suicide.

She turned to him. "So you think someone murdered Grace."

"I don't know." His voice was hollow. "I thought maybe you, with your experience, could . . ."

She looked at him curiously. He must suspect Bebe Hollo- well; she was the likeliest person. The woman was strong, and able—did Louise ever know that!—and emotionally skewed herself. Bebe had been in her room when Grace went or was taken from the inn. Could she have persuaded the delicate Grace to accompany her on a lethal little walk to the falls? The answer was yes. With a start, Louise realized Grace's kind heart had made her vulnerable to people who suffered. All Bebe would have had to do was apologize, give Grace a sad tale of how she missed her dead Ernie, and ask her please to go up that woodsy trail with her to the falls. There, they could honor his memory. Louise had been exonerating the very best candidate from all suspicion.

At that moment, she and Jim were passing a big patch of lacy, clawlike, blue flowers. Perfunctorily, for now she was thinking of things besides flowers, Louise said, "There they are—your flowers."

He looked without interest at the tiny-petaled blue blos- soms. "What are they?"

"Oh, I thought you'd know. It's love-in-a-mist." Grace had obviously been the only gardener in the Cooley house, but was it possible this man hadn't even *noticed* his wife's new romance garden?

She said, "That plant is in your new garden at home."

He doubled back on the path a few steps, leaned down, and peered at it. "Oh, yes," he said, "now I recognize it."

They walked a few more paces before she said, "To answer your question: If someone asked me to look into a possible crime, the answer is, of course, I would certainly try to help."

"Oh, God, Louise, I wish you could just make some sense of it . . ."

Again, he aroused her compassion. "But, Jim, even if there was foul play involved in Grace's death, I would have little to contribute. You know why?"

"No. Why?" The eyes had a waiting expression.

"Because it would be hard to find clues to a murder committed outdoors on a thirty-acre piece of property. If anyone is going to solve it, it's those troopers who are combing through the grounds." She thought guiltily of how she and her helpers were already snooping into the affair. "And Sergeant Drucker must have told you he's doing a background check on everybody who's been around the inn. That includes even you and me."

"He did tell me—I understand. Well, thanks, anyway, Louise. I just thought maybe if . . ."

"I wish I had something special to offer, Jim, but I don't."

And at that moment, she didn't.

Soggy cucumber sandwiches were the fare at the tea under the tent. Afterward, people headed back to the van to return to the inn, where they hoped for something better. Louise saw Jim again; this time he was meeting up with Frank Storm among the cheerless rhododendrons. Fiona Storm joined them, giving each man a friendly hug. They linked arms and walked down the wide path, looking like three sad musketeers. Well, at least Jim has his good friends, she thought. He was going to need them.

Quite a trio. The stern Frank. The stern Fiona. And Jim, stern, but with those friendly, rounded edges that made him a sympathetic figure, one who could be trusted. Musketeers, indeed: one for all, and all for one.

But the musketeers had gone no more than a few strides when they were intercepted by the omnipresent Bebe Hollowell, stomping along in her sturdy walking shoes, determined to break into the group. Louise could tell by their body language that they would rather be alone. After all, they knew, and Louise knew, that this woman could be a killer.

Chapter Sixteen

LOUISE HAD LOST TRACK of Bill and Nora, so she climbed into the van that would return them to the inn and hunkered down in one of the seats. A moment alone might give her the chance to sort out her tangled thoughts. She looked up just in time to see Bebe plopping herself down in the seat next to her. Not Bebe again!

"I'm sure your husband won't mind," said the woman tersely. "It's such a short trip." Louise stole a glance at her. The woman was really quite handsome, in her pantsuit and jaunty raincoat, though her bronze suntan somehow looked out of place on a rainy day. Her big green eyes were giving Louise a sideways glance. Louise tried to disguise a shudder, and shrank back in her own seat. Three miles to town, and no getting away.

The van filled up and they drove off. Bill and Nora were somewhere behind her. Leaning in toward Louise, Bebe talked in a quiet voice so the others wouldn't hear; Louise had to strain to catch the words. "Did you call him? Did you call my brother? Are you going to let the police do it all—have you no mercy?" She stared at Louise, and it was scary to see a woman so frightened, so angry. Even if Bebe had committed no crime, she carried an enormous amount of guilt—for something. And of course, if she had killed her husband last month, and Grace Cooley yesterday, she was a dangerous threat. Louise couldn't remember when she had felt more uncomfortable with a fellow human being; the woman's heady perfume, and even her mint-laden breath, seemed to surround Louise in an oppressive fog.

"Bebe, I promise I'll call him—I'll try to help you. Now let it rest." She slumped in her seat, realizing what she had done was totally wrong. Detective Geraghty had recommended her to the Litchfield police, and she was blowing it. It was completely inappropriate to promise to help a murder suspect. Her only reprieve would be if Bill could learn something about the woman from the hometown authorities that would set this all to rest. In the meantime, she would take care not to be alone with Bebe.

Louise leaned her head back against the plastic seat, closed her eyes, and tried to shut out the world, tried not to mind the smell and the sense of Bebe sitting next to her. She opened her eyes only when they reached the inn.

Without talking to her family or Nora, she went immediately to her room to complete her calls, first exchanging her wet tennis shoes for sandals. The "Big Five," as Janie had nicknamed them—the three Eldridges and the two Radebaughs—would meet again at noon to share the results of their inquiries, and to pass them along to Sergeant Drucker.

The message button on her phone was blinking: Charlie Hurd had called back. She quickly dialed his number from memory. "Louise, how'd you get mixed up with this outfit? Higher Directions: very hot, very cutting edge, very *successful*—but a little kooky. You have to give them a lot of credit, though. They've learned how to jam math into delinquent kids' brains, and as a little bonus, to teach 'em how to read."

"So I've heard," she said. "Did you get any details? Is there any dirt—you know, anything that's not strictly on the level?"

On the other end of the line Charlie paused. "Let me read you something here. Higher Directions is, quote, very highly leveraged. Read: several million in debt. They were banking on Federal funds which haven't materialized because of their religious component—"

"I know they're religious, but I thought it was non-denominational."

"It is. One of those fuzzy nondenominational churches with lots of personal agendas. You know—improving yourself in 'regular increments.' "

"Does that mean saying to yourself, 'Every day in every way I'm getting better and better'?" she joked.

"Yeah, and straighter and straighter: no lying, cheating, fornicating, or—if you'll pardon the expression—buggering."

"How do people view Jim Cooley and Frank Storm—and, for that matter, Fiona Storm?"

"They're well respected, all three of them. The only other problem they've had is the two kids who offed themselves."

"Killed themselves? Really?"

"Yeah. Kids who were banished from the school, or faced banishment—did I say that right? 'Banishment'?"

"Yes, but if you're more comfortable with 'expulsion,' you could use that, too."

"Louise, quit twitting me: I'm not some kid. So these two students, both of them about to graduate from their Brooklyn school, were found dead. OD'd on drugs. Story was vastly underreported, which tells me *someone* in Higher Directions has clout. Rumors were that both kids were gay, but nothing firm on that. The police did a long investigation, and there was even talk of it going to a grand jury. They finally concluded the school wasn't responsible, but there's still a lot of buzz about the incident."

"Suicides. How interesting." Louise thanked Charlie and gave him Drucker's phone number to follow up on the details. She knew Charlie would not rest now until he had the full story.

But then, neither would she.

Charlie's research showed that Jim Cooley was in financial difficulties. He might have had a reason to rid himself of Barbara Seymour so that he could inherit. But everything in Louise's being told her Jim was Barbara's protector, and not the one preying on her.

However, the suicides of the two students left her with a nervous feeling in her stomach. *So that's what tough love does for you,* she thought. Maybe the Higher Directions file should remain open.

She lay on her bed and rang Paul Warren again. No luck. She left another message, longer this time, tweaking his memory of Channel Five's *Gardening with Nature* program set at the botanical garden, and providing him with more detail on Grace Cooley.

But what could she learn from him that she didn't already know? That Grace visited the garden on a weekly basis? That she filched plants, maybe? That she bought pamphlets on plant culture, or took courses in how to raise dahlias?

Louise lay back and relaxed for a second. It took only that long, after the swim and the lengthy tour of Wild Flower Farm, to send her into a deep sleep.

"Tell me the truth."

He had avoided this moment, but at last it was here. "Sandy, dammit, there is no truth to tell."

"Mark, I know now you're not straight. You married me while living this great big terrible lie!"

He flailed his hands in the air, then slumped heavily onto the bed, wishing he could at least light up a cigarette. "I think you've gone crazy, girl. I am straight as they come."

She stood in front of him, arms akimbo, muscular legs spread wide. "Friday night, you left this room—don't tell me you didn't."

"Well, maybe I did, but what the hell do you think I was doing? I just couldn't sleep, so I went downstairs—fortunately I didn't nearly kill myself on them like our hostess—and then outdoors to take a little run down the road."

Her blue eyes smoldered. "In the rain? I'll bet. You can't stand being married—admit it. You can't even stand spending the night in the same room with me. Night after night. Now it's been, what, three weeks in Italy, and two nights here, with no more excuses that you're too tired because of climbing all over the Uffizi. I know what's wrong. You just can't bear the *proximity*." She shook her golden head. "God, even in Florence you had to get out of the hotel; I'd wake up and find you gone."

He bowed his head. "Sandy, I wish you wouldn't think this about me."

"I don't think it—I feel it. It's in your lovemaking. You're not there, Mark. So, like, where the hell are you? And why did you marry me in the first place?"

She turned away angrily and paced the room—the room reserved for newlyweds, or those celebrating wedding anniversaries such as the twenty-fifth or maybe the fiftieth, if anyone could imagine being married that long. Mark looked at his beautiful wife standing against the pink-and-mauve background and felt like screaming.

"Don't answer. I think I know why," she went on. She raised her hands in an imploring gesture, as if asking the gods to intervene. "A girl should listen to her father." She paced for a moment longer. Finally, she pulled up short in front of him, running a hand through her short curls. "I guess I shouldn't be so mad. Like, I should have known, the way you took after me at college, and then dropped me. God! That was like a challenge, since no man had ever dropped me."

"You found lots of other guys during those years—why didn't you marry one of them?"

"I *waited* for you to finish grad school, and then ran after you until I finally captured you. What an utter, complete fool!"

"You did it on your own," he said, in a low, defeated voice. "I didn't force you down the aisle of that church."

She reached over and touched him on the shoulder, and he flinched. "What happened back at NYU, Mark? Between you and Jeffrey? I wish you'd just admit it. I might even forgive you then."

He looked up at her with pained eyes. "All right. I admit that occasionally I've been attracted to—guys. And believe me—it's not a good place to be, because you're not welcome in the straight world, and you're not welcome in the gay world. But don't be so naive, Sandy. It happens more than you think. Sure I had a thing for Jeffrey. I thought even in your innocence back then you might have recognized it. I still think you did."

She straightened, angry again. "You were really fried, weren't you, when he dated me instead of you?"

Mark was cooler now. He gulped once, then decided what to tell her. "I thought he . . . returned the feeling. But it turned out he was straight after all."

She stepped back, and he could see she was trying to disguise her shock.

He stood up and confronted her. "You really believed we were lovers, didn't you? That we had a history together. That he was gay, and so was I?"

"Yes."

"Well, that's wrong. And Friday night, what did you think? That Jeffrey and I were back at the old stand? That I sneaked away and went into his room, and . . ."

"Yes, I did, as a matter of fact. I even saw the two of you—"

"How do you know, Sandy? You may have seen two guys, but not Jeffrey and me—"

"Oh, God, don't lie to me! How can I believe you?" Her mouth hung open in anguish.

"Sandy, you pushed Jeffrey off that summit, didn't you? We both know you're tough enough. It was really no problem, was it?" He stared into space. "Or was it during the CPR . . ."

She looked at him with fear etched sharply on her face. Then her eyes narrowed. "Wait a minute, Mark. *No,* you don't. I didn't push him off. *You* did, didn't you? This is just another bluff. You're the one who wanted him gone. You and he made love Friday night, and it was like old times, right? And then you realized how dangerous it was. You'd lose everything—because your father-in-law, for one, would never agree to bail out a nearly bankrupt husband of mine who was a complete liar!"

Mark shook his head. "I'm getting the hell out of here. I'll get a cab to take me back to Stamford. You can take the car."

"That's generous of you," she said bitterly, "seeing as it's my car anyway. But I wouldn't leave just now if I were you, Mark. You're in enough trouble. Do you really need the entire Litchfield barracks chasing you home?"

The Sexual Lives of
Plants and the
Disappearing Honeybee

PLANTS HAVE INGENIOUS SEXUAL lives. In fact, they are so blatantly sexual that some people are uncomfortable with close-up views of male anthers opening to shoot out their pollen, or female stigma lunging out to receive it. Immovable and unable to go to sexual partners, a plant cleverly dresses up, produces flowers in wild colors, stripes, or even polka dots, and lures a go-between—a bee, a bird, a small animal—to fertilize it. Thus, the plant achieves its goal of reproducing itself. Pines, ferns, and other cone-bearing gymnosperms don't bother with all that gimcrackery: They simply wear their old clothes and expose themselves to the wind to get pollinated. Some plants, failing to obtain pollen from their friends, self-pollinate, even though this is not as desirable genetically for the plant as getting its pollen from another.

But things are going on in the natural plant world that should concern us. One of our great pollinators, the honeybee, is threatened with extinction. Gardeners are beginning to notice and complain that their apple trees or their zucchini is not getting pollinated, because bees seem to be absent. And they are, both wild and managed bees. The beekeeping industry is in jeopardy, suffering a steep decline in the number of managed colonies. (Actually, bees don't need management—they do very well on their own living in a hollow log. Beekeepers are essentially providers of luxury condos for these valuable creatures.) Manmade and natural forces are responsible for the problem:

❧ Two kinds of mites, which represent a devastating scourge to bees;

❧ Pesticides, which are twice as abundant today as when Rachel Carson wrote the disturbing book, *Silent Spring;*

❧ Loss of habitat, as more wilderness land with hollow logs and stumps to hold natural hives disappears.

While managed populations are dropping from disease despite the best efforts to prevent it, the wild honeybees have been almost completely wiped out. Other species of wild bees are a separate issue. Their numbers have been decreasing since colonists came to America, and they continue to disappear. When beekeepers lost an occasional swarm of bees, it was a good thing: These strays would "reseed" the wild honeybees—thus keeping a good supply of pollinators in existence. Now, the luxurious quantity of bees that existed in the United States for more than three hundred years is gone.

Some see no way out of the bee crisis until it seriously affects agriculture. Even now, some agricultural growers import masses of bees to pollinate plants. Eventually, perhaps, another pollinator may have to step in and take the place of the valuable bee. That won't solve the problems, however, since some plants are "bee-specific," and designed by nature to be pollinated only by this benevolent insect.

Genetic engineering is doing its best, creating new type "BT" corn seeds and cotton seeds that lessen the need for heavy pesticides on crops. (It is estimated that fifty percent of all pesticides are used to treat U.S. cotton crops.) Pesticides, of course, affect not only bees, but the thousands of other plant pollinators as well: birds, butterflies, squirrels, foxes, mice, possums, bats, and lizards.

Many large growers and plant scientists scoff at organic farms and claim they can never fill the nation's and the world's need for food. But the price of using pesticides—and they are used heavily in farm fields the entire world over—is beginning to be understood.

Encouraging individual gardeners to raise bees is not considered a solution to the bee problem. Amateur beekeepers often lose their interest after a few years and neglect their hives: This can create a serious spread of disease to other neighborhood hives.

As it is, most of us don't appreciate plant sexuality the way we should. The creative source is pollen. Great clouds of this life-giving substance swarm over fields of crops and flowers, landing randomly, but often in the right place to effect the beginning of a seed. Pollen is the very basis of our lives. It initiates the seed or fruit or grain, assuring the continuation of plant species, and thus the food we eat. A corn plant, alone, needs pollination in what will become each kernel; this takes an estimated 25,000 pollen grains.

Some plants that used to grow in vacant fields are becoming rarities in the United States, and their existence needs to be cultivated by backyard gardeners. Surely, America's gardeners are committed, spending endless time and an average of about $400 per family each year. But percentage-wise, there are not that many devoted gardeners in the country. Witness the fact that on any given day at a botanic garden, a person may wander on the paths in complete solitude.

The USDA has a National Seed Storage Laboratory that attempts to preserve plant species. But it hasn't been able to stockpile viable heirloom seeds. That makes it all the more important for backyard gardeners to raise these endangered plants. Native flowers,

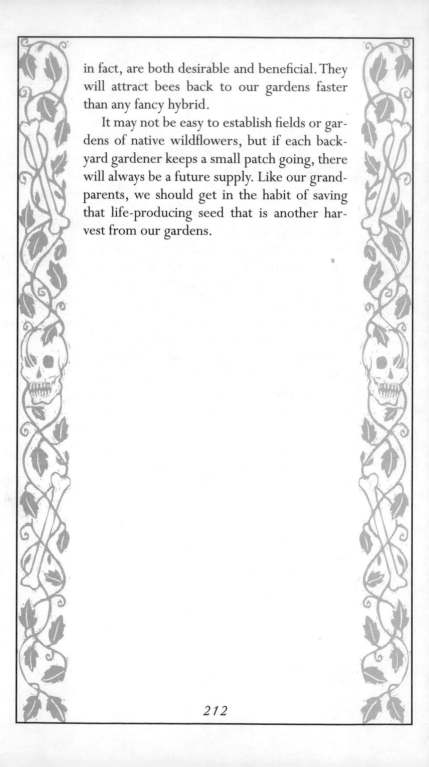

in fact, are both desirable and beneficial. They will attract bees back to our gardens faster than any fancy hybrid.

It may not be easy to establish fields or gardens of native wildflowers, but if each backyard gardener keeps a small patch going, there will always be a future supply. Like our grandparents, we should get in the habit of saving that life-producing seed that is another harvest from our gardens.

Chapter Seventeen

"Is this ever cool," said Janie, walking farther into the deep, tunnel-like pantry. It had a stone floor and was lined with shelves filled with canned and jarred foods and dried goods stored in square tin cans. At the end, where it turned the corner, there was a beat-up green recliner, sitting on a rectangle of gold shag carpet. "This chair is just like the one we got from my great-grandmother."

Teddy grinned at her. "Probably yours isn't quite so shabby—but I love it. This place is my lair. It's actually an old cold cellar that, if you follow it all the way, leads to the river where they used to have an ice house. But that's closed up now with a good old six-foot-thick Connecticut rock wall."

Janie examined his little bookshelf and the reading lamp on it. Under the lamp was an embroidered doily. "What a cute doily," she said, fingering it and casting him a sideways glance, teasing him.

Teddy's face turned red. "She gave it to me—Miss Seymour. Said it would refine the place. I told her I didn't need a refined place." Actually, Teddy thought, Miss Seymour would be surprised at how *unrefined* it could get down here.

The bookshelves held college textbooks he had picked up here and there. Between the bookshelves and the chair rested a keyboard. "Oh, a musician, too," his guest commented. Along the other wall, there was a set of barbells. Janie scanned these possessions and then she slid down in the chair, stretching back in it like a pretty yellow cat, and every male fiber in his body was alerted. She said, "Wow, comfort. Bring on a book." Happy for the distraction, he plucked one out and handed it to her.

"Psych I—so that's why you're so clever about understanding people." She smiled at him. He crouched down beside her and laid a forearm on the chair where there was a little space next to her leg.

"I never took psych—I just read this stuff. There're more interesting ones there." He picked out another. "See, *History of Revolutionary America*. I like that subject—I'd major in history if I ever went to college."

She cocked her head a little. "Don't you know the jobs are in technology and science, not the humanities?"

"Yeah," he said cheerfully, "that's what they say. *And* the service industry. Don't forget the service industry. I've got a job I like. I have a future here with Miss Seymour, whether it seems like it or not. I'll probably run this inn someday."

She shook her head. "You have more self-confidence than anyone I've ever met. Where does it come from?"

He shrugged his shoulders, hoping, perhaps, she would notice how broad they were getting. This was the opportunity he had sought: being near Janie, the magical blond girl from another world. Washington was not so far, really, not too distant for him to comprehend. His thoughts had drifted. What had she asked—about self-confidence, was it?

"Don't know where I got it. Small-town life. Consolidated county high school. Plenty of good teachers who encouraged me. And I help with the business at home."

"Your folks have a business?" Janie sounded as if the concept were totally foreign to her.

"Sure, lots of people around here survive on little businesses. My dad and mom have a grocery store at the edge of town. Good one, too, super meat, fresh produce. Competes pretty well with the bigger markets around." Teddy grinned, and he could see her examining, close up, his face with its crooked, orthodontia-free teeth. Her mind registering his heritage: a grocery store. That made him a grocery boy. So be it. He didn't have money, yet, to get those teeth straightened. And he couldn't change what his parents were and what he was—not that he had always been the most exemplary kid, either. But Janie didn't need to know that.

"That makes it a mom-and-pop store—and kid. Mom-and-pop-and-kid store." He delivered the line with a wholesome smile on his face, and Janie bought it, just as people always bought it. "I love that store," he said, really getting into it now, "because I like people—I really do. They don't make millions, but it gives you a good idea of how this country works. You know, they used to call England a country full of small shopkeepers. Well, New England was somewhat like that, too."

"So you may go to school one of these days?"

"Yeah. Maybe I'll go to Yale." *Sure, I'm twenty-one already, wasn't exactly the valedictorian of my senior class, and I'm going to Yale,* he thought cynically. But he knew how to name-drop, and why not drop the best names? He could never impress this girl by saying he intended to matriculate at the University of Bridge-port. "So, what is your friend Chris studying at Princeton?"

Janie rearranged herself in the chair, and he couldn't help staring at the way the long blond hair hit her cheek. "He's a science major. I don't know what he'll specialize in yet—I don't think he does, either."

"So, your mom is a TV garden lady, and a junior detective. How about your dad? State Department, huh?"

Janie looked at him quickly. Was he going too far with that "junior detective" stuff, or was it something else? *And what was it with your old man—was he a spy or something?*

"Yes, State Department. We've lived overseas a lot. My folks may even move there again, but I'll probably stay and go to college here."

He leaned in as close to her as he could without having some phony excuse. She was one of the prettiest girls he'd ever seen. "I like it that we're getting better acquainted." He smiled. "How about planning a date?"

She laughed. "Oh, but I won't be back here very soon . . ."

"I can *easily* make it to D.C."

"Well . . . I suppose you could come around Thanksgiving. Then Chris would be home from college." Her enthusiasm wasn't overwhelming.

"I'd love it," he said, pinning her down on it before she changed her mind.

She narrowed her eyes. "But I wouldn't call my mom a *junior* detective again."

"Gosh, Janie, I didn't mean—I'm sorry. I was just trying to be funny."

"I understand."

"But we'd better go now. I have a feeling Chris is going to be looking for you."

She reached out her hands and he pulled her out of the low-slung chair, and then she was standing right next to him. Their bodies were almost touching. He wished they could make love right now on the rug, as he and Ginger, the head waitress, had done a dozen times at least—though somehow he knew this wouldn't happen with Janie. Teddy reached out for second best, a kiss and hug she'd remember until Thanksgiving. Then they heard Chris calling.

"Okay, you two," called Chris, "I hear you in there somewhere. Come out, come out, wherever you are!"

Teddy grabbed her elbows, which was about as much as he could grab, considering the situation. He hated when people invaded his lair. "Janie, I sure do want to help you and Chris if you go out and do any investigating."

She looked up at him. Was she as aware as he was that this was a magical moment? She said, "It has to be soon, because in about an hour we leave for home."

Be sincere, and not too forward, he thought. *Don't blow it now.* "Then we have an hour. There's nothing I'd like better than to help you, Janie. You're one of the nicest girls I've ever met."

That much was as true as anything he'd ever said in his life.

Chapter Eighteen

AT NOON, LOUISE AWOKE suddenly and
realized she was due at the meeting in the library. She got down off the tall bed, ran a quick
brush through her long hair, and hurried out to
the hall and down the stairs. As she entered the
large room, Janie made a sweeping bow wel-
coming her, then snapped the door closed behind her. "You're late, Ma. Let's get crackin'."

They took seats on the big leather couches
near the fireplace, with Janie sitting next to
her mother. As they settled themselves, Har-

grave the cat rose to a sitting position in his basket and observed them solemnly, debating whether or not to give up his territory. Finally, he decided to stay, lying back down and resting his green-eyed gaze on Louise.

Louise gave the cat a conspiratorial wink.

Janie looked at her mother, slightly perplexed. "*I've* been petting him while we waited for you to come down from your room. How come he likes you best?"

Louise's mouth twitched in a smile. "Cats really know people, they say."

"Hmmh."

She patted her daughter's knee. "Just kidding. Actually, it's because I've spent more time with him than you have."

"If you two would stop discussing the cat," said Bill mildly, "we can get rolling. I'll go first. Now, about Jeffrey Freeling's fall—or push: I corroborated what the kids found out yesterday. Mark Post is roundly hated by his new father-in-law. He appears to be a corner-cutter—which in the computer business means he may have filched someone else's idea, refined it a little, and then sold it as his own. He has lawsuits against him up the kazoo. Some people think he married Sandy for her money—among them, Sandy's daddy."

Louise looked around the group and said, "Let me try a far-fetched theory on you. It entered my mind just this morning at breakfast, and it could explain Jeffrey's death." She told them all about seeing two men embracing Friday night, and proposed a scenario in which Mark and Jeffrey were secret lovers, with Mark killing Jeffrey to keep this knowledge from the upscale family into which he had just married.

"Whoa," said Bill. "That's a real stretch, Louise. And yet, what I have to remember, when I doubt your theories, is that you're usually right."

She smiled. "I know. I have a pretty good track record, haven't I?"

Nora, leaning forward in her chair, said quietly, "I saw them, too, Friday night."

Louise smiled with satisfaction. "There you are. Nora saw them, too. I think we have to keep that theory in mind."

Janie sat back, draped her arms along the back of her chair, and clasped her hands behind her head. "Why would a well-known guy like Jeffrey want to spill the beans about a thing like that? Why wouldn't he just want to keep it a secret?"

Bill scratched his head. "Not a bad point, Janie. I don't know. I also had the Gasparras checked out. Not much there, but they owe a big tax bill to Uncle Sam—they just haven't been making it lately. But no criminal record on either Rod or Dorothy."

"No wonder they were so angry when they thought someone stole their red iris," reflected Louise. She told them of her encounter with the couple and Fenimore Smith, the owner of Wild Flower Farm. "They could have paid off their debts if they had perfected the reddest iris of them all."

"So they didn't?" asked Janie.

"According to Fenimore Smith, their iris is not the Sacred Blood iris, but probably another one that's similar, just not that red. I suspect the Gasparras convinced themselves that someone had stolen their plants without any concrete evidence. Or it could be an example of people suing big outfits and hoping for an out-of-court settlement. Maybe they thought Smith would pay them off rather than go through the hassle of a lawsuit. At least they didn't kill anyone over it—or not yet."

Nora's eyes were bright with excitement. Louise realized how important it was for her friend to make a contribution here, if only to help her out of her terrible depression. She could hardly wait to take her turn. "I may have found out something terribly important about Grace," she said. "My poet friend teaches at several schools in the New York area. The class that Grace took from him is at NYU. He saw her just last week." She smiled. "What do you think of that? That gives us four people with NYU connections: Mark and Sandy Post, Jeffrey, and Grace."

"Hmm," said Louise. "And Grace and Sandy met each other in a poetry class there, too. Could Grace have known the others—"

"Louise, what's important is what this teacher said about Grace. She was an excellent student. Oh, of course he could tell she had problems— they came out in the things she wrote, as did her delirious love of trees and flowers. But her work was good enough to be accepted for publication in *Poetry Lore*. I can tell you from firsthand experience that any poet would love that. He said Grace was on a creative 'high' these days, and didn't believe she would consider taking her own life."

"Neither do I," said Bill. "The woman was a hopeless romantic. But not someone with the courage to throw herself over a waterfall."

"Good work, Nora," said Louise. "Bill, how about Bebe?" She wondered if it was time to reveal that Bebe had had her in a death grip last night in the hall.

Bill launched right into it: "I want you to picture a warm, bombastic, loving, belligerent, extroverted woman with twinkly dancing feet—"

"That's going to be a little difficult," said Nora dryly, "except for the dancing feet."

"What I'm telling you is that she's a woman of contradictory moods; she's made as many enemies as friends in Mattson. But there's nothing yet from the police on whether she was responsible for good old Ernie's death."

Louise noticed they talked about Ernie now as if they had personally known the wealthy old farmer. Bill had even committed to memory one of Ernie's favorite phrases, relayed to him by Bebe: "hissy-fit," as in, *That woman's having a hissy-fit!* Louise had a secret fear Bill would use it someday to describe *her*.

She sighed. "Then it's my turn, I guess. I haven't reached the botanic garden yet, but I did hear from Charlie Hurd. He says Higher Directions schools are going strong, especially with all the national publicity. The irony is that they've grown too fast, and they're terribly in need of money. And then there are the suicides." She told them about the two unfortunate youths.

"Two suicides?" said Bill. "That must have flashed red lights at Drucker when he checked out Higher Directions." He frowned. "Do you realize none of this gets us anywhere on Grace's death? It only implies that Jim Cooley and Frank Storm could have been in league with Neil Landry in trying to disable Barbara Seymour. It has nothing whatsoever to do with the two deaths."

Janie leaned forward. "Neil Landry loosened that carpet—no one else. He looks guilty as sin. The other relatives don't."

Louise stared thoughtfully out the big front windows. "No, Jim and Frank never look guilty. They're too righteous."

"Not very charitable, are we, Louise?" noted Bill. "It will be hard to prove anything about Barbara's accident. I ran a check on Landry. He's clean. Maybe the stair rod just popped." He arched an eyebrow. "If it were at our house, Louise, we wouldn't suspect foul play. We'd just suspect atrophy on the part of all physical things, especially houses with large mortgages."

Chris spoke up. "Janie and I talked to Teddy, who knows next to nothing. You'd think the guy would be more observant, hanging around here all the time. He said it would be hard for people to tramp over the lawn without someone from the kitchen staff seeing them."

If a kitchen staffer like Teddy was involved, thought Louise, *no one would consider him out of place.* She tried to recall the other thing about Teddy Horton that didn't set right with her.

Janie, her blond hair straggling into her eyes, gave Chris a sideways glance and he blushed, bowing his head. Louise wondered if there was some crisis she had missed among the three young people—for Chris, Janie, and Teddy had definitely become a triangle as the weekend progressed. Janie continued, "He did tell us one thing that has to do with Grace. But the police already know this, so it couldn't mean much: Frank intercepted Grace and Bebe's dinners when Teddy was about to deliver them. Frank delivered them instead."

"Why?" asked Louise. "Did he say?"

"Frank said he was going up, so he was being his usual helpful self—or so Teddy said." Louise remembered Grace's untouched dinner sitting on a dresser in her bedroom. The woman had not eaten a bite of it. "Oh, my," she said, "this is getting us nowhere."

Bill said, "We've come up with nothing new on Grace except that her poetry teacher didn't think she was suicidal. But so what? That was last week. Everyone since then has agreed she was a delicate vessel. And Bebe, the only one with opportunity, doesn't add up as Grace's killer. Now, on the matter of Jeffrey Freeling's death: Mark Post may have had a reason to kill Jeffrey. Revenge—or there's Louise's far-out sexual intrigue scenario. Let's see, I've lost track. Who else . . . oh, Gasparra. Not likely, I'd say—a blusterer, but not a murderer."

"It's not very substantial stuff," said Louise quietly.

"Not a sound theory in the bunch of them," said Bill. "We'll pass these fragments on to Sergeant Drucker when he gets here. Meanwhile, let's pack and get ready to go home. We've done our best. These two people were not killed. One fell, the other jumped. Right?"

Faintly, the others answered, "Right," except Janie, who stubbornly retorted, "Wrong."

Reluctantly, they adjourned their little meeting and dispersed to their separate rooms. Louise trudged up the winding front stairs, lost in thought. There was one ambiguous statement that had been dropped in a conversation this morning, or maybe even yesterday afternoon: something offbeat—the kind of thing a murderer might say to throw her off the track. In the confusion of conversations with more than a dozen people, she couldn't quite put her finger on the one that really disturbed her.

The phone call came when Louise returned to her bedroom to retrieve her suitcase. Paul Warren, listening to her long, detailed message, had done some legwork before calling her back. A practical man, the director of horticulture had gone right to the personnel at the front gates. "We have plenty of people there to eyeball the customers."

Yes, they did remember the woman, he said. Louise's description of a near-anorexic female, with rosy light brown hair, wide-set blue eyes, and poetic manner had rung a bell with more than one of the attendants. They remembered her as a studious note-taker. An alarm went off in Louise's head: She had forgotten that Grace's notebook was still missing—probably the most important clue of all. Drucker had said the evidence people hadn't found it.

Warren told Louise that this frequent botanical garden visitor was often accompanied by a person who appeared to be her husband. "Does she *have* a proprietary husband—a tall guy with light hair?"

"Indeed, she does."

"We might even have her on videotape."

"You have surveillance cameras in the botanical garden?"

"No, but we've had some problems lately—you'd be surprised at the nerve of people, who think they'd like to take home a small bush or plant from the garden. A security guard goes out with a videocamera during crowded periods. I can't guarantee anything, but if she's a regular, we've probably photographed her. Why don't you fax me a picture of the woman and

I can verify her presence here, at least—and her husband's. And then maybe I can fax you back a confirmation. The attendant said the reason she remembered them was that they were followed recently. That makes it all the more likely that they were photographed."

"Followed?"

"By a tall, dignified black man. Our security people noticed this and intervened with him—warned him about his behavior in the garden. At that point, he disappeared and hasn't been seen since. I'm sure *he's* on video."

Frank Storm, tailing Grace and Jim? But why?

Louise was trying to control her excitement and organize her thoughts. She made a mental note to ask Sergeant Drucker to fax a photo of Grace to the botanical garden. Another fantastic plot, almost as crazy as the scenario she built with Mark Post and Jeffrey Freeling, was forming in her mind.

She hung up the phone just as Janie burst in, happy to be going home. "Ma, this was a great trip, but too many accidents, and too rainy. Pick a better spot next time."

Louise sat on the bed and looked at the girl. Janie was one of the last people to see Jeffrey Freeling. There must have been something . . . "Janie, tell me one more time, because this is important: What did you and Jeffrey talk about on the way up the mountain?"

"He was cool, Ma. Told us about his genetic engineering. He was obsessed with plants and studying their molecular makeup, and how it resembles *human* molecular structure—as a plant person, don't you love that? Super guy, the kind who could almost convince a reasonable person like Chris to switch from organic chemistry to biology."

"Did he talk about anything personal—anything at all?"

"No."

"Nothing. Not his house? Just his work?"

"Not his house—well, he did tell me he lives in Briarcliff, in Westchester County. And he mentioned his garden."

Louise felt as if she had just reached Nirvana. "Tell me what he said about his garden." She pulled in a long breath.

"He was embarrassed about it, actually. He had what he called a 'romance' garden. It had love-in-a-mist, love-lies-bleeding, Sacred Blood iris—natch—and, I can't remember, rosemary, maybe. Stuff like that."

Louise stared out the window. "Gotcha!" she said quietly to the air.

"Ma, are you all right?"

The phone rang then, Chris for Janie. "Something's shaking, Ma," her daughter said. "Gotta run."

Louise didn't have a chance to tell the girl about her startling new take on the deaths in Litchfield County. She didn't even have time to tell her to be careful.

Chapter Nineteen

IT WAS NOT SILLY to do this by herself. Louise would be completely safe. After all, the yellow police tape outlined the crime scene where no one was supposed to tread. The worst that could happen was that she would meet the two patrolmen who were still scouting the grounds near the falls for evidence.

Passing the kitchen complex, she could not resist peeking in. For one, she was starved, and looking forward to a more substantial tea than the soggy one at Wild Flower Farm. She could imagine the scones served with clotted cream and jam. Whirlybird sandwiches with green-and-pink filling. Anchovy-paste sandwiches, just like Fortnum and Mason's in London. Pudgy cream puffs. Eclairs dripping with fresh chocolate frosting. Fruit tarts . . .

Her mouth was filled with saliva. Louise slipped into the kitchen only to find Barbara with Stephanie Landry, hovering beside her, helping to arrange tea snacks.

Barbara must have read her mind. She took a tart off the tray and proffered it to Louise.

"How did you know?"

"You looked hungry, my dear. And I wanted to thank you for the story in *The Litchfield Hills Sentinel*: That Tom Carrigan got it just right. The whole town's read it. I've had lots of calls supporting my position."

The lovely Stephanie looked only slightly abashed. "I guess the town didn't want a new development here, either," she said. "Neil and Jim and I were wrong." Louise wondered if the young woman would decide Neil was wrong for her. She thought it was significant that she hadn't laid eyes on Neil this morning.

"Altogether, I fear it's been a dreadful weekend," said Barbara, whose face was gaunt and gray.

Louise took a few steps toward them. "It must be particularly hard on you, Barbara," she said. "Especially Grace's death."

"Yes." The woman's capable hands placed tarts on a tray with lightning speed, and Louise realized the proprietor knew every job in this place, backward and forward. "Of course, I'm not that surprised, Louise." She looked up dreamily from her work, out the big kitchen window into the fog. "I knew somehow that we were going to lose her."

"But—how did you know that?"

"I saw Jim and Grace in April, and, surprisingly, she seemed so much happier. Her eyes *shone* with excitement. And yet— I had this feeling that it wouldn't last." Barbara turned her blue-eyed gaze on Louise. "Wasn't that a terrible thing to think?

She was so thin, so—emotional. And they were on another wavelength than she was . . ."

"You mean Jim, and Frank and Fiona?"

"Yes. Tougher than she, maybe too tough *on* her. They are all so competent that . . . it almost seems to destroy people. They showed Grace up for a weakling, or at least she thought so. 'Dilettante,' she once called herself. 'I'm just a dilettante who hasn't accomplished a thing in the eyes of my husband.'" Tears crowded Barbara's eyes. "Isn't that incredibly sad?"

Louise's voice was hollow. "Yes, incredibly." Sadder than Barbara knew, for the young woman *had* turned to something—something very dangerous—to make her feel better about herself.

Barbara, having finished one tray, moved it briskly to a side counter, dusted her hands on her apron, and turned to Louise again, businesslike now. "At least we'll finish off the weekend with a lovely tea. We'll be serving in half an hour."

Stephanie watched her aunt with concern. Louise thought how ironic it all was: It was Stephanie's husband, Neil Landry, who had probably made a crude attempt to disable her aunt. Stephanie had no doubt been convinced of this by Jim Cooley. *The righteous Jim Cooley always steps forward to make sure justice is done,* Louise thought.

Teddy stopped her as she circled around the kitchen garden. "Mrs. Eldridge—I wanted to say a personal word."

"Yes, Teddy."

With a beatific smile that would melt any maiden's heart, and might already have melted her daughter Janie's, he said, "You did good by Miss Seymour. But there's something else." His forehead wrinkled, giving him a puzzled, little-boy look beneath that distinguished cowlick. "These people dying . . . can you figure that out? I've tried, and so have Janie and Chris, but we've come up flat. You're so smart about these things—I bet you could get to the bottom of it." There was a distinct echo here, she realized, of what Jim Cooley had said to her at Wild Flower Farm.

"Well, thanks for the vote of confidence, Teddy. I'm still hoping for something. In fact, I've got a new slant on the whole thing. But I need proof, so I'm going out on a little hunting expedition."

He stood, arms akimbo, worried now. "You be careful, ma'am. There's police out there, but I suppose nothin' worse than that. And I hope Chris eventually forgives me."

"Forgives you? For what?"

He made a dismissive "aw, shucks" gesture with his hand, and said, "You'll probably find out about it from him. If not, I'll tell you about it the next time I see you."

"If there *is* a next time," said Louise.

"Oh, there will be," said the confident young man. "It's all set—I'm visiting at Thanksgiving." His pale blue eyes registered concern. "I—I hope that's all right with you."

Louise nodded absently. "Oh, of course." She conjured up a memory of Thanksgiving at the Eldridge house. Parents and family visiting. A nightmare of cooking that she always made worse by leaving everything to the day itself: pumpkin pies, with their excessive number of ingredients. Homemade cranberry sauce, the only kind Bill would eat. Candied sweet potatoes, which the girls insisted upon. Special sage turkey dressing, her grandmother's tradition. Even the defrosting of the turkey, which she invariably accomplished in the last two hours before baking time, by running a swimming pool's worth of cold water over the chilly beast in the kitchen sink.

Let's face it, Thanksgiving is hell—always has been since I've had to do it myself. Dismally, she recalled the contrast with the years growing up when her grandmother had them down to her farm for the holiday. Gram pulled off Thanksgiving like a professional. Food prepped ahead of time like any sensible housewife. Everything cooked or baked or canned so delightfully that even now Louise could taste the crisp exterior turkey meat, the dark, rich, fleshy pumpkin pies, the crunchy homemade pickles.

But a thought came to her, and she brightened, coming back to the present. Maybe Teddy would help her in the kitchen! She gave him a winsome smile, but even as she did, she wondered if she would regret it. "I bet you would love to help with that kind of dinner—all those fixings and everything . . ."

He seemed to get her message. "Ma'am, I'd be happy to spend all day in the kitchen with you."

"Thanksgiving it is," she said. Wondering, *Did he just con me, or was it the other way around?* As she walked off, she turned and took a last look at him, standing there in his white uniform shirt and black trousers, with his charming, snaggly-toothed smile. He was staring at her legs. A pleasant young man, and yet there was something about the way that his eye always lingered that she didn't like. . . .

Grace Cooley had possessed the most remarkable legs. And Teddy must have become acquainted with Grace during her visits over the past three years—the lonesome, vulnerable Grace. But no, it couldn't be. There was simply no motive—or was there? And then Louise remembered the other thing that was bothering her: the fact that Teddy would inherit from Barbara Seymour. Louise had made a mental note when she first heard about this from the elderly proprietress. Yet she had been so distracted by Jeffrey's and Grace's deaths that she had shoved the fact to the back of her mind.

Teddy Horton, always on the scene, was a young man who had a way of charming people. Louise could just imagine him flattering his way into elderly Barbara Seymour's heart. Could he have loosened that carpeting, hoping the woman would die and he would get his money? A future where the inn was closed did not augur well for Teddy—unless he knew about the inheritance.

And he hadn't even crossed her mind as a suspect in either the two deaths or Barbara's accident. Now Louise dearly wished they had done a background check on him. But of course Sergeant Drucker would know all there was to know about the young man, she thought. Louise reminded herself firmly that this whole investigation was not on her shoulders.

As she circled around the kitchen garden, her suspicions faded. Right now she was on a much hotter lead. And she expected to follow it right up the gray, misty path to Litchfield Falls.

She crossed the damp lawn to the flight of eight steps that led to the veranda. With one hand resting on the stair railing, she stared up at the side door, the one that gave access to the back stairs of the mansion. Then Louise turned around and gazed at the huge expanse of lawn.

Was anyone expected to believe that Grace crossed sixty feet of open space without being seen? For that was the distance between the inn and the path to the falls. Half a dozen members of the kitchen staff and any of the more than a dozen guests could have spotted her. Louise's high-flying hopes of solving this case began to flag.

Just as Grace might have done, she crossed the lawn, entered the open pine forest, and took the path to the top of the falls. As she walked through the filtered light, she noted the flowers growing in patches of sun beside the path: yarrow, stands of white daisies, and even an occasional drift of love-in-a-mist, in full but delicate bloom.

As she shoved her hands into her shorts pockets, it all became clear. Grace, killing herself? Never, thought Louise, especially not after the weekend Grace had experienced. Louise knew her in a way that others would never know her—as a passionate gardener, with all the requisite foibles. This special knowledge made Louise more certain that Grace's death could only have been foul play—not suicide.

If her theory proved right, it meant Grace had had strong

reasons to stay alive. But it would take a miracle to convince the prosaic, live-by-the-rules Sergeant Drucker. He would demand hard evidence. It would be nice to find Grace's notebook, but Louise knew the troopers would have spied that little red object. No, it was something else Louise was after. Evidence that the state troopers, as skilled as they were, might not recognize as such.

Her eyes searched the path carefully. Afraid she might miss something as she passed, Louise grabbed at a Sir Harry Lauder's walking-stick bush and ruthlessly wrenched off a branch. It was scraggly and dangerous, and perfect for pulling back the brush and examining the ground beneath.

After a few minutes' climb, the path took her over a rise and around a stand of hemlocks. Louise found herself looking down upon the trickling stream that constituted the headwaters of the Litchfield falls. Huge rocks crowded into the creek as if they were attempting to block the water from plunging over the cliff. Two more bloated granite boulders guarded either side of the falls, leaving only a two-foot entrance. Grace would have had to stand right there between them in order to throw herself off—or be pushed.

Louise clambered down the hill to the stream, her eyes still searching the ground, behind each rock, deep in each crevice. She discarded her branch because she needed both hands now to make her way over the first of the fat boulders. On the other side, she hopped down and maneuvered through the slippery stones in the shallow, steely-cold water, her sandaled feet growing numb. All the while she looked for the thing that would show that Grace had not come here willingly. She climbed onto the rock on the other side of the falls opening. The people—men, probably—who so colorfully named mountain peaks and rock formations would surely have called these two "The Breasts."

Peering over the edge of the boulder, Louise saw what she was looking for.

"Grace, you did it!" she exulted. It was no more than a bit of wilted vegetation with something smooth and brown attached to it, tossed among the ferns alongside the rock. Like Grace herself, it was slight, but it would be enough. Enough to start making people ask the right questions.

Louise reached out, holding on to a hemlock seedling for balance, then twisted herself around the rock like a contortionist. She could feel her heartbeat against the arm she held crushed against her chest. If she looked down at this point, she would certainly topple off the cliff. She kept her eyes fastened on her prize, pushing aside the delicate fronds to examine it more closely. Then she smiled with satisfaction—but didn't touch it. A trooper should collect this evidence.

Hoisting herself back up onto the rock left Louise red-faced and panting, and she crouched there for a minute to catch her breath. Then she stood up, steadied her feet, and felt, for a wild moment, like the king of the mountain. She considered beating her breast and giving a Tarzan-like cry of joy.

Instead, she smiled to herself and turned away from the falls to climb down. It was several seconds before she understood what she saw. She was looking into the scary hazel eyes of Jim Cooley. Cooley stood balanced expertly on the boulder opposite her, as if it were something he did every day. No longer playing the morose widower, he looked like an avenging angel.

She had not meant to do it again—put herself in danger with no apparent way out. But here she was, trying to solve things her own way, facing another life-threatening situation. And this one was too grave, too watery, to laugh off. Louise was afraid. The precipitous tumble that would take her to the deep pond or the rocks below was only moments away, unless she did something—like shout bloody murder. But she couldn't.

Being right was not satisfaction enough. She had to know everything. And she could scream later.

For the deadly mastermind was here: a modern-day killer standing on a prehistoric boulder not twelve feet away. Louise stared back at Cooley. He had on a navy blue anorak, with the hood tightened around his face. His cheeks were red from the effort of climbing, his eyes bright, his smile intact. He looked like a poster boy promoting the great Connecticut outdoors.

"You didn't kill Grace," she said.

"What makes you think Grace was killed?"

"Oh, I know she was—and so was Jeffrey." Louise didn't elaborate. The man hadn't seen what she saw alongside the boulder on which she now stood. "You might say, Jim, that Grace has spoken to us from the grave."

Intricate Design and
Easy Culture:
The Wonderful Iris

THE IRIS IS THE *Wunderkind* of flower design. It overshadows the simplicity of the Compositae—that is, the daisy, the mum, and the coneflower—and some say even the mighty rose. Its bold, sometimes bearded falls, graceful erect standards and crests, triangular stigmas, long stamens, and graceful, strappy leaves have put it not only on the map, but also on the flag. France's fleur-de-lis is, in fact, the yellow flag iris.

The flower has an early place in history. In 1950 B.C., Thutmose I brought irises home to Egypt from Syria as part of the spoils of war. The iris's image was carved on the brow of the Sphinx because Egyptians regarded the flower as the eye of heaven and a symbol of eloquence. Ancient Greeks almost deified the flower, and a nymph-goddess by this name was thought to be a messenger of the gods, traveling between Mount Olympus and mankind. The variegated colors of the flower's falls symbolized the colors of the sky through which she traveled.

Later, the iris was adopted by the Christians and became the Virgin Mary's symbol of purity, along with *Lilium candidum,* the Madonna lily. The pagan Clovis I of France acquired a shield bearing three golden irises on a blue field; it was thought to have been bestowed by an angel. He succeeded in battle after that, and soon converted to Christianity. Not only was the fleur-de-lis the royal badge of France, but also part of the British royal arms until Britain gave up its claims on the country in 1801.

The rhizomes of this beautiful plant were thought to be both medicinal and magical. Its use in medicine goes back to the earliest times; it has been used as a cathartic, an emetic, a cure for scrofula, and a relief for toothache. Dried rhizomes used to be strung into beads and hung on babies' necks for them to chew. Today, some irises are grown for their violet-scented fragrance, which is added to perfume. Few plants have attracted more names, or been more inspirational to writers and painters.

And yet, for all its illustrious history, the iris is of *such* easy culture that you might call it the courtesan of the plant world. Iris will grow almost everywhere, in varied conditions of cold and warmth, moisture and relative drought. As a gardener, your most important concern is not the *growing* of these delightful plants, but rather their unbridled spread. For if left alone in a benign environment, they will take over your garden world: Then there's a heavy digging job involved in removing them.

The gardener can have different varieties of iris in bloom for more than two months. The earliest are the six-inch-high bulbous dwarf crested iris, in lavender, blue, white, and yellow. They add a special element to woodland gardens. In May come the bearded iris, their bloom extending for four to six weeks. Then follows the beardless variety, Siberian and Japanese among them, which bloom through June and sometimes into July.

Iris are basically divided between two varieties, the **bearded**, and the **beardless**—which some wags call a "clean-shaven" iris. Bearded iris, in general, like sun, a raised bed with good drainage, and soil that is low in nitrogenous compounds and organic food, but high in mineral food from decomposed rock. The pH should be neutral to slightly alkaline. The small, bulbous types also like this environment. Beardless varieties are different: They can take wet feet, thriving and spreading in these conditions in moist swales and draws. They are gross feeders and like lots of manure-filled compost that is acidic. All varieties should be allowed to keep their foliage, except in the case of new transplants.

Since water gardens have become more popular, the beardless variety, *Iris pseudacorus,* is being sold in great numbers. This natural-ized iris will grow five-foot-tall foliage in or near a pond, and produce yellow flowers fol-lowed by handsome seedpods. But watch it! It forms a giant clump until the only way you will be able to move it is with a backhoe, so it is best put where it is going to stay.

Among the beardless iris are many natives. They include the pale blue *Iris missouriensis,* which is called blue flag in some parts of the country; *Iris virginica; Iris californica;* and probably the most vivid of this group, the Louisiana iris hybrids. They come in yellow, red, blue, rust, purple, and white. And if you put them in your garden, you might find that they tend to "walk." They have exceptionally long rhizomes, and are liable to spring up two feet away from where you first planted them. Boards placed in the garden will help keep them from wandering.

Of course, the Japanese iris, *Iris ensata,* is known and coveted by gardeners for its huge, lush flowers. Siberian iris (*Iris siberica*) is simi-lar and sometimes easier to grow. It has smaller flowers.

You must keep your eye on bearded iris. They will crowd themselves out if you don't. Dig them up and divide them every three to five years; otherwise, their blooms will grow smaller, and dwindle away.

Since they're easy to field-grow and cross-pollinate, there are thousands of varieties of iris. Colors and combinations of colors seem endless. You can develop some new varieties of your own with some simple cross-pollination.

This will produce seeds that benefit from cold stratification before germinating into baby plants. Within two years, you may get a bloom, but what kind of bloom is problematical. It's those mixed-up genes: As a grower said, "You may create a very ugly new baby. The iris has a lot of pretty mixed-up genes, so that when you get a cross, you're liable to get a big surprise." Most gardeners are content dividing the rhizomes with a simple whack with a sharp shovel. As always, beautiful and obliging.

Chapter Twenty

JIM COOLEY'S EXPRESSION CHANGED. The phony pleasant look was gone, replaced with what was in his heart: sheer cruelty. Louise realized she shouldn't have thrown those combative words in his face.

They watched each other like two kids in a dangerous contest—daring each other to step toward the nearby mouth of the falls. Louise cautiously pulled her hands out of her pockets. If she fell off the front of this rock, she would slip straight down to the pool and rocks below. But the same fate applied to Jim Cooley, and he knew it. These thoughts made her dizzy. She flexed her toes to clamp her sandals tighter on the curved surface of the boulder. If she did fall, she intended to do her best to fall backward into the stream.

"Louise Eldridge," he said airily, as if they were just meeting for the first time. "Can't I talk you out of this?"

"No, Jim, you can't. I suggest we act like the reasonable people we are, and go back down the trail to talk it over with Sergeant Drucker."

He laughed. "I don't know why I would want to do that."

She put her hands on her hips. Grace's deliberate attempt to lead them to her killer gave Louise a feeling of strength. Unlike Nora, she was not inclined toward extrasensory perception. Yet right now she felt as if the dead woman's spirit were there, helping her.

She needed to keep him at bay. "I'll tell you one thing, Jim. The police will never believe a second person fell off these falls. What do you take them for, a bunch of idiots?"

"Louise, consider the facts. The police haven't even connected the two deaths. And they never will—if you aren't around to tell them." He showed her his teeth in a big grin. "It's about the luckiest moment of my life to find you here—because I could tell you were hot on our trail, and I was getting very worried that the police would believe you. So I need to dissuade you from making such a big mistake."

"What makes you think the others—my husband, Nora, Chris, Janie—don't know what I know?"

That cat-that-swallowed-the-canary grin again. "Because I saw you all leaving the library a few minutes ago. Depressed. Frustrated. Resigned to the fact that Jeffrey fell, and Grace jumped."

The man was right. She hadn't shared her final scenario with anyone. Not even Janie. She hadn't had the chance. Janie had dashed from their room right after she had disclosed the vital information that Jeffrey Freeling had a love garden.

What a fool she'd been to keep this to herself!

"I—I left some hints with people. They'll figure it out."

"Contrariwise, Louise, your reputation *precedes* you. You're a derring-do, reckless woman who's been in bad situations before. Now, what would be more logical to the plodding, rather unimaginative Sergeant Drucker than for you to come up to the falls, snooping, and then slide off the rocks because in fact, Louise, they're slippery as hell in this kind of weather!"

"And what about you?" she asked.

"If I were to push you off the falls? I'd simply dash back to the mansion and into my room, the way I came. Frank and Fiona would be happy to say I've been with them the whole time."

Louise watched in horror as he jumped into the shallow stream and splashed across it. "Oh, God," she muttered, nearly losing her balance. She reached above her and grasped the limb of a hemlock that drooped over her perch.

"He-e-e-lp!" she screamed, repeating it over and over like a wounded, yelping dog. "Help, help, help!"

With the man now scrabbling up the rock on which she stood, Louise wished she still had her rugged Sir Harry Lauder's walking-stick branch in hand. Jim hoisted himself onto the boulder and took her by the shoulders, teetering. A desperate thought came to her. "Wait—you don't want to kill me." Her voice came out in a shuddering croak. "I'm the only one who can explain to them all why you did it in the first place. Make them understand."

"You, explain—explain what?" he growled and tightened his hold, preparatory to giving her a good shove forward. Her eyes widened, and she felt as if she were going to faint.

Then she heard the call. "Hello, up there. What's going on?"

Her heart leaped, pounding harder in her chest. "Please help me!" she screamed. Then she looked up at Cooley and said, with a wryness she hadn't known she could still summon, "Well, Jim, go ahead if you must. But someone is watching."

They both looked down through the mist to the base of the falls. Two state patrolmen assigned to search the grounds for evidence stared up at them from the edge of the deep pool twenty-five feet below.

"Sir, what's goin' on up there?" said one. The other was already sprinting up the trail toward them.

"Officers," Jim called out, in his smooth, baritone voice, "Mrs. Eldridge was in trouble. But I'm here now. And I'll help her down."

He released her, and she slid by him and jumped down into the stream, splattering cold water onto her bare legs, but not minding. In fact, she was loving the feeling of being alive. She scrambled to the other bank, up some rocks, not minding the bruising of her knees, and onto the pine-needle-covered path. Now it was safe to turn and look at her adversary. He was still standing on the rock where they had both been a moment ago, looking calm and in control.

"Come on, Jim, we have to go back down that trail and talk to some people."

He hopped off the boulder. "Coming. And I was glad to be of service here, Louise. You'd really gotten yourself in a bit of a jam, with both your wild imagination and your dancing on those rocks."

She thought, *What a peculiar group we make, the four of us, Jim and I walking in front of two grim-faced troopers as if we were prisoners.*

The troopers had treated both her and Jim as lawbreakers,

and indeed they were—both were wandering around inside the taped-off area secured by the police.

When he saw her coming across the lawn, Bill ran down the porch stairs and gathered her in his arms. "Louise, my God, where've you been?" When she didn't immediately answer, he looked at Cooley and the troopers in bewilderment. "Have you four been out together? What's going on?"

Louise murmured close to his ear. "Please don't ask me right now. I'm in a lot of trouble here."

One of the troopers said, "Is Sergeant Drucker inside?"

Bill turned to him crossly. "He's talking to Mark Post at the moment, but he damned well better get out here." One trooper escorted them to the veranda, while the other strode quickly into the mansion.

In a moment, Drucker appeared. He looked at Louise carefully, as if checking for signs of violence. Seeing none, he couldn't resist a little joke. That crinkly smile took over his face. "Well, well, I hear you two were up at the falls, hugging. What were you doing, trying to reenact Sherlock Holmes and Moriarty at the top of Reichenbach Falls?"

Jim Cooley broke out in his rich laugh. The man was smooth as silk. "Hardly as confrontational as *that*. Louise climbed up on the rocks there. I don't know how she did it, but knowing how dangerous it was, I trotted up after her—"

"Wait a minute," protested Bill, sensing something wrong with this story.

Drucker put up a hand to urge him to be quiet. "And then what happened, Mr. Cooley?"

"She was up on one of those big boulders. I guess she was trying to figure the angle of Grace's fall." He looked at Bill, his eyes wide with innocence. "I do know the woman has a reputation as a kind of daredevil detective—"

"Watch it!" cried Bill, stepping closer to Cooley. But Drucker grabbed his shoulder, holding him steady.

"So I thought I'd better try to keep her from doing anything too dangerous."

"That isn't the way it was," said Louise quietly. "Ask the troopers."

One of the men shrugged his shoulders. "Like we told you, sir. We couldn't tell exactly what was happening." Drucker looked perplexed. The troopers saw only a man and a woman on top of the falls. They could have been doing anything, just up there for the fun of it, maybe. Jim Cooley had just revealed himself to Louise as a guilty man, but he had not revealed himself to the world. Right now, he stood chatting with Sergeant Drucker, a benevolent but slightly sad smile on his face, perfect for the bereaved widower and champion of foolhardy damsels.

Well, the son of a bitch was not going to get away with it. "Sergeant Drucker," she called out, "when you're through talking to my savior, could I have a private word with you?" Then she turned to the tall trooper hovering near her. "This is important," she told him, fixing him with her gaze. She gave him specific directions to her important discovery behind the boulder at the top of the falls. "And now I need to talk to my husband for a minute." The trooper nodded toward Bill, and her husband approached her. Leaning her head briefly against Bill's shoulder, Louise knew that the trooper could neither see her mouth moving nor hear what she asked before her husband gave her a quick kiss on the forehead and hurried off.

Drucker finished talking to Cooley and took Louise by the arm, wordlessly guiding her into the mansion. He stopped in the library, where he ceremoniously closed the door. He might have been about to give a child a salutary scolding. He stood there looming above her, declining to sit down; this meeting would take place by the door, and it wasn't going to take long. First, a brief, disgusted shake of his head. Then he said, "I never thought, when I solicited your help, that you were going to put me in the position of having to fish another dead body out of that pond."

"I'm sorry, but—"

"Never mind apologies. Let's get down to more important things. You got a fax, Louise." And he handed her a paper on which there was a blurry picture of two familiar-looking people.

She gasped in horror. This man and woman now lay dead in the local morgue, and they had died in the name of love.

Chapter
Twenty-one

WHEN LOUISE ARRIVED IN the library, only the cat was there to greet her; the guests and staff were not yet there. "Hi, kitty," she said absently, wandering about the room, thinking hard.

As she passed to the right of one of the big leather couches, she nearly stepped in a pile of broken vase pieces on the floor. "Oh, oh," she exclaimed. As she remembered it, the expensive-looking, flower-bedecked object had stood well back of the couch, on the wooden pedestal that now lay beside it on the floor.

The vase was reduced to so many fragments that Louise was sure it was beyond repair.

She put her hands on her hips and looked at the cat. "*Harg*rave."

Hargrave sat in his box—a wise, impertinent look on his face.

Crouching down to touch the biggest piece, she began to have second thoughts. If anyone could find an artisan to put this thing back together again, it was Barbara Seymour. "Naughty kitty," she chided. The cat blinked his eyes, shirking all guilt. Louise tipped her head at him, assessing. Hargrave was not a kitty. Not really. He was a seasoned tomcat who obviously knew how to conduct himself around a house filled with precious objects. It was very strange to think that the cat was responsible.

She would call the housekeeping staff in a minute, but first things first. She had a feeling about this library, and she had to pursue it before the others showed up. She was sure there was another clue here somewhere. *Of course, dummy,* she scolded herself, *you could try the fireplace, the only place in the whole house where a murderer could openly destroy evidence.*

She went over to the wide stone opening and knelt down. The slate hearth was cold against her bare knees. She stretched forward to see what she could see. The embers were lifeless and gray, a clutter of little shapes. Then, she detected a movement in her peripheral vision.

Hargrave, who had watched all this from his basket, now sprang up. He crowded his large cat presence directly in front of her and proceeded to rub the side of his head vigorously against her forehead. Louise burst out laughing. "What an opportunist," she said, "waiting until I come down on your level."

Then he stopped rubbing and just sat there, looking at her. Green cat eyes staring deep into her hazel ones. Sending a message.

She smiled. "You're definitely trying to tell me something, aren't you, old boy? Don't tell me you broke that vase just to call attention to this room! Or was someone else pussyfooting around in here last night? Well, I'm definitely getting it; actually, I got it even without you." Not the least abashed that she had just had a one-way conversation with a cat, Louise sprang to her feet, went to the door of the library, and called out for help.

Sergeant Drucker's men had come in and moved the library furniture into a large horseshoe shape, with an open end at the fireplace. There were seats for twenty-one: Jim Cooley, Frank and Fiona Storm, Mark and Sandy Post, Rod and Dorothy Gasparra, Bill, Nora, Chris, Janie, Neil and Stephanie Landry, Barbara Seymour, and her staff of six, including Teddy Horton. Four were still empty, with Bill, Janie, Chris, and Teddy unaccounted for. Louise knew what had delayed Bill. But her heart raced as she feared for Janie's safety. Then she realized all the people she distrusted were in this room.

They all sat down, except for Jim Cooley, Drucker, and the four state troopers on Drucker's crime squad. The troopers stood in their drab gray uniforms, unrelieved except for blue-and-gold Connecticut state police patches on either shoulder. Their presence attested to the fact that this was more than a little social chat with the sergeant.

Yet Jim Cooley was in a state of denial. He stood near the fireplace with two troopers, conversing as casually as if this were a cocktail party. Louise found his bravado unsettling. Was Jim going to get away with all this?

Well, at least the cat seemed to have his number; Louise had a good view from her seat nearby. Cooley was standing right next to the wicker basket where Hargrave was resting. The cat watched Cooley's legs with concern, his ears flat against his head and his tail twitching back and forth, as though he might reach out and attack him with a claw or a tooth. Instead, he rose, looking disgusted, and slunk away behind the couch.

Over on the other side of the room, Sergeant Drucker also appeared unhappy. Face stormy, he stood at the library door with arms folded and feet braced wide apart, quietly chewing out a trooper. Louise assumed he was upset because his squad had not been able to locate four people—extra-tall people at that—on the grounds of the inn. After issuing a final order to the trooper, who immediately rushed out the door, the sergeant strode to the front of the room. His tall, grim presence brought the library to silence, and Cooley to his seat.

Once he had arrived at the fireplace, however, Drucker looked out at the crowd and smiled. Louise was perplexed: He had slipped back into his usual good humor as easily as he would slip on his coat. Was this lightning switch in mood just part of his act?

In a light, almost jovial tone, he said, "This shouldn't take long, ladies and gentlemen. I know you're anxious to enjoy that wonderful tea Miss Seymour has set up. I also want you to know how much I appreciate your cooperation with this investigation. It has been a bit puzzling, and as I told you all at the outset, it was a question of ruling out foul play. So, through the able assistance of my crime squad, and of a special helper, Mrs. Eldridge, I believe we've reached some conclusions. And I must inform you, that just as a formality, this session is being taped"—he nodded his head to one of his men standing at a nearby library table—"by Trooper Barnes."

Drucker took a step toward them and grinned in a friendly fashion. He continued: "You must realize we know a lot more about you than we did yesterday—having run you through the police computer. This, plus other cross-checks in your local communities. So, without revealing any secrets or confidences, let me share with you a few of the things that I've learned." He tossed out a hand in a nonthreatening gesture. "Consider this a kind of review. We want to set your minds to rest. I know you've been living in each other's pockets for three days now, so most of what I tell you will be no surprise. But it will help you put the facts straight and eliminate gossip and rumor. That way, you can all go home and get a good night's sleep."

What a warm, fuzzy guy he was, Louise thought—but not really. He held a small notepad in his big hands. He looked down at it. "All right. Let's take the victims, first. Dr. Jeffrey Freeling. Several of you noted he was a bit grouchy. He had that reputation, too, at NYU: a demanding teacher who wouldn't stand for any slacking off. A public reputation for bickering with other scholars about his research breakthroughs"—he smiled boyishly—"a fact I picked up in an article in *The New York Times*." He glanced around at their faces. "We lost a talented man here, when he took that misstep at the top of Bear Mountain."

Jim Cooley nodded. "We knew that, Sergeant. So now, what *of* Freeling's accident?"

The sergeant smiled at Cooley. "Let's leave that until later." His face sobered. "Now, your wife, Mr. Cooley, a lovely young woman, not even forty. Taking college classes in an attempt to get a degree. Botany, poetry, her favorite subjects."

Jim Cooley reddened, then bowed his head. Louise watched him in disgust. What a faker.

"Mrs. Cooley, then," the sergeant went on, "was a somewhat nervous but well-met person with few connections in her life outside of her immediate family in Brooklyn. Her parents are deceased, and she had no sisters or brothers. Many noted her tendency to—well, how will I say it?—get down in the dumps."

He flipped over a couple of pages in his little pad. "Mrs. Hollowell, now . . ." Bebe looked up nervously. "A grieving widow. Your husband Ernest passed away only a few weeks ago. As we all know, you've been pretty upset about these deaths, and talking to all of us quite a lot about them." What an understatement, thought Louise.

That was all he said about Bebe; then he turned abruptly and faced Sandy and Mark, meeting two sets of anxious eyes. "The Posts. This young couple lives in Darien, and Mark works in Stamford. Both knew Dr. Freeling, and apparently had some bad feelings toward him over something that happened at NYU some years back. However, they appeared to have made peace with each other."

He stared at Rod and Dorothy, who sat on one side of the circle, edgy but silent. "Mr. and Mrs. Gasparra work hard at their Pennsylvania nursery business. On this trip, they've encountered some friction with local people, notably the owner of Wild Flower Farm. They also publicly expressed a grudge against Dr. Freeling; they had no dispute, however, with Grace Cooley."

His brown eyes touched on Stephanie and Neil Landry. "The Landrys were conspicuously absent at the time of these deaths." He gave Neil Landry a pointed glance. "There has been some demand that we also investigate the tumble Barbara Seymour took down the front stairs Friday, in case it's related to the other deaths. Our conclusion is that it's not related, and at the moment we lack evidence to prove that anyone meant Miss Seymour harm."

Barbara stared at the floor. Louise was sure she wished they weren't talking about her. Stephanie grabbed her aunt's hand and whispered something in her ear. Neil Landry sat apart from the two women, his aloof expression further separating him from them.

"Now the two hardworking individuals involved with Jim Cooley in the very successful educational enterprise, Higher Directions—Frank and Fiona Storm. They have spotless reputations, and so do their schools, for the most part. The only shadow on them is the case of two students from the Brooklyn facility who committed suicide in May—just before they were supposed to graduate."

"I wish you wouldn't throw things like that into the conversation, and not allow us to explain it," said Frank. He sat next to his wife, proud and immovable.

"Go ahead," Drucker said amiably.

"The two young men in question were probationary students," said Frank. "Their graduation was in doubt during the entire semester. Then, they unfortunately fell into a vortex of evil."

Drucker lifted an eyebrow. "Homosexuality, I hear. That's a vortex of evil, in your opinion?"

Storm didn't like his tone. "To Higher Directions, homosexuality is a sin, and it should be eradicated from society."

Drucker said, "I suppose the same goes for adultery."

"It does," Frank agreed fiercely. "But those boys were deep into trouble according to witnesses. They began the usual downward spiral that accompanies this kind of behavior: lying, smoking dope, slacking off in their schoolwork, hanging around bad companions, staying out after curfew—the whole nine yards. Before you knew it, they were known to be depressed, self-absorbed, and—"

"—candidates for suicide," finished Sergeant Drucker.

"Exactly. That's what the police concluded, Sergeant."

"Thank you for that explanation; it was very informative. Now your partner, Mr. Jim Cooley, with whom many of you have become friends this weekend, occupies quite a prestigious place in the ranks of educators. He heads a business that runs three private schools with a total of about fifteen hundred students. Mr. Cooley has told us his wife was—upset. Miss Seymour told us the same thing of this niece by marriage, though Miss Seymour mentioned that Grace had seemed to perk up lately. In the absence of any other evidence, we could say with assurance that Mrs. Cooley took her own life, in this dramatic and rather poetic way."

Fiona Storm slowly shook her head, as if to say, What a shame, poor girl. Tears came to Jim Cooley's eyes. Frank Storm looked stolidly ahead.

Drucker looked triumphant. "However, we do have some other evidence." He strode over to where Louise was sitting and gave her an unreadable look. "Mrs. Eldridge?"

Everyone turned and stared at her, and she caught her breath. What had she gotten herself into? This was dangerous territory she was entering: a virtual jungle, a dense thicket filled with truth—and lies.

Jungle: The New Look in Gardens

PEOPLE WHO LIVE IN the tropical outposts of the United States are almost blasé about the ease with which they can grow things. It is nothing for them to go out and pick bananas, avocados, or exotic fruits from their own trees, and grow lush poincianas, gingers, and plants that gardeners in colder zones have never seen or heard of. But now, the tropical look has invaded the consciousness of northern gardeners, and the jungle effect is the hottest new thing in garden design.

It isn't that easy, and some predict the fad will evaporate quickly once gardeners experience the labor involved. Think about digging up all those canna, dahlia, begonia, and caladium tubers, and wrestling that enormous banana tree root out of the ground, swathing it in burlap, and shoving it into cold storage! Imagine yourself spending half the year tripping over extra houseplants such as cyperus, giant Mexican tree ferns, delicate bamboos, or brilliant, strappy-leaved cordylines.

In spite of these drawbacks, the jungle look is definitely in. Sometimes it's found in crowded urban gardens. While most of us would deck these gardens out with polite plants and vines that hug fences and stay out of the way, a London garden designer has destroyed that convention. In his small city garden, twenty by fifty feet, he has created a tropical forest with Australian tree ferns, huge-leaved *Gunnera manicata* that grow eight feet wide, bamboos, and several varieties of palms. He simply brushes aside the massive plant leaves as he walks through them. The place is such a hit that he now designs such gardens for others.

This jungle garden is a world away from your grandmother's pastiche of pastel garden borders. Again, throw out the conventional advice that plants should match or blend. Think Gauguin: Go ahead and mix hot colors, stripes and speckles, and surprising leaf textures, and let the results speak for themselves. What they will do is excite the eye and lead it deep into the jungle's interior. If your soul trembles at the sight of bright red next to bright yellow, then separate the two with an arbitrator: a neutral, gray-toned yucca.

So that you don't encounter backbreaking labor in the fall, this out-of-place jungle gar-

den should be a combination of both hardy and tender plants. Among the tender ones, none is bolder than the banana tree. Its drooping leaves are the classical emblem of the tropics. Yet it's an easy-to-grow plant that's fun for both big and little kids. Just be prepared for that wrestling match with either the root or the plant itself in the fall.

Fluffy, umbrella-topped cyperus soaring above the level of the flowers will add grace and lightness to this tropical array. And the garden definitely calls for gaudy cannas: Try the variegated-leafed varieties. Fiery-colored dahlias, the castor bean plant, red orach (*Atriplex hortensis* 'Rubra'), and the majestic datura are other good choices. This garden probably won't be complete without the flamboyant, often speckled, green, pink, or red leaves of the annual caladium.

There are many sturdy perennials that will add brilliance to your jungle. They should be the permanent structure into which you place the more tender varieties. Use hardy bamboos, striped grasses such as *Miscanthus*, red-hot-poker plant (*Kniphofia*), spotted ligularia, yucca, fern, and even a low gray beauty not usually thought of when we contemplate the hot tropics: *Artemisia* 'Powis Castle.' Consider another grass that is like an echo of the umbrella-topped cyperus, but hardy to zone five: palm sedge (*Carex muskingumensis*). It is densely tufted and would make a stunning lower story in a tropical-motif garden. *Polygonum bistorta* is a useful plant with long-lasting pokerlike flowers in pink or red. And if you let the tall blue annual verbena seed itself within these beds, it will be as useful as a perennial. Its color and rangy form make it a perfect foil for the hot reds, pinks, and oranges.

Like a traditional garden, your jungle needs trees. The underused golden catalpa is not only winter hardy, it is also exotic, with drooping, bell-shaped white flowers, serpentine seed pods, and big, heart-shaped leaves that shine golden in the fall. Others are the golden black locust, with black trunk and filigree yellow leaves that go orange in autumn, and the katsura tree, with its splendid ovate blue-green foliage.

These are practical tree choices. But if money is no consideration, "rent" a bit of jungle—namely, the noble palm tree. That's what some East Coast gardeners do. They lease twenty-foot palms for a seven-month season for $400 to $500. At the end of October, they merely call up the supplier and have the trees redug and put into winter storage. In other words, they put away the trappings of their tropical paradise until the snow melts and spring comes again to turn their thoughts to things equatorial.

Chapter
Twenty-two

Louise stood in front of the fireplace, trying to ignore her quickening heartbeat and the tightness in her chest. She said simply, "My family and friends and I have been able to uncover some small details."

Looking around the room, she instantly met the poisonous gaze of Jim Cooley. It sprang out at her like the fangs of a snake. Frank and Fiona Storm stared at her with equal venom.

And to think not a minute ago the three of them thought they were home free.

She was glad she had rattled their cage: Somehow, it made her feel more confident. Now, all she had to do was lay out the evidence in a logical way, so people would believe her.

Momentarily lost in thought, she put one hand on her chin and paced the length of the hearth. Then she turned toward her audience and gave them her opening shot. "Two hours ago, I began to believe that Grace Cooley was murdered." She paused to let that sink in, then continued: "I was walking the paths at Wild Flower Farm with Jim Cooley. He asked me if I would be willing to help solve the case if it turned out Grace's death was foul play. My heart went out to him, because I think he truly is suffering. But eventually I said to myself, Why is a bereaved widower telling me this? If he suspects foul play, why doesn't he press the police to take action? I realized it must be a smoke screen to allay any suspicions I might have."

She looked around nervously. Where were Bill and Janie? She had no choice but to go on without them, so she moved to the next point in her argument: "And we all noticed the affinity of Jim for Frank and Fiona Storm. If they talked to you on the subject of Higher Directions, you know how close they are philosophically. They'd have to be, to make such a success of their schools. The schools are heavy with debt, not unusual for enterprises like theirs. But there was something more insidious: the two student suicides. Certainly this somewhat alters our view of Higher Directions."

Realizing they were now facing open warfare, Jim, Frank, and Fiona put their heads together and whispered vehemently, but when Louise resumed talking, they grudgingly stopped.

She opened her hands. "Strange things happened after the deaths. Guilty people began to act out." She avoided looking at Bebe when she said this. "And I thought to myself, Jim and Frank *never* look guilty. Jim is like everyone's conscience, always stepping forward when there is *justice* to be done.

"Then Saturday night, the night Grace died, Frank intercepted the kitchen employee and asked to take her dinner up to her. Frank knew her well, and knew Grace would never eat while feeling so ill, since she ate like a bird at the best of times. One has to ask, Why bring the woman a dinner she couldn't eat? Was it so the kitchen staff wouldn't know she was missing from her room?"

Frank seemed to be examining his hands. Her voice got a little louder. "Nora Radebaugh has a friend in New York City who taught Grace in a poetry class. He told Nora that Grace was not suicidal at all, in fact, just the opposite. The woman was on some sort of creative high, and even going to get some of her poetry published." Her mouth stretched out in a grin. "What writer kills herself on the eve of publication?"

She paced back and forth in front of them to work off nervous energy. "Also, Grace had just redone the yard of the Cooleys' lovely brownstone in Park Slope and put in a romance garden." She turned her hands palm-up in a gesture of bewilderment. "Now if any of you garden, you know what I'm saying is true: A new garden is a sign of hope and renewal, not death." She raised two fingers. "Two reasons for Grace not to commit suicide. But the question was still: Why would someone want to kill her?

"A red flag went up when I learned Grace's husband didn't even recognize one of the major flowers in the garden: love-in-a-mist. No, this garden wasn't a celebration of her romance with Jim Cooley."

"What are you *saying*?" demanded Cooley, leaning forward. "Some damned romance garden shows I'm a murderer?"

"Easy does it," said the trooper, stepping forward and standing there until Cooley resumed his seat.

"Grace was a romantic," declared Louise. "Jim was not. Bereft of romance in her own marriage, she found it one day at the New York Botanical Garden."

"How would you know that?" growled Cooley.

"Oh, there's proof. Grace had frequent rendezvous there

with a man she grew to admire and love. Just minutes ago I received a faxed photograph of them together." Out of a shorts pocket she pulled the grainy picture of a man and woman walking. They were leaning into each other as if they were the only two people in the world.

The assembled guests gasped, and began to talk to each other. The only silent ones were Jim Cooley, the Storms, and the Posts.

Continuing to hold the photo up for display, Louise said, "This man was so smitten with Grace that he planted a romance garden that is a twin to hers, in his own yard."

Jim Cooley sat as if frozen, first examining the photo, then looking resolutely off into space. But it was Sandy Post's face that held Louise. From beneath her cherubic cap of blond hair, she stared with eyes that seemed permanently set in the wide-open position.

"Yes, *there* was the hidden connection: Jeffrey Freeling was the man Grace loved. They embarked on a quiet, innocent friendship that grew into romance. She needed both of those things: friendship and romance." Louise spoke directly to Jim Cooley: "As someone who knows you well has told me, *Grace was living in the shadow of people who destroyed others with their competence.*"

"I said that to you, Louise," interrupted Barbara Seymour in an angry, shaking voice. "But I didn't mean that Jim *killed* Grace . . ."

"No," said Louise. "And Jim didn't kill Grace, Miss Seymour." She turned back to Jim Cooley. "You sensed that your wife had a new, secret friendship, because she was suddenly happy, after being unhappy for so long.

"That's why you forbade her to visit the botanical garden. But we discovered the couple was followed, at least once, by a man that fits the description of—Mr. Frank Storm."

Jim was halfway out of his seat again, all six feet two of him, and his physical presence made Louise's heart start pounding. Trooper Barnes stood right next to him, with another officer moving close on his left. Cooley maintained his calm. "Just as Aunt Barbara said, this doesn't prove a thing, except that Grace had a friend she met in a garden. I already knew that. I just didn't know it was Jeffrey Freeling."

"Yes, but you were startled Friday night when your wife left your bedroom in the middle of the night. And you followed her. I was there. I—I was suffering from insomnia."

She cast a self-conscious look at the group, and then realized she had no time for embarrassment. In a low voice she added, "I heard those unmistakable sounds of a couple embracing. So did the others who were out in the hall—and who knows how many of us were out there, listening? I also saw two men in silhouette, talking with one another, with their arms around each other. At first, I thought it was a sexual liaison, but now I realize one was consoling the other because of a loss one of them had sustained."

She extended a dramatic hand. "That loss, my friends, was the loss of Jim Cooley's wife to Jeffrey Freeling."

Barbara Seymour gasped and stared reproachfully at Louise. But even if she lost the older woman's friendship, Louise was obliged to continue with the story.

"Jeffrey and Grace came together that night, made love for the first and last time. In the eyes of Jim Cooley and Frank and Fiona, Grace's adultery was disloyalty of the worst kind. You can read it in their motivational manual."

Fiona sat forward, livid. "You are merely guessing."

Louise rushed on, ignoring her. "Your husband Frank was with Jim after Grace disappeared from their room, and when her treachery was confirmed by the sound of the lovers moaning. It was Frank who comforted Jim: He put a friendly arm around his shoulders and embraced him."

"No, no, no," Jim droned, shaking his head.

"But, Jim," Louise said, "I'm sure you were in that hall Friday night, because you mentioned hearing the 'bumps in the night' at breakfast the next morning."

"So *what?*" demanded Cooley.

"You couldn't have heard those bumps, if you hadn't been out in the hall, spying on your wife. Those rooms are silent as tombs, with their soundproof walls, and doors made by a master carpenter."

His eyes blazed, but he remained silent.

Louise stood to one side of the fireplace, for effect, and to gather her thoughts. "So, let's chalk up a third reason Grace wouldn't kill herself: She was in love, for the first time in years."

The group was spellbound now. "When the friendship between Grace and Jeffrey was discovered by Grace's husband— and what a shock to find your wife's secret lover staying in the same hotel for the weekend—his pride would have it no other way than to kill the happy couple."

"Bullshit!" bellowed Cooley, grasping the arms of his chair with either hand. "I'm going to damned well sue you—"

"What the police needed was the evidence," explained Louise, keeping her voice from trembling with an effort. "But there was none. As I told Sergeant Drucker, Grace's notebook would have been a gold mine of evidence—it was a catalogue of her thoughts and emotions. But it's disappeared. Yet I still found something she left behind."

When she continued, her voice was hushed. "I went up to the falls an hour ago, because I sensed that Grace would try to tell us what had happened to her. And I remembered what she said yesterday on the garden tour about picking flowers. Bebe, you remember," she said, turning to the woman.

Bebe nodded solemnly. "She never picked flowers," the widow said.

"I went up the trail, inside the yellow-taped crime scene,

thinking I would be safe, since the troopers were out there, but no one else. The area was sealed. I was looking for something that wouldn't have looked like evidence to anybody else, and I found it—an obscure little bunch of vegetative matter. Flowers, in fact, that Grace picked as she was being forced or cajoled up that trail to the falls."

"But she didn't *pick* flowers," said Bebe. "It was part of her religion, or something, *not* picking flowers."

"Exactly. In fact, she wrote a poem about it." Louise took a piece of paper out of another pocket and unfolded it:

> " 'The pulse of life in the iris red
> Is the passion that makes my blood flow fast.
> Oh pick it not, this perfect flower,
> For, like desire, we must make it last.'

"But she did pick these flowers. We have to ask ourselves, why? To show us she wasn't going up the falls of her own free will. She told us Saturday, 'Over my dead body would I pick flowers.' Unfortunately, that is exactly what happened!"

Louise let that sink in for a moment, noting again Frank Storm's rigid countenance.

Trooper Barnes handed an item to Louise. It was now protected in a transparent evidence bag. A limp bouquet, an insubstantial little gathering of love-in-a-mist, yarrow, and wild daisies. It was secured with Grace's tortoiseshell hair clip. She raised it so people could see it.

"Anyone could have put it there," snarled Jim Cooley.

"How did it get attached to Grace's hair clip, then?" Louise challenged.

Frank said, "That's a pretty anonymous-looking hair ornament. It could have been dropped behind that rock weeks ago—years ago."

And this was a break she hadn't counted on.

"So, Frank," she said quietly, "you knew she threw her little bouquet behind a rock. You thought it was just a few dead flowers that would look like plant debris. But only the person who took Grace up that path would know it was thrown behind 'that rock.' "

If he was ruffled, Frank didn't show it beyond the faintest tremble in his voice. He said, "I guessed—because the police didn't find it, and you did, it had to be behind a rock. Now, tell me this, Mrs. Eldridge." His tones were clipped and cold as ice. "There was a whole cadre of kitchen employees running around this place Saturday—it was a big dinner night at the inn. How do you think someone could strong-arm Grace across the grounds and up that trail without being seen? From what I understand, neither she nor this phantom assailant was ever seen going across the lawn."

Louise felt a flush rising in her cheeks. She had known it would come to this question, and she had no answer for it. How did Grace and her assailant pass through the yard without anyone seeing them? Was it just good luck on the part of the murderer?

There was a leaden feeling in her stomach as she realized she might have proven adultery, but had certainly not proved murder. What did a silly little faded bouquet mean? If only someone else had found something. . . .

Just then, as if in answer to her prayer, into the room came Bill, accompanied by Janie, Chris, and Teddy. The young people were panting, as if they had been running. Their eyes, like Bill's, were filled with excitement.

The excitement of the chase, thought Louise delightedly. These cohorts of hers had found or done something, she knew, to slice through the jungle of muddled facts and solve this mystery. They stood together at the front of the group, hardly able to wait to tell their story.

"I stumbled on these three," Bill explained, nodding his

head at the young people. "And Janie, Chris, and Teddy have confirmed some new information. They found out why Grace wasn't seen on the side or back lawn Saturday afternoon."

Jim Cooley glared at them. "You kids know? How the hell would *you* know?" He looked straight into the cunning face of Teddy Horton.

Teddy grinned, and shifted nervously from foot to foot, hands clenched by his sides. "We've been exploring, Mr. Cooley. Now, I've worked here three years, and I knew darn well that the supply tunnel was blocked. But Miss Eldridge here—the lovely *Janie* Eldridge, that is—was more inquisitive than I was. She's the one who said we should check the tunnel out good, from both sides. So we did. And it *was* blocked—'til recently, when someone tampered with the wall. The cops who saw the scene wouldn't know the difference—although Miss Seymour would have known, since she knows this place like the back of her hand. And, of course, she hasn't been walking around the grounds much since she took her flyer down the stairs." Calmer now, he winked companionably at the elderly woman. Barbara beamed back.

"Go on, son," said Sergeant Drucker.

"So whoever did this closed the tunnel up, but built it only a fraction of its former thickness of six feet and supported it with a piece of three-quarter-inch plywood. That left a pile of extra rocks, but who thinks anything of a stray pile of rocks lying around in Connecticut?" He paused to give them a big grin. "Well, to make a long story shorter, it would have been easy to open the tunnel the rest of the way and let people through. What's more—well, you take it from here, Chris."

Chris pulled a little package out of the pocket of his tight-fitting jeans. "We found something unusual at the very end of the tunnel, stuck behind a rock, right near where it exits through a kind of earth cave near the river."

He held the little package up: a red notebook in a plastic evidence bag. A gasp went around the room. "Finding this proves Grace was forced through that tunnel. If she went *voluntarily,* why would she ever leave her precious notebook behind?" He broke into a smile. "And you should see what it *says.*"

Bill took a step toward Jim Cooley and looked right at him. In a commanding tone, he said, "It was stunning—you might say *amazing*—how Grace managed to jot down the name of her killer while being dragged to her death—"

Cooley's eyes had grown dark with anger. "Eldridge, you're a *liar*! You're *manufacturing* evidence. That *couldn't* be Grace's notebook."

Louise sauntered toward him. "And why not? Only someone involved in killing her would know that, Jim. It can't be Grace's notebook, can it, because you burned it!"

At that, Cooley's nervous gaze was drawn to the big fireplace; then it returned to Louise's face.

Louise said, "That's right, in this fireplace. With a trooper on guard inside the mansion all night, it must have driven you mad—you couldn't retrieve the metal binding. But we found it in the ashes here." On cue, Trooper Barnes held up the little bag containing a metal spine with three rings attached to it.

"Good *God,* there's no way I could have killed my wife," bellowed Cooley. "My movements are *totally* accounted for. And I didn't kill that prick, Jeffrey, for God's sake—I tried to *save* him." He looked around frantically, his eyes lighting on Frank, who was sitting beside him. His friend looked back at him.

Cooley jerked forward involuntarily in his chair, his sweaty palms squeaking along the leather chair arms. His voice was raspy, desperate. "Maybe Frank did it, but certainly not with *my* blessing. Even if you do think I had a motive—even if my wife *was* committing adultery under my nose—you'll never pin these murders on me."

Frank looked over at Jim, his entire demeanor a rebuke.

He said harshly, "What a friend you are. What loyalty. I'm not taking this rap alone." With great dignity, he rose from his chair.

Fiona Storm reached out and caught his sleeve. "Frank, *no,*" she pleaded. "No one's proved *anything* yet." But he pulled away, giving her a mournful look. "Sergeant Drucker, let's end this. We need to talk."

Chapter
Twenty-three

"HE CONFESSED."

"Thank God."

"As we grew to suspect," said Sergeant Drucker, "it was a conspiracy. Frank admits to murdering Grace at the behest of his friend, Jim. He told us Jim shoved Dr. Freeling off Bear Mountain, although Cooley won't own up to it yet. They planned it Friday night, after they discovered the two lovers were makin' out in a room right down the hall. Mrs. Storm could be involved—though Frank's trying to keep her out of it."

"I'm sure he is. After all, they have a family."

"It was quite sly how Grace exposed her murderer," said the sergeant. "Frank apparently felt a lot of sympathy for Grace, so he honored a kind of last request as he forced her up that hill. He let her pick out a couple of flowers—knowing, of course, how addicted she was to gardening. When he wasn't looking, she pulled her hair clip off and attached it to the little nosegay. He saw her drop some debris next to a big rock, but didn't notice the clip. He thought it was just a harmless handful of flowers."

He looked down at Louise with a frown. "And it was quite sly how you had your husband run out and buy that substitute red notebook at the local Shopko's—"

She smiled. "You didn't approve?"

"It served its purpose: Cooley showed his hand, and it brought both him and his accomplice down."

"Solving this thing must give everyone a sense of relief, especially poor Bebe."

He chuckled. "I just got a call back from the Mattson police. The lab reports are back, and she's pretty much cleared of any wrongdoing in her husband's death. In fact, the chief said she's up for a Volunteer of the Year award for her work at the Bonne Chance Retirement Home. Like she told us, those old folks never lost faith in her."

"What a momentous waste of emotional effort," said Louise, laughing. "The poor woman was sure she was going to be accused of serial murder. She was throwing emotion around like Pollock flinging paint. You might say she was having a *hissy*-fit."

Drucker grinned at the homey expression. "And now she's going to go back to get a plastic plaque and become a local hero. Sometimes things work out." But then he shook his head and gave Louise one of his brown-eyed, hangdog looks that invited sympathy. "Yet I don't want you to think it's always this easy to solve murders, Mrs. Eldridge. Sometimes there's no physical evidence. No little limp bouquets. No burned note-book spines. No confessions."

"Isn't it ironic that Frank and Jim just barely escaped blame in the suicides of those students, and then they get themselves in much deeper trouble." She looked at Drucker anxiously. "It *is* pretty certain that Jim will be convicted along with Frank?"

His eyebrows came down in a frown. "Can't say for sure. The case against Frank is stronger."

"I'd hate to see Jim get away with Jeffrey's murder," said Louise, "especially since he was probably the mastermind of the whole plan." She stared out the front door of the mansion, into the misty rain.

"I was wondering, Mrs. Eldridge . . ."

"Wondering—what?"

"Well, to tell you the truth, Mr. Cooley's been talking about you. I think he considers you the personification of some-thing—unholy." Drucker chuckled nervously. "I know this sounds corny, but he thinks he's an agent of *God,* and you're some sort of representative of the *devil.*"

"Oh, *swell,*" she said, angrily shoving her hands into her shorts pockets. "Is the man totally crazy? What did I do to de-serve this? Or I should consider it a compliment, since he's a bloody killer. That makes *me* a *saint.*"

"It's wild, I know. But would you be willing to come over to the barracks with me and talk to him?" He looked at his watch. "Provided, that is, that you have the time."

"I have the time."

The state police barracks' interrogation room was small, about six by six, with stark white walls and a small window. Louise wriggled a bit to try to make herself comfortable in the wooden chair, then sat stock-still and gathered her thoughts. Sergeant

Drucker was counting on her to break through Cooley's reserve, but he hadn't supplied any particulars. He had only looked down at her with a twinkle in his eye and said, "You'll figure out what to say to him."

Cooley was brought in by a trooper and sat down opposite her. She was relieved to see the guard standing at the closed door, but Cooley had no handcuffs on, and probably would have liked to reach over the table and strangle her. Instead, he spoke, his rich baritone voice resonating in the bare room. "Mrs. Eldridge, the instrument of my destruction. You've come."

"I heard you wanted to talk."

"I swear I didn't kill Jeffrey Freeling. I wish you could persuade Sergeant Drucker of that."

Louise sat back in her chair and just looked at him. Much to her discomfort, she could swear the man was telling the truth.

"Then you're saying it was really an accident."

He looked down at the table, ran the fingernail of his right thumb casually back and forth over the cuts in the Formica, then gave her a calculating look. "Someone might have pushed him, but it didn't kill him. Afterward, I was right there, giving him mouth-to-mouth . . ."

Louise remembered the story. "And then Sandy took over when you got tired." She had an image of Sandy, sitting in the library with the others, her eyes wide with panic.

"Yes," he said, hope in his eyes now. "Sandy took over—and *she* killed him. I saw it happen. They all saw it, but they didn't realize what they were looking at."

"But . . . why didn't you stop her?"

He stared at her for a long time before he answered. "Because, of course, I wanted that man dead. That's a statement I will make only to you."

It was a delicate moment. Quietly she said, "Tell me how it happened: Sandy stepped in to help you . . . and she deliberately suffocated the man?"

He looked at her with guarded eyes. "I knew from the shouts

of the climbers down below that something was wrong. I came down as quickly as I could and began CPR, but I was running out of wind, what with having to scramble down that hundred feet of rock so fast. Jeffrey appeared to start breathing again when Sandy stepped in and insisted on relieving me. She told me and the others to step back, because in the close, rainy air, Jeffrey Freeling was going to need as much oxygen as he could get." He extended his hands in a wide gesture. "So everybody moved way back, out of the line of vision. When he got worse, not better, I figured out what the little minx had done."

"What?" asked Louise hoarsely.

"Pressed two strong thumbs against his trachea. Why, the autopsy would have shown it, if someone was looking for it: specific bruising at the trachea. So there he was, a traumatically injured person on the verge of resuming breathing, who instead is deprived of a crucial oxygen supply."

Louise slumped back and gave a loud grunt. "My God, what a mess." She looked over at Jim. "Why on earth would she do that?"

He shrugged. "I don't have the faintest idea why Sandy did it, except I can tell by his odd behavior that Mark Post knows something happened. *He* might know why. I'm telling Drucker, and my lawyer. He's got to get me off the hook for *that* one . . ."

She shook her head. "The only way you can clear this up is to confess—if you did push Jeffrey."

"I . . . I'll admit I *wished* him dead with every fiber of my body."

She stopped him. "Listen, this is between you and Sergeant Drucker. But if you tell him everything, it might leave you free of one murder charge, and only up against a conspiracy to murder your wife."

Cooley was thinking about that. "Yes. That might be the way."

She looked at her watch, then at the devastated man sitting across from her. Here was a person with a set of ethics, even if the ethics were sadly distorted. What could she say to him to cause him to do the right thing? It was a responsibility she hadn't asked for, and didn't want. She had no magic words. Finally, she told him the practical truth. "I absolutely have to go. We have to get to the airport and catch a plane. I won't wish you good luck, exactly, Jim. I only hope you have enough goodness left inside of you to tell the truth. That would help everybody, and it might atone a little for the vicious things you've done." She started to get up.

He reached a hand out and lightly touched hers. "Wait. Louise, you're a woman of principle, even if your principles are too diluted and liberal for me. I'm an evangelical of the old school. I believe we have contrary states within us—the state of nature, and the state of grace. The state of nature merits eternal wrath, the other merits eternal happiness in heaven."

"So Grace and Jeffrey merited God's eternal wrath . . ."

"But Louise, this is not so strange to you. You, too, possess a fervent sense of justice."

She looked at him, and the words scared her. Indeed, justice was her overriding passion.

"Justice is allied with vengeance," he continued. His eyes were bright with the torment of his inner thoughts. "Back even before Christ, they used to stone women to death who committed adultery. No one questioned it."

"Yes, and then Jesus came along and changed all that. He said, 'Let him who is without sin cast the first stone.' "

He persisted, as if he needed her approval. "But what would you do if your husband were untrue to *you*?"

She shook her head slowly, and thought of her beloved Bill, and how such disloyalty would break her heart. She said, "I know I wouldn't kill him. I'd try to talk him back home."

He sighed again. "Maybe you're right. I did love Grace as best I could. I *tried* to take care of her, but she was a strange, needy woman—and I couldn't, or maybe I was too busy to even understand what she needed." His voice rose in desperation. "I never knew what the devil was going on in her *mind*! Then recently, she blossomed, just like a flower. I read her notebook one day. It had this smarmy love language in it, each little passage with a date on it. I remember some of it. Just a couple of weeks ago, she wrote, *He told me*— '*It takes so very little—just your hand warm against mine and our fingers entwined, and I feel as if I'm connecting with your very soul*.' "

Tears sprang to her eyes. "How beautiful."

"Oh, *yes*," he said sarcastically, "isn't it, though."

"But, Jim, maybe she just made it up—maybe it was her own poetry . . ."

"*Somebody* was saying things like that to her. She was so different. I forced her to tell me what it was all about. She finally admitted she was seeing another man. Just an innocent friendship, she swore it. And she promised me she would quit going to those gardens and end her running around."

"When was that?"

"Just last week. To reward her, I planned another trip up to Litchfield to stay with Barbara. Grace was very fond of Barbara. The garden tour was the big attraction this weekend." He got a faraway look in his eyes. "Something about her manner when we arrived Friday got me suspicious. Not of Jeffrey—I didn't suspect him at all. I don't know what it was—maybe the way she looked . . ."

"I remember she acted as if she felt weak."

"Yes, and her face and eyes were all lit up. I didn't take my usual pill at bedtime—it knocks me out immediately, and God knows I need the sleep—"

"What pill?"

He laughed in embarrassment. "It's only melatonin, but it works. Then, sure enough, she got up about two o'clock, and I followed her. I *heard* her, moaning as she fell into somebody's arms. Frank was out there, too and he could tell which room they dodged into. It was the professor's." Cooley's eyes blazed with jealousy, as they must have in that dark hall Friday night.

"You think she planned this? I suspect Jeffrey was the one who planned it; he was probably desperate to see Grace again."

"Whoever planned it, it was a terrible betrayal." He hit his breast with his open hand. "It hurt me, right here. It was as corrupt and subversive as anything I've ever known—my own wife cuckolding me right under my nose! And the final irony: She might actually have become impregnated that night . . ."

"But I thought you two couldn't have children."

"Oh, not her," he said bitterly. "It was me who couldn't beget. Ironic, isn't it, that in eighteenth-century America, Cotton Mather preached that a woman's inability to have children meant she had fallen out of favor with God. Think how badly off Grace would have been back then—and all on account of people's ignorance." He gave a short laugh. "No, Grace was perfectly healthy, except for being too thin. Her spirit was ready, her body was ready. My childless wife was like a plant, with a passionate desire to be pollinated."

Louise had a horrifying flashback to the broken, bruised Grace at the foot of the falls. She looked at Jim. "And that was the unkindest cut of all, wasn't it?"

He sat there, head bowed, stripped of pride. "Yes."

"What are you going to do, Jim? Let Frank take the blame? Try to pin Jeffrey's death on Sandy Post? Let it go at that?"

"I don't know anymore what's right. When Grace died—and I knew when she died; I could tell by the look in Frank's eyes when he returned to the veranda—I began to realize how wrong I was. I thought of an old folk song I used to play when I was young. And believe me, I thought I had put all that romantic stuff away for good. But knowing Grace lay dead somewhere up that hill—that brought it all to the surface again."

For a moment Louise didn't think he could go on. But he did. "The song was called 'Mattie Groves'—about an English lord who cuts off the heads of his wife and her lover." He raised his head and gave her a lopsided smile, and she could see his big, sad eyes were wet with tears. "Penalty for adultery, of course."

278

He sat there at the dismal Formica table and sang the last verse of the song. His baritone voice was even hollower than usual.

" *'How now, how now—my merry men . . . why stayed you not my hand? For I have killed the fairest pair—in all of Eng-a-land . . . in all of Eng-a-land.'* "

It had begun as a somber narrative in the lower registers, but it finished in a high, despairing flurry of notes that caused Jim Cooley's voice to crack. Louise bowed her head and tried to restrain her sobs.

When she finally looked up, he was staring at her. He said, "I was arrogant, playing God, administering justice. I was so arrogant that I thought you'd never catch me. I've done terrible things, but you have to believe that I *loved* that woman."

After a long moment, she said, "I guess you did. But now you have to set things right."

Vegetables: From Utilitarian to Aesthetic

VEGETABLE GARDENS HAVE A spartan reputation, for, after all, they are the legacy of the days in America when most people were farmers and crops were raised in a no-nonsense style. Today, when many fewer Americans farm, there still is a leftover set of nuts-and-bolts rules for growing vegetables. But some people are overturning that tradition, with surprising results.

Vegetable growing attracts us because we know exactly what we're getting. Provided we refrain from spraying or treating the garden with chemicals, we can bring organic produce and fruits to our tables on an almost daily basis during the growing season. Later, we can freeze or can the leftovers to feed the family healthfully during the off-season.

Some will say the easiest way to manage a vegetable garden is to have long, narrow, utilitarian beds, through which a Rototiller can be guided with ease. But there is another scenario. Crops can be grown with the same ease in raised beds set in attractive designs that make them fully as engaging as gardens full of flowers. Some gardeners are placing these beds in their front or side yards and making them into show-stopping beauties. Home owners do this either for design's sake, as in the case of a prestigious New York clothes designer, or more often because they are tired of wasting their front yards on lawns.

"Raised" bed is a key phrase. Raising the soil eases the gardener's work and encourages greater harvests. You can lift your bed six or so inches above ground level without supporting its sides with wood or other materials, but some vegetable gardeners construct wooden sides as high as twenty inches or more. Wheelchair gardeners usually work in beds about two feet high—so that they can reach directly over from their chairs to cultivate the plants.

These deep beds have advantages. They are never walked upon, so the soil—deeply tilled as it is—stays fluffy and requires minimum cultivation. The work is easier, because the gardener has less bending. Vegetable beds,

raised or not, should never be wider than about four feet, so that they can be worked on easily from either side.

For years, people were using pressure-treated lumber to build flower beds; after much debate, it has been shown fairly conclusively that this wood has harmful substances that leach into the soil, and thus into food we raise in that soil. Nontreated timbers should be used instead.

The believing organic gardener does not use chemical fertilizers on the garden, especially not the vegetable bed. People who have access to compost can fertilize their beds adequately with it, particularly if it has some manure added. Then, a little extra food may be needed from time to time—for instance, in the planting hole for tomatoes. It goes without saying that these gardeners maintain a compost pile of their own, throwing into it all appropriate table scraps and the green and brown waste products from the garden itself. (One gardener who couldn't get a crop of melons to bear fruit was delighted to find the Rocky Ford cantaloupe seeds that reached the compost pile not only sprouted there, but gave the family its only melons for the season.)

Vegetable gardeners are having fun with heirloom vegetables, which are easier to obtain than they used to be. They are accessible through seed companies and seed exchanges. The large, tangy Brandywine tomato, for instance, is an heirloom variety whose popularity has swept the country, and some believe the heirloom variety of spinach called 'Madagascar' is more flavorful than newer types.

Getting fancy with a vegetable patch is not hard. The French have done it for centuries, labeling such a garden a *potager* or "kitchen garden." This can be an assembly of edged rectangular beds four feet wide, set in an interesting pattern, or a more intricate design—an arrangement of corner gardens emanating from a circular garden in the middle of which you can place a sundial.

Again, cultivation will be remarkably easy if you *keep your feet out of the garden*. What has always distinguished the *potager* is the edging for the beds. You can use lettuce, decorative kale, mâche, herbs, or even flowers—globe-shaped plants being favored. *Colorize* the garden with edible flowers: nasturtiums, pansies, violets, and even marigolds. Flowering kale (*Brassica oleracea*) can be used with great effect in this type of garden. *Corner* the beds with accents of rosemary or lavender plants. You can sink pots of these herbs into the ground in the summer vegetable bed, and later winter them over inside the house.

Some vegetables could join the Plant Hall of Fame for their beauty—eggplant, artichokes, pepper, kohlrabi, kale, and okra among them. By giving them a few judicious haircuts, even homely fellows like tomatoes can be kept tidy during the growing season and contribute to the beauty of the decorative, edible vegetable garden.

If that is not enough for you, then create a Secret (Vegetable) Garden by erecting hedges

around it. You can festoon this privacy hedge with unobtrusive fencing to discourage omnipresent deer.

Whether we plant a straightforward, farm-type truck garden or a decorative bed, our vegetables have the same needs. They will profit from systematic watering. Especially in dry climates, take the time and effort to put down drip irrigation systems in these beds and attach them to a timer. You will do the plants a favor, and save yourself work and higher water bills.

As for pests, most backyard gardeners will not be much bothered by them, because of the variety that usually exists in a small vegetable bed. Marigolds and patches of dill also help in their control. But cabbage and broccoli, two popular vegetables, are often afflicted with cabbageworms, aphids, and root flies. There is a solution: A plant study showed that underplanting these crops with clover reduces the *Brassica* pests by ninety percent.

The vegetable bed is another place where people can and do use conceits and follies. Nicely designed bean "towers." Gracefully constructed bamboo "igloos" to support tomatoes. Creatively designed lattice walls on which to grow peas. Some artistic gardeners even deliberately plant vegetable vines near their compost pile, to swarm over and disguise it from view. So use all your garden wiles and learn to raise healthful vegetables in settings that are veritable works of art.

Chapter
Twenty-four

WHEN SHE WAS DELIVERED back to the
mansion, Louise went in to find Bill reading
in the library. She came over and gently
touched his hair. Without looking at her, he
reached up and grabbed her hand, and delivered a status report. "You're back—good.
Your hand feels like ice—I think you need to
go home. Kids are ready. Nora's up in her
room nursing a headache 'til we're ready to
leave. Suitcases are near the door. Chris gassed
up the car." He angled a suspicious glance up

at her. "And from *Janie* I accidentally found out about Melissa McCormick."

"Oh, yes, I guess I didn't have a chance to tell you. Melissa will arrive on Saturday and probably stay—a month or so."

"My dear, just what kind of commitment . . ."

"Bill," she said quietly, "this little girl just *lost* her parents. Do you mean you don't want to accept her into our home?"

Tapping an impatient finger against his book, he seemed to be weighing the various options: a little argument with his wife, or more book time? They exchanged one more long look; then he sighed and dropped his shoulders. "I can feel it coming now. Three daughters. Martha—who's gone so much she's like a stranger. Janie, who's so feisty that it's more like having a sparring companion than a daughter. And now Melissa. Compliant and thirteen, you think?" He nodded his head solemnly. "That little redheaded person reminded *me* of the Artful Dodger. But it's okay. You just take her in and you'll find out."

"I *will*. I'd love to. *Thank* you for understanding, honey." She rubbed his shoulder affectionately. "Now I have to tell you something that's pretty important."

He had already sunk back into his book and was paying scant attention. She tried stroking his hair, thinking that would help. Quietly, she said, "I found out something new from Jim Cooley. It's about Sandy Post . . ."

He was as obsessed with his book on Connecticut history as another might be with a racy novel. She could have insisted that he come out of his reverie, but he looked completely endearing as he sat with his glasses poised on his nose, his body nestled snugly into the fat old chair. Why should she disturb him, when this was his first moment of relaxation all weekend? Her minor concerns could be put off for a few more minutes.

Meanwhile, Louise turned her attention to the cat, who was a good deal more responsive than her husband. Hargrave seemed to sense that she was leaving, winding around her legs to be sure she knew he was there. He must have experienced the departure of many guests, so she was flattered that he was coming over to give her a special farewell. "Goodbye, old boy," she said, and reached down and scratched behind his ears. He raised his head, closed his eyes in ecstasy, and hoped it would never end. She would miss this little creature.

Then Bill was ready with another nugget of information. "Y'know," he told her, "this place is intriguing. It's amazing the people who came out of here. Inventors. The intellectuals who inhabited Nook Farm, who of course included Harriet Beecher Stowe and Mark Twain. This state was like a fermenting brew— lots of ideological conflict. There were the evangelicals—the kind you never relate to. People like Jim Cooley and Frank and Fiona Storm. And then there were the more intellectually inclined—"

"Bill," she interrupted, "I know you're on a historical journey here, but we have to—"

"I know, but just listen to this: Did you know that Lyman Beecher was a liberal in his social views, but a staunch, diehard Calvinist when it came to religious practice? At the same time that he was head of Litchfield Congregational, a young fellow was being raised on a farm outside Litchfield who grew up to be very important in the church—Horace Bushnell. He came down hard on the fire-and-brimstone ways of Calvinism. Said it destroyed people. And just to show you how things change, one of his chief followers was Lyman's son, Henry." He smiled up at her. "Ironic, huh?"

"Henry, the adulterer." She rolled her eyes. "Very interesting, especially after the weekend we've been through. Think of all the adultery that must have been committed in Connecticut over the years. Good thing they all didn't have to pay with their lives, like Jeffrey Freeling and Grace Cooley." She looked at her watch. "But, really—"

"Here's what you'll like," he said, slanting a glance up at her as she stood fidgeting by his chair. "This Horace Bushnell was roundly chastised for being a 'Romanticist.' "

"Oh?" she said, her interest perking up.

"Yeah. He studied Romantic poets like Coleridge, and developed a kind of mystical theology that involved both logic and intuition. He talked a lot about the divine forces in nature—does that remind you of anyone?"

She stared out the multiple-paned front windows of the inn. "Yes—Grace Cooley. She was always looking for God in nature. Maybe she would have done better if she'd lived in the late nineteenth century—contemporaneous with this Bushnell fellow."

He looked thoughtfully at Louise. "One more geological footnote. Bear Mountain is part of Connecticut's northwest highlands, and it's made out of tough bedrock—schist and gneiss. They're from the Paleozoic Age—a mere five hundred million years old. But this mansion property we're on, with its falls, is different. It's part of what they call the 'marble valley.' And though marble may appear hard, it isn't. It's limestone-based, and when it erodes, it carves the landscape and creates . . ."

"Waterfalls?"

Bill nodded. "Waterfalls. Pits. Pools."

"The waterfalls over which Grace was thrown."

"Yes," said Bill, "and that deep pit of a pool in which we found her body."

"So Jeffrey died in the highlands, and Grace died in the lowlands, in a marble valley. It's so sad—they couldn't even die together."

"That's right," he said, staring dreamily into space. Then he came out of it and clamped his book shut. "Louise, we have a plane to catch."

"Yes, dear."

"I'll alert everyone."

"You do that. I'll be with you in a second. I have a little unfinished business."

"With Barbara Seymour?"

"Yes. I have to try to make her understand."

She went first to the veranda, in hopes of finding a leftover cup of coffee and a sweet. But the tea things had been cleared. Her glance turned longingly toward the kitchen, where she could still smell coffee. In the doorway, Barbara Seymour stood, wearing an embroidered denim dress which Louise guessed was normal Sunday afternoon attire.

Barbara's expression was grim, aimed at keeping her at a distance. But Louise was determined not to lose the woman's friendship. "I was hoping no one had emptied the coffeepot yet."

She and Barbara were the same height. They looked levelly at each other. "I saved you some in the kitchen. Come on."

Louise followed her. The kitchen's gleaming stainless steel counters were now cleared, and the dishwasher was humming quietly. On a counter was a small tray with a few sandwiches and tarts, a small insulated thermos, and a pitcher filled with cream. "Oh!" she said, "for me?"

"Yes," said Barbara solemnly. "I'm not blind, you know: I saw Sergeant Drucker come back and fetch you over to the barracks."

"Jim wanted to talk to me."

Barbara focused her eyes on an imaginary spot on the stainless steel, scratching her fingernail against it, avoiding Louise's eyes. "He is one of those true believers who can't be persuaded they're wrong. It harks me back uncomfortably to some of my Calvinist ancestors. Yet when I heard about the deaths of those two students, and then think about the deaths here in Litchfield"—now the woman turned her gaze on Louise—"it's almost more than I can comprehend!"

"There's no real evidence that those students' deaths weren't suicides. Barbara, Jim and Frank had already been cleared—by the time they got themselves into real trouble. But I think Jim's going to do the right thing now."

"So he did plan this, didn't he? A punishment right out of the Old Testament." Her pained eyes looked at Louise. "It's a wonder he didn't have Frank stone her, with the stones from that wall they dismembered!" Tears flowed from her eyes and down her lined cheeks.

"Oh, Barbara." Louise went over and took the elderly woman in her arms and hugged her close. "This must be killing you."

Louise could feel the woman's wet cheek against hers move downward and up again, in a nod. Yes, thought Louise, those nearest and dearest to us could also do us great harm. Barbara surely was a living example.

"I loved Grace," Barbara said, "and she loved me. But she'd never confide. Those big, scared eyes just presented a barrier, whenever I inquired about anything—personal. Because she knew Jim was my own blood, and she would do anything to keep from hurting me. And I feel sad that all her little poems are gone."

Barbara extricated herself from Louise's embrace. "But we'll always have the one that's going to be published. That was so important to her. And life goes on, doesn't it? And you must eat, for you've been working hard. Come sit down." She beckoned her to a small pine worktable where there were two chairs. They sat there, under a window with crisp, embroidered cotton curtains. It provided a nice view of the kitchen garden, from which the mist was clearing. "Here, let me pour you a cup of coffee."

Strengthened by the quiet conversation and the food, Louise felt as if a fog were lifting from her mind. Jim Cooley and Frank Storm were in custody, and Sandy Post probably was by now, too. Barbara told her that the noxious Neil Landry had been routed from the mansion by his young wife. The atmosphere around the place was beginning to improve. Louise felt relaxed and secure, the way a person should while visiting a country inn glowing with fine New England tradition. She had said her good-byes to Barbara, and promised to stay in touch.

She took the shortcut toward the front hall, because she knew her family and friends must be waiting. It was an isolated corridor that led from the end of the kitchen hallway to the lobby, but she strode fearlessly into its deep gloom, feeling the history of the mansion, sure that the ghosts were gone from this place.

Her footsteps echoed on the stone floor as she reached the darkest point of the hallway, the point where the corridor inexplicably bent again, the product of some early architect's quixotic dream. Her pulse quickened, and she recognized that same uneasy feeling she had been living with for the past three days. Sweat broke out on her body, as the phantoms of the mansion surrounded her in a final attack.

Then she heard a sound behind her, and all the imaginary fears became real. It was Sandy Post, her blond hair shining even in the dimness of the hallway. She stood silent and strong, a lethal little powerhouse ready to launch an attack. She was wearing a no-nonsense jogging outfit that made the bulky dress purse slung over one of her shoulders look out of place. The white running shoes on her feet almost seemed like weapons in themselves.

Louise had seldom felt so helpless. "Ai-ee!" Her little yip of fear and her faltering step backward told Sandy all she needed to know: Louise had learned the truth. She recovered her balance and then did her best to cover up. "Oh, *God,* Sandy, you gave me a start, coming up that way behind me."

"Stop right there, Louise." Sandy spoke in her normal little-girl voice. She would not have been threatening at all if Louise hadn't just heard Jim Cooley describing how this woman might have snuffed out Jeffrey Freeling's life with her determined little thumbs. *Might* have, indeed—she *must* have done it. There had to be a reason she was demanding Louise's attention in this hidden-away passage.

Louise's eyes focused on the object in Sandy's hand. A large gray pistol, pointed straight at Louise's stomach. It had a metal extension that Louise guessed was a silencer. Any kind of gun would be lethal in Sandy's hands, and this one would do the job soundlessly. Her stomach constricted as she speculated on how long it would take someone to find her dead body with a hole blown through her middle.

But instead of fear, she was surprised to feel anger growing inside her. Why had this happened to her? Surely the wheels of justice could grind faster than this. She had briefed Sergeant Drucker a half hour ago, so why hadn't they picked the woman up for questioning? Yet it wouldn't do to get excited; Sandy was too good with guns. "I'm stopped," said Louise tersely. "Now what do you want?"

"Always the cool one, aren't you?" Sandy said. "You just know it all, don't you, Louise? You went over to the jail, and I bet Jim Cooley told you all sorts of strange things."

"What would he have told me?"

"Things about me," she said petulantly. Louise could see her eyes smoldering in the semidark. "I guess you don't know how awful this whole thing has been for me."

Louise remembered her own suspicions that Mark Post and Jeffrey Freeling might be lovers, and it dawned on her that Sandy must have believed this, too. There was her motive for snuffing out Jeffrey's life, a life only precariously held, after his fall from the peak of Bear Mountain.

"Yes, it must have been awful, suffocating a man and then finding out he had done you no harm. Jeffrey wasn't Mark's lover—but you must have thought so. You thought you were re-moving the embarrassing evidence of your husband's homo-sexual history."

"But you see, Jeffrey could have been his lover, if Mark had

292

only had his way. Mark's, like, not what he told me he was when we married."

Louise kept her eyes on the young woman. "And I bet your daddy told you that right from the start."

"Yes, Daddy did, in fact. But I had to have him—he was so hard to get."

"And then, of course, it wouldn't do to have people know that your new husband was inclined toward the opposite sex. So you had to remove Jeffrey, who you merely *suspected* was involved with Mark. How pathetic. How utterly pathetic."

They were the wrong words to say to such a privileged young woman, the apple of her father's eye, and an Olympian to boot. "God damn!" she said. "Don't patronize me, you— middle-aged gardening snoop." She pointed the gun directly at Louise's head.

Louise put up her hands in a double fan effect in front of her face, as if she had the power to stop bullets with her bare hands. "Just a minute, Sandy," she said, in a voice she reserved for stern talks with Janie. What did she have to lose at this point by inserting a little motherly reprimand? Maybe that was what Sandy had lacked all her privileged young life. "Another murder isn't going to do you any good, my dear. You're going to end up strapped to a table with a needle in your arm. Just let that sink in for a minute."

The younger woman said, "What do I have to lose, getting rid of you? Then it's only Jim Cooley's word against mine—"

Suddenly Louise pointed down the hall. "Someone's coming . . ."

Sandy sneered. "You're not pulling that old trick—" But she couldn't resist a quick look, even though she kept her body and her gun carefully pointed at Louise. Louise didn't delay an instant. She swatted the young woman's hand smartly forward and sent the gun flying. It clattered on the stone floor of the hall, out of sight in the semidarkness.

"*Damn* you," Sandy hissed, stuffing her hand in her big purse.

Oh, God, Louise thought. *What else does she have in there?* And then a voice yelled, "Police!" Sandy jerked her hand out of the bag. Empty. Louise sighed with relief. "Hold it right there, Mrs. Post," the trooper called. "Don't move. And put your hands up."

Sandy stood there, well balanced on legs held slightly apart. Without haste she slowly raised her hands. She would have fooled them into thinking she would surrender, but her eyes gave her away. They were calculating and cold, defying Louise as she must have defied anyone who had ever presumed to tell her what to do. Sandy still gripped the handbag, and Louise knew she was just waiting for the right moment to pull out the second weapon she had reached for a moment ago. Then the woman would be in a perfect position to wheel around and open fire on the troopers coming down the hall.

Louise took in her breath sharply. Sandy was an Olympian, but what the heck, Louise was not in bad shape herself . . .

Without giving herself a chance to think further, she lunged toward Sandy and quickly twisted a leg around the other woman's, pulling forward with all her strength in a startling example of bungled karate. This toppled them both off balance, and they hit the floor awkwardly, grunting loudly. Then, like two scrapping animals, they began grappling for the purse and the weapon inside it. The bag had fallen free from Sandy's shoulder. Louise had body length on her side; she laid herself on the purse, as if protecting a living being. She heard the pounding footsteps approach, and yelled, "God, hurry!"

Before Sandy could make another move, the troopers had arrived. They bent down on either side of Sandy and hauled her up. One held her while the other handcuffed her. A third trooper helped Louise to her feet and asked if she was all right.

Rubbing her knees where she had struck them when she tumbled onto the floor, she looked up and gave him a reproachful look. "Not really. I'll be a lot better when I get out of this place."

Louise was through trying to exorcise the demons of Litchfield Falls Inn. All she wanted to do was go home.

Chapter
Twenty-five

IT WAS COMFORTING TO be back in Washington. The heat wave was over, and the night so balmy that it invited the world to join it, not hide from it. Bill turned off the air-conditioning and opened the car windows. Traffic on the George Washington wasn't bad for a Sunday night, and in just eight miles and about twenty minutes, Louise would be home, slipping into a bath, and then into bed.

Bill took his eyes from the wheel for an instant and gave her a worried look. "You must

be sore as the devil, Louise. I can't believe you tussled with a woman who's been trying to be in the Olympics."

Janie piped up from the backseat. "Yeah, Ma, pretty good for a wimpy woman who names her pillow 'Puny.' "

Louise pursed her lips, then said, "I hadn't thought of myself as a wimp."

"Oh, I'm just kidding," and the girl reached forward and patted her mother on the shoulder. Louise reached up and put a hand on the girl's.

"I will say my knees hurt where I fell," Louise said, "and my neck, where Bebe Hollowell throttled me." The conversation in the car had of course been all about the crimes. But Nora didn't take part, staring out the car window in a silence so deep it was as if she weren't really there.

"So Sandy Post actually killed Jeffrey," said Bill. "And Jim Cooley won't admit that he *meant* to kill him by throwing him off that cliff."

"Not yet," said Louise, "but I think he will eventually. Sergeant Drucker said it would help with the other charges against him if he cooperates."

"Such a deceptively friendly kind of guy. Didn't he tell his wife anything after Jeffrey's accident? Didn't he say, *'Your lover's dead, and you're next,'* or something like that?"

She laughed. "No, or Grace would have taken off like a gazelle. Jim dosed her with a couple of sedatives in their room before they returned at teatime. That made her less resistant when Frank came along to abduct her. Certainly she needed some sedation: Her lover had died—possibly been murdered. Jim says he never told her he knew of her disloyalty. But she figured it out, of course, the minute Frank came to her room."

"When did Grace write the poem she never finished?"

"She had started it, but was interrupted by Frank. Then he hustled her down the back stairs to the basement, and out that tunnel to the trail that leads to the falls."

"What strikes me is the amount of bad feeling floating around the place," said Bill.

"Bad vibes everywhere, that's for sure," said Chris, leaning forward against the front seat. "I knew something heavy was goin' down with those newlyweds—and here it turns out that Sandy's a murderer. They'll both probably end up in jail—one for murder, one for computer fraud."

"Then there's Rod and Dorothy Gasparra," said Bill. "For all we know, they may still be there, plotting against Fenimore Smith."

"Good grief, I hope not," said Louise. "Since I was a witness to their argument in the nursery, I think Dorothy, at least, has come to her senses."

"But how about that *Bebe*!" said Janie. "The town gossips of Mattson, Massachusetts, nearly ruined her. It makes me want to never live in a small town."

Louise silently remembered Bebe for a moment. Then she said, "I like it that she's going home to receive an award from the old folks. And Barbara Seymour—she's safe now. She can close the inn and turn it over to the Connecticut Trust."

"Or else she could sell it to an eager billionaire," said her husband. "One thing for sure: Stephanie's marriage will never be the same. I gather she's staying with Barbara for a while. That ought to help them both."

"Ho, Stephanie won't have any problem," chuckled Chris. "I bet she can find herself another man in no time flat."

"Oh, really?" said Janie airily. "Any woman can, if she tries."

"In the meantime," Louise said, "it's going to be awfully hard on Barbara to watch what happens to her nephew." She shook her head. "What a weekend. Rainy weather. Two murders to avenge adultery . . ."

"Adultery, let's face it," said Chris, "causes an awful lot of trouble."

Louise continued: "An attempt on the life of Barbara Seymour. Marriages gone sour: the Posts', the Landrys', of course the Cooleys'. And a malicious attempt to blackmail the country's top nursery . . ."

"And one maligned widow who was exonerated," said Bill, "but will probably never stop talking about it."

"It's quite a story." Louise struck her forehead. "*Story*—damn. I promised to call Charlie Hurd. He's probably home biting his nails waiting for the phone to ring. Or else he's shown some initiative and called Litchfield barracks on his own. I have a feeling he may get beaten out by Tom Carrigan."

She turned to the passengers in the backseat. "You know, we never would have made any sense of these murders if we hadn't worked together."

"Let's not get all mushy, Ma," said Janie in a sarcastic tone she used when sentiment reared its ugly head. "Though I thought Chris was *really* great."

"Thanks," said Chris.

The girl added mischievously, "But I like Teddy, too. And if I were going for the *money,* well, I hear Teddy's going to be very rich someday."

"Oh, so that's it," protested Chris. Janie slid closer to him and put her head on his shoulder, and his objections were silenced. Louise noted that though Teddy might be charming, Janie had not changed the object of her affections.

Nora was in her own world, staring out the window as the lights of the parkway swept by like lasers, and ascending airplanes buzzed over their heads.

Soon, Louise felt as if she and Bill were alone in the car. "You know, darling," she told him, "I hate adultery. And I dislike books that make it into the most romantic of all pastimes. They elevate it into something almost holy."

"Yes, but, honey, you had a lot of sympathy for Grace and Jeffrey. Don't tell me you didn't."

"That's because they were decent people. Even then, they could have been more honest about it. They could have maintained a friendship . . ."

" 'Just say no' to sex, huh? How was she supposed to cultivate a friendship with a man with that autocratic husband breathing down her neck?"

"They could have done it. They could have met once in a while—"

"For what, tea?"

She looked over and could see he was grinning, not taking her seriously.

"They could have corresponded, say, through a private post office box. Discovered whether they truly were in love. Then, she could have filed for divorce, and that would have been doing it properly. Or else she could have stuck with Jim and tried to change him."

"Change him? Come *on*. What we have to remember is that Jim Cooley was a hard case, a really hard case. She couldn't reform that guy."

"That may be, but cheating's not good for one's health."

They looked at each other and laughed. Bill said, "Very bad for Grace and Jeffrey's health."

Then, embarrassed, they fell silent, remembering Nora in the backseat. Through the rearview mirror Louise could see her neighbor, still brooding. Nora's ears must be burning: She'd been there, done that.

They traveled the next few miles in silence, and the noise of the airport subsided. Then Louise turned to Bill. "I know the final line."

"The final line?"

" '*That you are not dead.*' That's the conclusion of Grace's poem. If Grace had only had a chance to finish it, we might have figured out much faster that she was pining after the dead Jeffrey Freeling."

"Huh," said Bill. "So how does it go?"

Louise had been over it so frequently that she knew it by heart.

> " 'It is all gone now, since last we kissed
> Our precious flowers, our love in the mist
> My love lies bleeding, near the Iris Red
> And my pulsing heart is pleading that you are not dead.'

"What do you think of it?" asked Louise excitedly. They were turning into Sylvan Valley now. She could smell the lovely, familiar mold of the Virginia woods, almost see her house set amidst the trees. "Isn't that it? That has to be it. The words fit perfectly."

"The passion's there," said Bill nonchalantly, "but it doesn't scan terribly well."

Nora had an unbelievable headache. Perhaps it had come on because she hated the thought of going home. Chris was going to be either at work or over at Janie's house, so she would be essentially alone. Ron wouldn't be back for a week. That meant at least a week before she could even try to mend her marriage.

And there was another reason. She felt a guilt so heavy that it hung about her shoulders like the massive ceremonial shrouds worn by heads of state. Chinese empresses. British queens. Except she was no queen, being celebrated by her people. Quite the opposite: a woman of questionable intentions, questionable integrity. A woman whom Louise might describe as not taking her marriage vows seriously.

Just barely, she could hear Louise in the front seat talking of adultery. But she forgave her friend, who had no idea of the biological imperatives that drove some humans. Like Nora.

While Louise mingled with many men, and admired some, and even possibly entertained a sexual twinge or two, Nora was different. Her body, her psyche, and her spirit were highly charged, and sometimes there was very little she could do to control it. She seemed to emit pheromones, like moths in heat. So it wasn't only her fault, it was also the way men were attracted to her.

Granted, it was a tiny bit better as she grew older, although menopause had recently created a setback. It heightened her sexual desires again. While Ron loved this, he knew he wasn't always enough for her, and it grated on him. And each of his many absences put her at risk.

The irony of this weekend was that the man who had caught at her heart and her loins—who had the look of someone who *needed* love, needed her—was already taken. A cruel joke for both of them.

She had waited. God knows she had waited Friday night, until when—one, one-thirty? And then Jeffrey had come downstairs from his bedroom, and she had risen from the chair on the veranda, and approached him. Reached out to him, her mouth filled with soft words of longing.

But he had held her rigidly, at arm's length, and said, "It's best you go to bed, my dear. Best for both of us."

Without more words, she had left him and gone upstairs, through the lighted hall, to her corner bedroom. A few minutes later, as she was getting into bed, her bedside lamp went out. There was so much psychic energy outside her door that she arose and opened it.

Utter darkness. Someone had interfered with the lights in the upstairs hall as well. As she stood there, she could detect the faint chemical odor of Jeffrey's tweed jacket, as if he had not quite rid himself of the smells of his beloved laboratory. There followed a confusion of sounds—muffled footsteps on the stairs, a moan, right there in the middle of the hall.

Then she saw the faint shadow of two men standing in front

of the nearby window, caressing. She was cold with shock, not understanding at all. Jeffrey, with another man? Since Louise had also seen the men, Nora was spared the humiliation of bringing it up after Jeffrey's death. She, too, thought he and Mark had unexpectedly found themselves thrown together at an isolated country inn, and were bidding each other good-bye forever. After all, Mark was now a married man.

And yet it had not been Jeffrey and Mark at all.

Friday night had been so dismaying. Jeffrey had preferred Grace's arms to hers, and what a deadly decision that had been!

The cloak of guilt fastened tighter. If only Nora had had the power to lure Jeffrey, to bring him to *her* room . . .

That would have left Grace, the sad, disappointed Grace, stumbling aimlessly about the hall, but forced eventually to return to her room. Making some little excuse to her suspicious husband, and then going safely to sleep.

Oh, if only she had been able to entice him to her bed. It would have saved both lovers, and such fine people they were. They would have lived to love another day. And she would have had her man—at least for *that* night.

About the Author

A former newspaperwoman, ANN RIPLEY now spends her time organic gardening, reading about politics and geology, and writing mysteries. She lives with her husband, Tony, in Lyons, Colorado, where she has completed her fifth gardening mystery, and has launched a sixth.